"I won't hang around while you look through the garage. Unless you want me to, Ms. Marshall?"

She would have laughed, if her mood had been better. "You'd be here for the next two weeks."

"Call if you need me," the man said, then shook hands with Tony Navarro and strode to his car, undoubtedly relieved to have escaped.

Tony didn't move. He wasn't watching the attorney's departure; he was looking at her.

"Do you need the key for the side door?" she asked. "Let me get my purse and I'll give you mine."

"No." A hand on her arm stopped her. "Actually, yes, thank you, but there's something else I'm hoping you'll do for me."

"That *I'll* do for you?"

He rubbed his jaw. "Is there any chance you could take more time off work? I could use some help going through the stuff in the garage, and on the lawn." When she gaped, he grimaced. "The truth is, you'd recognize something that doesn't belong, or should be there and isn't."

She shook her head in disbelief. "I'm supposed to use up my vacation days to help you go after my father?"

He cocked an eyebrow. "You'll have a chance to point out evidence leading to someone else."

And he was right—this offer would make her part of the investigation. What could she do but accept?

Dear Reader,

Writing a novel has a lot in common with putting a jigsaw puzzle together. Bits and pieces that have been floating unconnected in my brain suddenly fit. That's never been truer than for this book.

I read a long time ago about a man who just wanted the neighbors to leave him alone, so they did. Years passed, and vines grew over the house. I suppose the neighbors assumed he'd moved. Eventually a kid decided to sneak into the house...and found the man, whose remains had mummified, sitting in his chair watching a TV that had presumably died many years before. Bet that poor kid never got over it!

I write often about family ties, and have pondered the difference between the increasingly modern American family, with kids who have moved far away from parents and see them only occasionally, and the extended families once more common, where lives are tangled, sometimes annoyingly, but no one in need goes without help. In this story, both hero and heroine are part of the second kind, for completely different reasons. Both love the closeness even as they chafe at the demands of their families.

Add in another theme that has always drawn me: what happens to the family and friends left behind when someone vanishes. The effect is more profound than if that same person had died, allowing everyone to grieve. What's left behind instead is anger, grief, of course, fear and a lot of questions.

I had a moment of complete satisfaction when these and other pieces clicked together in my head and, hallelujah, there it was: a story.

Good reading,

Janice

USA TODAY Bestselling Author

JANICE KAY JOHNSON

—

Back Against the Wall

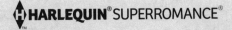

HARLEQUIN® SUPERROMANCE®

Recycling programs
for this product may
not exist in your area.

ISBN-13: 978-1-335-44906-1

Back Against the Wall

Copyright © 2018 by Janice Kay Johnson

Printed in U.S.A.

An author of more than ninety books for children and adults (more than seventy-five for Harlequin), **Janice Kay Johnson** writes about love and family—about the way generations connect and the power our earliest experiences have on us throughout life. A *USA TODAY* bestselling author and an eight-time finalist for a Romance Writers of America RITA® Award, she won a RITA® Award in 2008 for her Harlequin Superromance novel *Snowbound*. A former librarian, Janice raised two daughters in a small town north of Seattle, Washington.

Books by Janice Kay Johnson

HARLEQUIN SUPERROMANCE

The Hero's Redemption
Her Amish Protectors
Plain Refuge
A Mother's Claim
Because of a Girl
The Baby Agenda
Bone Deep
Finding Her Dad
All That Remains
Making Her Way Home
No Matter What
A Hometown Boy
Anything for Her
Where It May Lead
From This Day On
One Frosty Night

More Than Neighbors
To Love a Cop

Brothers, Strangers

The Baby He Wanted
The Closer He Gets

Two Daughters

Yesterday's Gone
In Hope's Shadow

The Mysteries of Angel Butte

Bringing Maddie Home
Everywhere She Goes
All a Man Is
Cop by Her Side
This Good Man

Visit the Author Profile page at Harlequin.com for more titles.

CHAPTER ONE

FLANKED BY HER brother and sister, Beth Marshall stared at the pile of boxes blocking the side door into the detached garage. She hadn't a clue whether she was looking at some of the oldest stuff jammed in here or the most recent. If there was such a thing as logical layering, say from front to back.

She almost snorted. *This is Dad,* she reminded herself. There would be no logic in how he stored anything.

Beside her, Matt groaned. "'Give me a weekend,' you said. This could take *weeks.*" He sounded so appalled, she was reminded that neither he nor Emily had so much as glanced inside the garage in, well, years. Beth had tried to prepare them, but obviously hadn't succeeded.

Matt was not an enthusiastic volunteer. Or a volunteer at all, really. He might still love their father—she wasn't sure—but Matt harbored a lot of anger, too. He made no effort to see Dad except for holidays, which he and his wife, Ashley, apparently considered obligatory. Or, at least, she did and had her ways of persuading him to show up and behave himself.

"Quit whining," Beth ordered, refusing to let herself be annoyed by his attitude. So what if he hadn't wanted to help? He was here. He'd contribute some muscle she felt sure they'd need.

"Do you promise Dad won't come out?"

She rolled her eyes. "Can you imagine it crossing Dad's mind that maybe he should help?"

He sighed heavily. "No. Okay. Why didn't I see a Dumpster?"

"Because I wasn't sure we'd need one. I'm hoping most of what's in here is good for a thrift store, at the very least."

He gave her a look she recognized from their childhoods.

Ten or fifteen feet separated the detached garage from the house where they'd all grown up. It would be way more practical to raise the street-facing garage door and gain a wash of daylight instead of depending on the two sixty-watt bulbs high on the ceiling, but none of them wanted neighbors to see the disaster inside. They'd debated parking their vehicles to block the sight line—but what was to stop a neighbor from strolling up the driveway to investigate what they were doing? Fortunately, a wood fence and gate that ran between the house and garage kept anyone from seeing what they were up to.

The truth was John Marshall had become a pack rat. Her word. Her brother called him a hoarder. Beth's younger sister, Emily, just looked anxious.

The garage was only the beginning, although it was the most jam-packed space in the house. What Dad used to call his den was piled with things he didn't know what to do with as well. The other rooms were just...cluttered.

"It's not like it's going to rain. I'll order a Dumpster if we need one. What I was thinking was that we could hold a garage sale, too," Beth said, trying for an upbeat note.

"We?" Matt leveled a look at her.

Of course, she would be the one borrowing tables, pricing and arranging. She could probably persuade Emily and some friends to help on the actual sale days.

"Let's just get on with it," she suggested.

They all went back to staring at the piles that nearly blocked the doorway.

"I guess we have to carry the boxes outside," Emily said.

Like there was a choice. But Beth steered clear of sarcasm.

"Sure. I already labeled the empty ones I brought." A blind person could see them—*Keep, Thrift, Garage Sale?? Toss*—but she hadn't given up on the aren't-we-going-to-have-fun vibe. Although, truthfully, even she felt daunted by the sheer quantity of *stuff* in the garage.

This being her idea, she stepped forward and grabbed a rubber tote, carrying it the few feet into the backyard, where they could make piles that wouldn't get in the way. Her brother and sister followed suit. Beth had already peeled the lid off her tote. "Huh," she said.

In the act of opening a cardboard box, Matt glanced over. "What?"

Beth wrinkled her nose. "I think these are student papers Dad graded. But wouldn't he have handed them back?"

Silly question. Maybe, admiring the literary excellence, he'd asked the students to return them to *him.* So he could store them in his garage.

She almost wondered aloud whether they should consult Dad about something like this, until she saw the date on one of the papers on top. 1987. She dug through, finding graded tests, multiple copies of articles he must have photocopied for student use and either never handed out or requested back so he could use them again. It didn't surprise her at all that he hadn't remembered he had them. He could easily have photocopied the same article a year later with no memory of having done so before.

Yes, that was her father. Super smart, and completely vague. He'd been teaching philosophy at the community college for thirty-something years. He either had no ambition to teach at a four-year university, or he couldn't take the possibility he would be rejected if he applied or... Yet another unanswerable question where Dad was concerned. He had this weird disconnect.

Beth sighed, hefted the box again and carried it around the corner of the garage to the recycling container parked in the narrow space between the wall and the six-foot fence. There was a thump as the heaps of paper hit the bottom.

One box down.

THEY HADN'T BEEN at it an hour when the first quarrel erupted. Beth didn't count the usual low-level bickering.

"Ooh!" Emily breathed. "Christmas ornaments. Remember? We never found the ones—"

"Give me those." Matt grabbed the box from her, stared into it with his face flushed dark, then carried it to where the garbage and garbage containers were parked. Both of his sisters raced after him.

"Don't do that!" Emily cried.

"Matt, *stop*," Beth snapped. "Just because you—"

He nudged the lid of the garbage can off with his elbow and turned the white cardboard box upside down before she could finish her sentence. Glass shattered.

Mouth open in outrage, Emily rushed forward to stare into the can. "I wanted those!" Swinging around, she punched Matt. Ineffectually, but still.

He only stared at his sister. "Why would you want anything that was *hers*?"

Then he stormed toward the backyard.

Emily's big blue eyes filled with tears. "That was *mean*!"

Yes, it was. Frustrated with Matt, Beth nevertheless understood how he felt. Their mother had walked out on them, not even bothering to stay in touch. Beth had been fifteen years old, Matt seventeen, Emily only twelve. Beth understood why Mom had left Dad. It was a miracle she hadn't years sooner. She must have thought she was marrying a gentle, sensitive man, who instead was both helpless where daily life was concerned and weirdly oblivious to the real people who also lived in the house. Even Beth sometimes felt like his mother. Witness today. What was she doing but rescuing Dad again? Imagine being *married* to a man you started seeing that way?

But Emily had been especially close to their mother, and was still childish in many ways. Would it have been so bad to let her have the Christmas ornaments Mom had hung on the tree every year? The ones they'd later replaced with standard-issue red and gold balls?

Emily raced after Matt to yell at him. Beth peered into the garbage can, thinking she might be able to rescue a few ornaments, but *eew.* Dad had dumped some disgusting leftovers straight into the can without bagging them first.

She backed away, then made herself pick up the lid and put it on.

She marched up to Matt, poked him in the chest with her index finger and said, "That was *not* your decision. Nobody asked you to take those ornaments home and treasure them forever. If they meant something to Emily, she had the right to keep them. Smashing them in front of her was cruel."

"I told you!" Emily cried.

His mouth tightened, and he glowered at Beth but after a minute nodded stiffly.

Are we having fun yet?

Behind her brother, the French door to the dining room opened, and Dad stepped out onto the patio, looking surprised to see them.

"Did I know you were going to be here today?"

Matt snarled and retreated out of sight.

"Yes, Dad." Beth made herself smile, go to her father and kiss his cheek. "I told you we were going to unbury the garage. Just think, you might be able to park inside it."

His forehead pleated, giving his narrow face a concerned look. "You won't throw away anything important, will you?"

"Of course not." She hugged him. "Anyway, how important can it be if you haven't seen it in ten years or more?"

"Well…" A bright and charming smile grew on his face. "You have a point." He greeted Emily absently, gazed at the open door and the shadow of his son inside with apparent perplexity, then said, "I'm working on something. If you need me…" He was already fading away. Beth had no doubt that five minutes from now, he'd have forgotten his children were here. If their voices caught his attention again, he'd probably remember, puzzle over why they'd want to waste time on such a tedious task and go back to his reading.

"Is he gone?" Matt hissed.

"It's safe."

Emily smirked. "Olly olly oxen free."

Cautiously reappearing, Matt said, "Brat."

"Jerk."

Peace restored. Temporarily.

SUNDAY MORNING, Beth ripped tape off the top of a big cardboard box she'd dragged from beneath the long-forgotten workbench and folded back the flaps to see clothes inside. This wasn't the first—

JANICE KAY JOHNSON   15

they'd found countless boxes of children's clothes, neatly folded and presumably saved by Mom for the next baby. Beth was beginning to think Mom had saved every scrap Matt had ever worn, certain she'd have another boy. There were girl clothes, too, but they'd been handed down once, and Emily had worn some of them out. Why hadn't Mom realized at some point that, nope, she wasn't having another kid, period, and maybe she ought to get rid of all the tough-boy toddler-size overalls and sweaters with tractors and rocket ships decorating the front?

Huh. Maybe this disaster wasn't totally Dad's fault. Maybe Mom had had her own pack rat tendencies. Beth remembered stories about how poor her mother's family had been when she was growing up. Maybe that kind of upbringing ingrained in a person the belief that it was best to hold on to anything that might conceivably be useful later.

This box, though… The clothes had just been dumped in it. Beth poked a little and realized that not only were these adult-size but each garment was still hooked on a clothes hanger. She reached in and lifted out a blouse. Pale pink with subtle white stripes. Mom had loved pink. She wore a lot of it. Petite, blonde and blue-eyed, like Emily, Christine Marshall had embodied femininity.

Beth was vaguely aware that Matt was slowly turning to her. "I remember this blouse," she whispered.

He swore and took a couple of steps to look into the box. He started to reach for a dress but pulled his hand back. "It's the clothes she didn't take. Dad must have wanted them out of sight."

Beth's stomach tightened. Even her father had emerged from his alternate world briefly when his wife disappeared. She'd left Word open on the computer with a note explaining that she was leaving him and she'd be in touch when she was settled. After that…nothing.

Dad had called the police, who hadn't been interested. Christine had taken her purse, her birth control pills out of the medicine cabinet, some of her makeup and jewelry. Obviously, she'd left voluntarily.

Beth, Matt and Emily had refused to believe she would do that. Leave Dad, sure. She'd taken to yelling at him a lot. But she wouldn't have abandoned her children. She, of all people, had known how inadequate he was as a parent. For a long time Beth, at least, had held on to the belief that Mom would fight for custody once she had a new job and someplace to live.

"She loved this blouse." Beth could hardly take her eyes off it. "Why didn't she take more of her clothes?"

"Because she left in a hurry?" Matt suggested, old anger roughening his voice. "Maybe she thought she'd try a new style for a new man."

"Maybe." Seeing her sister's distress, she shook herself. "Well. This is sort of creepy, but I can see why Dad didn't want to get rid of everything."

"I'll bet I'm the same size she was." Emily stepped forward. "There might be clothes I'd like."

Not even thinking it through, Beth dropped the blouse back into the box and slapped the flaps closed. "No."

Looking indignant, her sister said, "What do you mean, *no*?"

Matt turned on her. "Don't you speak English? She means *no*. *N.O*."

"Don't talk to me that way."

Beth shut her eyes and sought her equilibrium. A couple deep breaths, and she was back. "Emily, I hate the idea of seeing you in some shirt I associate with her, and obviously Matt feels the same."

"Dumpster," he said, sounding hard.

Beth shook her head. "Can we just set this aside? Keep it for now?"

"Why?"

"I don't know. I just…don't want to make that decision yet. Anyway…" She hesitated. "Her clothes were nice. When we do get rid of them, they should go to a thrift store or maybe a women's shelter." She didn't include *garage sale*. What if she breathed in the faint scent of her mother while she was handling her mother's clothes. Attaching little price tags. The idea made her shiver.

He frowned at her but gave an abrupt nod. "Up to you." Matt went back to the box of books he'd been looking at one by one.

Logically enough—if anything about this was logical—Beth found half a dozen more boxes filled with her mother's stuff in the same vicinity. Shoes, too, of course, but mostly clothes, including one that had lingerie on top. She closed that box really fast. Even the thrift store wouldn't want old, used panties and bras. She was tempted to write *Toss* in big black letters on the side but knew she ought to dig deeper in the box before she did that.

Matt and even Emily stayed away from the section of the garage where Beth was working. Emily kept stealing wary glances at her, and no wonder. She was used to a calm, competent, I-can-solve-all-problems sister, not one who freaked at the sight of a pink blouse.

Beth uncovered Mom's jewelry box and couldn't resist peeking inside. Tangled chains were jumbled with earrings and bracelets. Mom had obviously taken some of her nicer pieces, except…was that a *real* diamond in a stud earring? Beth didn't remember her mother wearing those. After a moment, she put the box back, setting it on top. She'd want to go through this later. Eventually. There might be something in here that Emily would like as a keepsake. The rest...well, anything that wasn't too familiar or particularly valuable could go to the thrift store.

A wave of exhaustion and discouragement hit her. After a full day yesterday, her muscles ached, too. Her back to Matt and Emily, Beth leaned against the workbench. What happened to her plan to go through everything, make brisk decisions, be done with it?

Speed bump, she told herself. They'd been moving along pretty well. She'd been right that most of what they'd found would be useful to someone. Matt had agreed to ask his wife if she'd like to go through the boxes of children's clothes before they passed them on. She was pregnant with their first baby.

The next box held things Beth didn't really recognize but guessed to have been from Mom and Dad's bedroom. She opened a stiff portfolio to find unframed art prints. Worth looking at later.

Finally, she shoved all the remaining boxes associated with Mom back under and on top of the built-in workbench, which her father would never use. Home repair was not on his list of skills. She'd left the window above the workbench unblocked, making a mental note to come back with some glass cleaner. Even so, the light falling through the window helped.

Pulling herself together, she decided to tackle the things piled against the wall beside the workbench next. An ancient Weedwacker. Could it have come with the house? Several fans on stands, wrapped in white plastic trash bags, must have been out here forever. A folded stepladder. More boxes.

Beth sighed.

Wallboard had covered the garage walls as long as she could remember, which meant it was discolored and battered. Nobody had ever taped or spackled or painted out here. She could just see wall-hung shelves on the other side of the garage. Probably *that* was where the oldest stuff was. Anybody would fill shelves before starting to pile junk on the floor, right?

Strange, though—the one sheet of wallboard in front of her looked a little different from the rest. Not really clean, but clean*er*, except for some gross but long-dry stains at the bottom. None of the dings, either. Maybe Mom and Dad had had it replaced at some point. If so, it had to have been put up shortly before the piles grew in front of it, protecting it. Except for a big hole bashed into it six or seven feet up. Something had probably smacked it. The extension ladder lying on a sheet of plywood suspended from the ceiling in the middle of the garage, right above the tracks and motor for the automatic garage door opener? Maybe. It would have been awkward to maneuver.

She doubted her father even knew he owned a tall ladder. He certainly wouldn't have any use for it. Once upon a time, Mom had nagged him into occasional tasks like painting. Later, if something obviously needed doing, he hired someone. Well, Beth hired someone. He'd look surprised but pay the bill without complaining.

Back to work.

Fans—thrift store. Or garage sale, if she had one. Stepladder—who didn't need one? If Dad didn't want it, she'd take it. The Weedwacker? It could probably be recycled, even rusty.

For some reason, the gaping hole kept drawing her gaze. Matt and Emily had moved their squabbling outside. They wouldn't see her give in to an inexplicable compulsion. She unfolded the stepladder and climbed up on it.

A flashlight would have helped, but at least the window was close. Beth angled her head to see down inside the wall. Her heart began to drum at the sight of something…

She screamed, lurched back and tumbled off the step stool.

TONY NAVARRO ADDED gas to his lawn mower, carried the can to the garage, wiped sweat from his face, then pulled the cord to start the damn thing again. Not too far to go, which was good. July in eastern Washington was hot. He should have gotten the mowing done during an evening this week, when it was cooler. Keeping up with his own yard and his mother's and often one or even a couple of his sisters', though, that got time-consuming.

A vibration in the pocket of his jeans had him sighing. *Please, not work.* He needed the day off. Bad enough he'd already caught shit from his mother for not going to church.

He let the mower die and pulled out his phone. Unfortunately, he knew the number all too well.

"Navarro. Isn't there anyone else who can take this?"

"I'm afraid not, Detective." The dispatcher sounded genuinely regretful. "Detective Troyer is on vacation, and—"

"Beck isn't back to work yet. I know." With a broken leg, David Beck wouldn't have to mow lawns, either. Jack Moore…no, he was caught up in a messy investigation. Tony sighed again. "What do you got?"

"This is a strange one," she said. "Somebody noticed a hole in the wallboard in their garage and took a look in it. He says they can see a human hand. Kind of…withered. His words."

Tony swore. "It didn't occur to this guy it's probably some discarded Halloween decoration?"

"I don't know. He was pretty shaken up."

Thus, she hadn't sent a uniform to check it out. She'd called *him*. What could he do but commit the address to memory?

Glad he'd been mowing his own lawn and not another family member's, he was able to go inside for a quick shower and change of clothes. Badge and weapon. Out the door.

The address he'd been given wasn't half a mile from his house. Homeowner was listed as John Marshall. Caller had been a Matt Marshall.

He could get in, he calculated, look, soothe the homeowners and be home firing up his lawn mower again in forty-five minutes, tops.

To his dismay, in that half mile, he passed from the neighborhoods made up of ranch-style homes, mostly built from the 1960s to the '70s, to those with older houses. These weren't as fancy as the ones close to Wakefield College, a private, very expensive, liberal arts school. Those had been handsomely restored. The bungalows on this block weren't rundown, but homeowners hadn't done much but keep up the painting and neatly mow the lawns. Still, they were constructed differently than newer homes. A two-by-four really *was* two inches by four inches, for example, rather than the current, abbreviated size still called by the misleading dimensions. Walls might be even deeper than that, the supports farther apart than in modern construction, too. He'd been counting on the fact that stuffing a body in a typical wall of a house like his was next to impossible, unless it was child-size. Here…he couldn't say *impossible*.

He spotted the right number on a white house accented with a bland beige. 1940s, at a guess. The lawn in front was brown—no one here had bothered watering. The detached garage was set back a little farther from the street than the house. Tony had expected the garage door to be open, but it wasn't. Two vehicles filled the driveway, and two more were parked at the curb in front of the house. A six-foot fence and gate blocked his view into the backyard.

Tony parked in front of a neighbor's home, grabbed his flashlight and walked up the driveway. Before he could veer toward the front door, the gate swung open and a young woman appeared from between the house and garage. Brown hair was starting to straggle out of a ponytail. Dirt streaked one of her gently rounded cheeks. Her nose, too—no, those were freckles. Maybe her hair was more chestnut, with a hint of red?

"Oh! You're not…" She spotted the badge and holstered gun at his hip and faltered, "Are you?" She blushed. "I mean, are you a police officer?"

"I'm Detective Tony Navarro, Frenchman Lake P.D. And you are?"

"I'm sorry." She shook her head. "I'm rattled,

and—" Breaking off again, she shook her head. "I'm Bethany Marshall. Beth. This is my dad's house. He teaches at the community college."

Tony nodded, still at sea but figuring she'd get to the point soon.

"Dad…well, he's a typical absent-minded professor. It had gotten so the garage was so crammed full of stuff, you could hardly set foot in it. So my brother and sister and I are spending the weekend sorting and getting rid of things. You know."

It had to have been the brother who'd called, then. "Where's your father?"

She looked surprised. "He's in the house. He's not much good at this kind of thing."

Okay.

"You see, we found…" She visibly stumbled over what they'd found. "Well, I guess I should just show you."

Now, there was an idea.

"Let's do that, Ms. Marshall," he agreed and followed her lead through the gate and alongside the house, past a garbage can and a recycling container.

He let himself get a little distracted by Beth Marshall, who had a truly womanly body. No matchstick arms here. He wouldn't describe her as plump, though, just curvy. He happened to like his women curvaceous instead of the currently

fashionable stick-thin, so he savored the sight of
her while he could.

Two people waited anxiously in the backyard,
along with mountains of packed boxes that had
been labeled *Thrift*, *Keep* and the like. The man
said, "Beth?" and then saw Tony behind her.
"Somebody came." He sounded stressed. Tall,
lean and handsome in a way that might be polished if he weren't also sweaty, dirty and disheveled, this had to be the brother. His arm sheltered
a young woman, a cute blonde with blue eyes that
were puffy and a scattering of freckles across her
nose. The youngest of the three, Tony guessed,
and probably considered prettier than Beth by
most people.

He introduced himself again and got their
names. Matt Marshall and Emily Marshall. Were
neither of the sisters married? He let his gaze slide
to Beth's left hand. No ring. Did any of them still
live at home?

"Okay, let me take a look," he said.

Matt started to move, but Beth shook her head.
"I'll show him."

"You should sit down."

"I'm okay." She gave an unconvincing smile.
"Just bruises. Really."

"Bruises?" Tony asked, once again following
her, this time through a side door into the shadowy confines of the garage.

Glancing over her shoulder, she wrinkled her nose. "I fell off the stepladder."

"Ah." He hated to envision her creamy skin blotched with the ugly colors of bruises.

Concentrate. He looked around. The siblings had cleared close to two-thirds of the garage, assuming it had been completely full to start with. Boxes and what looked like a lot of crap were still packed against the far wall. Tony mentally transferred the piles out in the backyard into here and thought, *Holy shit.* Beth had been understating the problem. Which made him wonder what the interior of the house was like.

Not his problem.

He saw the stepladder right away, and took in the single sheet of wallboard that subtly didn't match the rest. Stains at the bottom, where bodily fluids would have pooled. Instantly snapping into cop mode, he had a bad feeling he wasn't wasting his time after all. Didn't look like he'd finish mowing his lawn today.

Beth hovered behind him as he mounted the ladder. He was careful not to touch the wallboard and snapped on the military-grade flashlight he carried in his left hand. It lit a slice of the interior between two-by-fours.

Despite what he'd seen in his years as a cop, the mummified human hand made his skin crawl. He could see some of the wrist—and the top of a head, the hair blond, stringy, dull but still attached. The size of the hand and arm bone and the length of hair made him believe he was looking at a woman.

How long had she been walled up in the garage of this house? And who was she?

CHAPTER TWO

BETH SAW THE detective go utterly still. When he finally stepped down and faced her, his expression had been wiped clean, but she could feel his tension.

"I need to make a call or two," he said. "I'd appreciate it if you'd wait outside, Ms. Marshall."

However pleasantly phrased, it was an order. She nodded and hurried out into the sunlight.

"What?" her brother demanded.

"I don't know. He looked, said he has to make calls and asked that we wait out here."

"Damn, it's hot," Matt muttered.

Beth saw how pink Emily's face was. Her own face felt too warm. They should have long since renewed their sunscreen. After putting it on first thing this morning, she'd dropped it in her tote bag, currently sitting on the workbench. "We could go inside, get something to drink," she suggested.

"Make conversation with Dad?"

"Would that be the worst thing in the world?"

His mouth tightened. "Let's just sit in the shade."

"I'll get the cooler. We can at least have drinks."

While a police detective decided what to do about the dead woman encased in the wall of the house, she thought, semi-hysterically. Whoever she was, she might have been there the whole time Beth and the others had lived here. As a kid, she'd never have noticed that the wallboard looked a little different. Although…didn't she used to leave her bike there? Often letting it tip over and bash the wall?

When she went into the garage, she saw the detective's broad back and his phone at his ear. Somehow he heard her, though, because he swung around, his dark eyes locking onto her.

Until now, she hadn't fully let herself notice how handsome he was. Coppery-brown skin stretched over some impressive cheekbones and a strong jaw. A lot of the Hispanic farmworkers she saw in town were stocky and on the short side. The detective had to be close to six feet tall and athletic in a broad-shouldered, lean way. As his name suggested, he had black hair and the darkest eyes she'd ever seen.

He also carried an alarmingly large gun at his hip.

Trying to hide her shiver, she scurried to the small cooler, lifted it for his inspection, and waited for his nod before retreating outside with it. Matt and Emily had pulled folding lawn chairs against the back wall of the house, where the sun, high in the sky, granted them a meager two feet of shade. Since there wasn't a third chair—they'd come across these in the garage yesterday—Beth sank cross-legged onto the stiff, brown grass and opened the cooler.

"Who wants what?"

Emily peered over her shoulder. "Diet cola."

Matt took an energy drink, Beth water. Her body sighed in relief to be sitting, but she became more aware of the painful spot on her butt where she'd landed on the concrete floor, and one almost as bad on her shoulder. Plus, her nerves felt as if they were being stretched on a medieval rack. What was the detective saying? When would he come out to talk to them? Meantime, she prayed her father hadn't noticed the new arrival, wouldn't emerge to see what was going on. It was bad enough to imagine Detective Navarro interviewing Dad, but Beth didn't need the stress of dealing with him right now.

Matt stared straight ahead. Beyond him, Emily curled forward, clutching her drink and seemingly studying the grass, or maybe her feet. Beth's gaze darted from her sister and brother to the corner of the house that hid the side door into the garage, to the brick patio, then back to start all over again. What probably wasn't more than a couple minutes felt like an eternity.

Detective Navarro appeared, even more intimidating than he'd been when she first saw him. Beth wished he had a more expressive face.

Emily straightened and stared at him.

Matt stood. "So?"

"I'm confident enough those are human remains that I have a CSI team on the way. I don't want to touch anything until they photograph and fingerprint the section of wall that will have to be torn out."

On a shudder, Beth hugged her knees. She'd known but still hoped he would say, "I don't know what we're looking at, but it's not human."

"I'd like to talk to you individually, but first, let me ask a few general questions."

Nobody said anything.

"How long has your family been in this house?"

It was Beth who said, "Something like thirty years."

"Do any of you still live here?"

Matt shook his head. "Of course not. We're adults. I work in the Admissions Department at Wakefield. I'm married and own my own home."

"I work for the county agency dealing with long-term care and aging," Beth said. "I rent a townhouse a few blocks from downtown."

His gaze shifted to Emily.

"What *difference* does it make what we do for a living?" she burst out.

"It probably doesn't. I'm trying to get a picture of your family, that's all."

She sniffed and, looking remarkably childlike, swiped the back of her hand beneath her nose. "I work at a chiropractor's office. Dr. Findley. I'm a massage therapist. And I have an apartment near the community college with some friends."

His eyes met Beth's. "I gathered from you that your father lives in the house. What about your mother?"

THE SEEMINGLY INNOCUOUS question froze all three people, who suddenly had a deer-in-the-headlights look that sharpened Tony's interest.

Beth and the brother glanced at each other. She was apparently elected to answer.

"Our mother left Dad when I was fifteen, so… thirteen years ago. Obviously, we stayed with him."

A man she'd described as a typical absent-minded professor. Apparently, a man incapable of keeping his own home organized in any minimal way, who was, in fact, indoors at the moment, not even lending a hand. Because—how had she put it?—*he's not much good at this kind of thing.* Yeah, that was it.

"Did you maintain visitation with her?" he asked.

"No," Beth said, so softly he just heard her.

Horror showed in her eyes before she looked down at her hands. She knew what he was think-ing. "Mom just…went. When she didn't call or anything, Dad reported her missing. The police thought it was clear she'd chosen to leave."

"On what basis?"

Matt answered, his tone curt and edged with old anger. "She left a note on the computer. Took her purse, some of her jewelry and I guess some clothes."

"Birth control pills and toiletries," Beth added.

"Car?"

They all shook their heads at once.

"Was a suitcase gone?"

Matt and Beth looked at each other again, leav-ing Emily out. With reason, Tony realized. She'd have been eleven or twelve, maybe, when their mother had run away.

"I don't know," Matt said. "I don't remember anyone saying. I mean, why wouldn't she have used one when she packed?"

Did he really not get it? "I presume your father can tell us," he said.

He was beginning to find those silent exchanges irritating. He should have separated the siblings from the beginning.

"I sort of doubt he'll remember," Beth said. "He's…kind of vague about details. You'll see."

Mentally ill? If he was still teaching at the college level, could he be? Tony's curiosity about the man grew.

"I should speak to him next," he said.

Beth jumped up. "Let me get him for you."

He moved fast, staying right behind her when she dashed for the French doors. She cast him a startled glance when she realized how close he was, but damned if he'd let her warn her father in any way.

She pushed open the door, letting cool air spill out, and called, "Dad?"

"Beth?" A pleasant tenor voice preceded the man. "That you?"

"Yes, there's someone here to see you."

As soon as he saw her father, Tony had to discard preconceptions he hadn't realized he'd formed. The guy didn't have a receding hairline, reading glasses perched on the end of his nose or narrow, stooped shoulders. No sweater vest or corduroy jacket with leather patches on the elbows, either. If he smoked a pipe, Tony couldn't smell it.

Instead, the man was tall, thin, handsome, his brown hair graying at the temples. He hadn't shaved today, and his stubble was clearly gray. Tony saw a resemblance to Matt, in particular, and perhaps to Beth in the bone structure and shape of the eyes. Only Matt's coloring—blond and blue-eyed, like his younger sister—kept him from being the spitting image of his father.

Tony couldn't help recalling the straw-yellow hair he'd glimpsed inside the garage wall.

"Bethie?" Perplexity had her father looking from his daughter to Tony. "Who's this?"

Tony stepped into a comfortable family room with aging carpet and furnishings. Floor-to-ceiling, built-in bookcases covered one wall.

"Mr. Marshall? I'm Detective Navarro with the Frenchman Lake Police Department."

"Police department? Are you a friend of Beth's?"

"I'm afraid not, sir. I need to talk to you about something your son and daughters found in the garage. Perhaps we could sit down."

Appearing bewildered, he sank onto a well-worn recliner that faced a television. "Certainly, but... I don't understand."

"Dad, we found something upsetting—"

Tony laid a hand on her arm, silencing her with a shake of his head. "Ms. Marshall, if you wouldn't mind, I'd like to speak to your father alone."

Alarm flashed in her hazel eyes, but she subdued it enough to nod and say, "I understand."

Her father watched her go outside with a concerned expression he transferred to Tony. "Is something wrong?"

How was it possible that not one of his three adult children had gone into the house to say,

Hey, Dad, we found something strange? Especially given that this was *his* house. *His* garage.

Tony went for blunt. "We've found what appears to be a human body behind wallboard in your garage."

John Marshall only stared at him. "Did you say a *body*?"

"Yes, sir."

"But…who found it? How?"

"There was an old hole in one sheet of wallboard. Beth took a look in it and called us. I agree that it does appear to be human remains. Crime scene investigators will be here shortly." Undoubtedly as thrilled as he was to lose their Sunday off. "In the meantime, I need to ask you some questions."

"I don't understand. Nobody has gone into the garage in years. How could someone have gotten in, or—" Even he boggled at the unlikelihood of a killer getting around decades' worth of accumulated belongings to stash a body.

"I suspect the remains have been there for many years, Mr. Marshall. The body appears to be at least partially mummified, which can happen under some circumstances in a dry climate like ours." Insect-free circumstances, as this would have been until the damage opened the hole, likely much later. He paused. "Because you reported your wife missing, I need to ask about her."

Obviously perturbed, Marshall said, "The police were convinced she'd left on her own."

"I understand you found a note."

"Yes, when I sat down at the computer that evening and moved the mouse, I found that Word was open to a document she must have created. It was brief."

"Do you still have it?"

He shook his head. "We've replaced that computer several times since. I'm sure I printed it for that police officer, but I didn't need to for myself." Old pain parted the curtain of vagueness. "I could tell you what it said word for word."

Tony preferred to locate the printout in a file at the station. On an investigation, he rarely trusted anyone.

"Did the police fingerprint the computer mouse?" he asked.

"It was only one officer, and he didn't suggest anything like that. He really wasn't here very long."

Tony understood. People went missing all the time. Law enforcement response was quite different when a child disappeared, but adults most often did turn up later.

"We thought she'd call."

"Had you quarreled right before she disappeared?"

"Right before?" he said in apparent surprise.

"Well, I don't know. That was a long time ago. She'd been annoyed with me, but I hoped whatever was bothering her would pass."

Tony barely refrained from shaking his head. How could this guy fail to grasp the implications here? *Well, sure, she and I weren't getting along. Save the note on the computer? Why would I do that?*

"*Did* you hear from her?" It was conceivable he wouldn't have told his kids, depending on what was said. Or that he'd choose to lie now.

"Never a word." He sounded puzzled. "Didn't seem like Christine, but... Bethie was old enough to take over helping her sister and making meals, so nothing changed all that much."

Unbelievable. His wife vanished into thin air, but in his view, nothing much changed because, hey, his fifteen-year-old daughter stepped up and kept the family running. Either John Marshall was the most self-centered human being Tony had ever encountered, or he was guilty as hell. Maybe both.

The conglomeration of stuff in the garage made sense now. Tony was willing to bet a pile of boxes had started growing at that exact spot in the garage shortly after Christine Marshall had run away from home. There was a good chance, in fact, that her husband had immediately made sure the one stretch of wall wasn't visible, in case the police actually troubled to do a walk-through of the house.

Tony rose to his feet. "Thank you for your time, Mr. Marshall. I need to ask you to stay out of the garage. We'll block both doors with yellow tape."

A look of glazed bewilderment was all the response he received.

As he went out the French door, he heard a spate of voices. The department's two crime scene investigators must have just come around the side of the house, both suited up in white Tyvek and carrying a toolbox, camera and more. Matt and Beth had obviously hopped right up, while the baby sister didn't bother. Arms wrapped around herself, she had summoned an expression that was a cross between pouty and distressed. Was self-centeredness hereditary?

"Jess," Tony said, nodding. "Larry."

They both appeared grateful to see him. Their job didn't usually include a lot of interaction with victims' families.

He looked at the Marshall siblings. "You might want to wait inside with your father."

"Can't we go home?" Emily blurted. "Do we *have* to sit here?"

"Do you all have your own cars?"

Nodded heads.

"That's fine, then. Let me get phone numbers and addresses first."

Beth's chin jutted out. "I'm not going anywhere."

"Neither am I," her brother said, suddenly belligerent.

Tony raised his eyebrows but only said mildly, "That's up to you."

He jotted down Emily's contact info. She fervently hugged Matt and Beth, then fled.

No loss.

Tony stepped into the garage to join his team. Individual interviews with the siblings could wait until he knew what he was dealing with.

BETH WENT TO check on her father, to find him sitting in his recliner, staring into space. He must not have moved.

"Dad? Are you all right?"

He turned his head. "How could this happen?"

"You mean, us noticing something was off and checking it out?"

"No, that the detective asked questions about your mother." His fingers bit into the arms of the recliner. "I don't understand."

"I don't, either," she admitted, going to perch on the upholstered arm of his chair, where she could give him a quick hug.

More agitated than she'd ever seen him, he didn't even seem to notice her embrace. "Are they *sure*?"

"I don't think so, yet." Although, Detective Navarro wouldn't have called a CSI team if he wasn't reasonably sure.

CSI. In our house. The idea was unreal. In those white getups, they actually looked like the swarm of investigators in the background on TV shows like *NCIS*.

"I guess we'll find out," she added. "Can I get you anything?"

He shook his head and, after waiting for a minute, Beth went outside to join Matt, once more planted in a lawn chair. She picked up her drink, which already felt warm, and sat in the other chair.

"I freaking can't believe this," he muttered.

"Me either."

He turned a look of pure hostility on her. "You and your bright ideas."

Beth's mouth dropped open. "This is *my* fault?" Except, she thought guiltily, it kind of was. Her idea to clean out the garage, her curiosity that led her to look inside the hole.

"What if they open the garage door?"

Surprised, she said, "They haven't?"

"One of them went out and got a couple of portable lamps." He snorted. "Like everyone on the block and everyone driving by hasn't noticed two police vehicles out in front of Dad's house."

She frowned. "I don't actually think the detective came in a police car. He was driving a pickup truck."

"Oh, that means no one will ever hear about this," Matt said sarcastically.

"*That's* what you're most worried about?" Although why she was surprised she couldn't have said. Appearances had always mattered more to Matt than to her. Still. "What if that's *Mom*? What if she's been dead all these years, and we thought she'd left us?"

"What if our father gets tried for murder?"

The air left her lungs in a rush. "That's ridiculous! How can you think for a *minute*—"

"Who else, Beth? Use your head, for once."

"For once? What are you talking about?"

"You live in your own damn dream world, just like *he* does. Everybody is *nice*. Well-meaning."

Her mouth fell open. Did she know this brother, mocking her so cruelly?

"Nobody ever abuses a frail old man, do they?" His voice rose. "Nobody steals, beats her kid, cooks meth and sells it. And nobody ever murders his wife!"

Matt was yelling by the end. Beth wasn't at all surprised to see Detective Navarro stepping into sight. Eavesdropping, of course, but he couldn't help but have heard.

"You shut up," she said fiercely to her brother. "You've never been fair to Dad. Do you think he can *help* being...being..."

Her brother's lip curled. "Out to lunch?"

"Don't say that!" Even though, God, it was true.

He made a scoffing sound and looked away, which meant he, too, noticed the detective. "*What?*"

Navarro's dark eyebrows twitched. "You've lost your shade."

No wonder she was roasting. She should retreat to the house—but she couldn't stand her father's company right now.

"Ms. Marshall." His voice was unexpectedly gentle. "You're getting sunburned."

Of all moments to realize how attracted she was to this man. Noticing his looks wasn't anything like this intense awareness of his body, and hers, too. Her cheeks burned even hotter at the even remote possibility he might see what she was thinking. And...how could she feel anything like that *now*?

"I...my tote bag is in the garage. I have sunscreen in it."

"I'll get it for you." He disappeared for barely a minute, returning with the waterproof bag she usually used for her swimsuit and towel.

She started to push herself to her feet, but the detective came right to her, handing over the bag. Almost touching her. He studied her with those deep brown eyes. "You really should get out of the sun."

"I know. It's just..." Beth trailed off.

"You want to stay in case your father needs you."

"Yes," she admitted. "But—" She couldn't continue. *That doesn't mean I can sit in the silence of the house and pretend nothing is wrong.* She sighed.

He nodded, the understanding on his face enough to make her want to crumple. Which she didn't do. She was the strong one in this family. She'd never minded being a prop for the rest of them.

"There's some shade under the tree," he pointed out.

"We'll move." She summoned a smile for his kindness, lifting the tote bag a little. "Thank you for this."

His hardening gaze moved to Matt. Which Matt totally deserved.

She watched Detective Navarro go into the garage, then stood. Without a word, she slung the tote bag over her shoulder, grabbed the chair and the cooler, and marched across the crunchy lawn to the huge old crab apple tree. Beneath its branches she sat down. She looked up from digging in the bag for the lotion and saw Matt carrying his own chair over to join her.

"I'm sorry," he said, voice low. "I shouldn't have said any of that. This is just…" His gesture was meant to encompass this completely terrible day.

"I understand." She squirted a white glob on her hand and offered the tube of lotion to him.

Quiet now, they both rubbed lotion into their faces, necks, arms and hands. Beth dabbed some on the tips of her ears. They hadn't been outside that much, but the day was really hot, and she burned easily. Matt had more of a tan. He and Ashley were both runners and liked to hike and backpack, too. He also had yard work to do.

"Did you call Ashley?" she asked.

He thrust his fingers into his hair. "I should, but... Man, I keep thinking this will all go away."

"Maybe it won't turn out to be a body."

"Sure. That's why they've been in there for—" he pulled his phone from his pocket and checked the time "—almost forty-five minutes."

Had it really been that long? Heartsick, Beth gazed at the garage and tried not to imagine what was happening in there. The ridiculous attraction she'd felt for the man who might this minute be examining her mother's dead body? There could be any number of explanations. She latched onto heatstroke. That was as rational as anything else.

TONY WATCHED AS Jess and Larry eased the contorted remains away from the constricted space between the two-by-fours, wrapping as they went to keep it as intact as possible, using the open black body bag as a tarp to be sure they didn't

lose anything that fell out with the body—or *off*
the body—some of which was down to bones. He
couldn't look away.

Like most cops, he'd seen his share of dead people. Vehicular accidents could do hideous things
to a human being. Domestic violence, strangling,
gunshots, he'd seen the effects of all of them.
None compared to these remains that were more
disturbing by a long shot than finding only bones.

He'd seen photographs of Egyptian mummies,
unwrapped to display withered brown flesh. He'd
even read about a couple of cases where deaths
had gone unnoticed until someone found a mummified body sitting in front of a television.

None of that had prepared him for the reality.

Once they had begun cutting the wallboard to
remove it, he'd locked the door and taped coverings
over both the window and the pane of glass in the
door. He hated the idea that any of this woman's
children would ever see so much as a photograph
of what she looked like now.

That was assuming this *was* Christine Marshall, but he didn't have a lot of doubt. Missing
woman? Body found in the same house? As his
own father used to say, it didn't take a rocket sci-
entist.

This woman was petite. If she'd been any bigger,
she couldn't have been squeezed into such a narrow space. Even so, the angle of the feet—skeletal

except for some gristle—suggested the killer had broken her ankles to make her flat enough to cover with wallboard.

The blond hair was suggestive, too, as were her teeth. They didn't look like a young woman's, displaying a number of metal fillings on molars and at least one crown. She still wore a polyester blouse that was apparently indestructible, as were nylon panties. No trousers, shoes or socks. His guess was that she'd been killed as she started to get dressed, maybe after sex. She could have been surprised from behind.

Jess and Larry laid the bag and body on the cement floor. She stood, staring down in pity and the horrified fascination Tony suspected was on his own face.

Crouching beside the dead woman, Larry shook his head. "I don't know whether the ME can deal with a body in this condition, or whether we'll have to hunt down a forensic anthropologist."

"Morgue van on the way?" Tony asked.

Jess glanced at him. "Yes. It'll mean opening the big door, you know."

He did. So far, they'd shuttled whatever they needed from the van to the side door, hoping to avoid awakening too much interest from neighbors. What they'd found wouldn't stay a secret for any length of time, though.

"Once that's done, I'll go talk to the family again. Get her dentist's name."

"Bitch of a scene," Jess said sympathetically.

"No shit." And it was barely the beginning of the investigation.

CHAPTER THREE

MATT DEPARTED FIRST, which didn't surprise Tony. Figured he'd leave his sister holding the bag. It was clear he and his father didn't get along—maybe didn't even speak. Tony wondered how Beth had talked him into helping with the great garage cleanup.

Something else had occurred to Tony, too. Matt would have been nearly an adult when his mother disappeared. Seventeen or eighteen. He'd have towered over her. What if he'd come home unexpectedly and caught her with a lover, say? Words could have exploded into rage.

Leaning against the back wall of the house, Tony shook his head. He was being premature. Tomorrow, they'd know from dental records whether this was Christine Marshall. Until he had that confirmation, there was no use doing too much speculating.

Beth slipped out the French door, looking surprised to see him. "I thought you'd gone."

"I was waiting for you."

"Oh. Why?"

"Couple of things." He'd been worried about her, but he couldn't say that. Keeping an eye on her the way he had today, that had had nothing to do with his job. What he'd seen was a strong woman holding up under painful circumstances, still able to be supportive to the rest of her family. At this point, he couldn't afford to like her too much. "I don't want anyone touching the stuff you packed that's out here. Can I depend on your father to keep his hands off?" He'd debated moving it all into the garage, but that wouldn't protect it from his main suspect. At least in this climate, at this time of year, he didn't have to worry about rain.

"Yes. Good heavens! Even if he wanted to find something, how would he be able to figure out where it is?" Beth's laugh was sad. "I don't think he cared what we did with anything in the garage. Why would he now?"

Because his dead wife's body had been discovered?

"People panic." He watched her. "He didn't try to put you off tackling the garage? Or ask you to keep hands off anything?"

Her eyes briefly narrowed, but she answered with a no before hesitating. "The only thing he said when we got started was not to throw away anything important."

Though tempted, he didn't say, *What about*

your brother? Did he try to put you off? Maybe agree to help so he could steer you away from that part of the garage?

If that's what Matt had had in mind, he'd failed in a big way, hadn't he?

Beth looked at the fruit of their weekend's labor. A strip of yellow crime scene tape now wrapped the pile. "Will *you* have to go through it all?"

"Very possibly." Considering how much was still in the garage, too, he almost groaned. "It depends what was out here, how you reorganized it."

"We've already dumped some stuff in the garbage can," she said suddenly. "And the recycling container, too."

He sighed. "I'd better take a look in both before I go."

"I was going to order a Dumpster tomorrow."

"Hold off for now. I'll let you know when it's okay to go ahead."

She nodded, looking more drained than upset, which was understandable. He'd been lucky today to have her cooperation, to have her answer questions. That didn't excuse the way his body stirred at the sight of her.

"You ready to go?" he asked.

"Yes. I got Dad to eat a bite. I suggested he spend the night at my place, but he's set in his ways."

A spark of irritation reminded Tony of what her

JANICE KAY JOHNSON 53

father had said earlier. *Bethie was old enough to take over helping her sister and making meals, so nothing changed all that much.* Maybe he shouldn't admire her for enabling her father's selfishness.

She'd probably say she loved him enough to overlook some flaws. Tony grimaced out of view. God knows, he kept performing chores for his mother that she could afford to pay to have done. Of all people, he should understand.

As they walked the narrow passage alongside the house, Beth slid a glance at the window, covered with sheets of newspaper, before she looked determinedly away. Tony touched her back.

"Try to think about something else."

She gave a broken laugh. "I never drink, but I'm reconsidering that. I go right by the liquor store on my way home."

He smiled at her. "Might help tonight, but you'd be guaranteed a hangover in the morning."

She wrinkled her nose. "One reason I stay away from even beer and wine. My stomach doesn't handle alcohol well."

"Your father likely to drown his worries tonight?"

"I doubt he has so much as a beer in the house. He's never been a drinker either."

"Maybe you inherited the weak stomach from him," Tony suggested.

He stopped long enough to take that look into the garbage can and the recycling container, verifying what she'd said, before following her to the front of the house.

Beth stopped at the white Civic parked in the driveway. He guessed it to be ten years old or so. The brother drove a shiny black Kia Sorento that looked new. The other car at the curb earlier was an older Volkswagen Golf. Emily's, he presumed. Apparently Dad owned the Buick sedan, showing its years. Tony wasn't much surprised that John Marshall didn't bother to regularly upgrade what he drove.

Beth opened the driver-side door but, instead of getting in, gazed anxiously at Tony. "Will you be coming out right away in the morning?"

"Likely," he said. "If this isn't your mother… well, that leads to other problems, but it's clear we're looking at murder here."

"Could you tell, um, what happened to her?"

"You mean, what killed her?"

Unhappy, she nodded.

"A depression at the back of the skull is a possibility, but it could have occurred post-mortem." Somebody—say, her father—had had to haul the dead woman out to the garage, probably drop it on the concrete floor. Or it could have been dented when the body was forced into the narrow space. The rest of the scenario he was still playing with.

Could there have been construction materials handy out here? That was a question he'd have to ask but, for now, he held it in reserve. Otherwise, the killer would have to have driven to the nearest lumberyard and bought a single sheet. How had he unloaded it and gotten it into the garage without being noticed? After all these years, would anyone remember something so seemingly insignificant? Of course, anyone but the homeowner carrying the wallboard in would likely have drawn more attention from neighbors. Yet another reason to focus on John.

"The medical examiner might be able to spot something else," he said. "After so long, it's sometimes impossible to pinpoint cause of death. What we do know, though, is that she didn't wall her own body up in that garage."

"No. I…understand." Beth smiled weakly. "You probably had things you'd rather have been doing today, huh?"

He gripped the top of her car door, smiling again. "I was mowing my lawn when the call came. Wondering why I hadn't waited until it had cooled down."

Her smile was the most genuine he'd seen yet, adding a radiance to a face some might describe as plain despite translucent skin, a pretty mouth and eyes that were a soft gray-green with hints of gold.

"Still," she said.

He grimaced, conceding the point. No, this wasn't the way he'd have chosen to spend what was supposed to be a day off. On the other hand, he'd sought the promotion to detective because he liked puzzles.

If not for the call, he'd likely never have met her either.

The thought startled and dismayed him. She wasn't a suspect, but she was part of this investigation and, therefore, taboo.

Tony let go of the door and took a step back. "You take care, Beth. I'll let you know what we learn in the morning."

Whatever she'd seen on his face drained her of that momentary vitality, letting exhaustion and anxiety take over again. He ignored his pang of regret, watching as she slid into the car, buckled her seatbelt and fired up the engine, all without looking at him again.

SHORTLY AFTER THE dental office opened the next morning, Tony was able to talk to Dr. Hugh Koster, a short, pudgy man who explained that his X-rays hadn't been digital thirteen years ago. He'd have to send someone to search records stored in a back room.

Not an hour later, he called back.

"I'm looking at them right now. I received the

X-rays from the medical examiner's office, too. Do you want to see them side by side?"

Since he did, Tony drove right over.

He already knew from the heaviness in the dentist's voice that they were a match. Once they stood in front of a light box where the last full-mouth X-rays from Christine Marshall were displayed right above a computer monitor showing the new ones. Even Tony could see that the fillings and crown were in the same places. The dentist also pointed out a crooked eyetooth and a hollow in a molar, which he'd noted should be filled to prevent inevitable decay.

"No question this is her," he said, snapping off the light.

Tony leaned a hip against the counter in the exam room. "I'm not surprised. Do you remember Mrs. Marshall, Dr. Koster?"

"Yes, she was in here often," he answered readily. Seeing Tony's raised eyebrows, he said, "She had three children, also all patients. And her husband was, and is, a patient as well."

"How did she strike you?"

"She was a lovely woman." He smiled crookedly. "I'm happily married, but not blind. Her youngest looks a lot like her. Petite, blonde, a few freckles across the nose. My impression was that Christine had more force of personality, though."

"She and her husband seem like an odd fit."

Dr. Koster assumed a polite facade. "I don't know him well enough to say. He's a quiet man."

Tony thanked him, accepted the X-rays and delivered them to the ME's office.

Instead of starting his car right away, he rolled his head to loosen tight muscles and thought, *Crap.* There were reasons *not* to make this call—but he'd promised.

BETH'S LEGS GAVE OUT and she dropped onto the sofa, clutching her phone. "Oh, my God." She shouldn't be surprised but somehow was anyway. Or maybe the straightforward news had just offered a fresh injection of shock. "All those years…" Her throat clogged.

Over the phone, Detective Navarro's velvet, deep voice sounded as sympathetic as it had in person. "I'm afraid so."

"I need to let Matt and Emily know." Her mind spun. "And Dad…or have you already called him?"

"Please don't call him," the detective said, the order thinly disguised. "I'm on my way over there now."

"I'd like to be there when you talk to him."

"I need to speak to him alone. I'm sure you understand."

Of course she did. "Should I call an attorney for him?"

"I can't advise you on that," he said stiffly. "Surely he can make that decision for himself."

It would never cross her father's mind. Did he understand that he had to be considered a suspect? Beth knew he was incapable of an act of violence, and even more so of having the presence of mind and practicality it would have taken to hide the body.

Battling nausea, she thought, *Not* the body. *Mom.*

"I shouldn't have called you," Detective Navarro said, an odd note in his voice. "I need to ask you not to contact your brother either."

"Matt? Why?"

The little silence that followed let her know how naive she sounded.

"He was the oldest, likely to remember the most," he said finally.

That wasn't it. What he meant was *Your brother was nearly an adult. He lived in the home. I have to look at him.*

And to think she'd let herself feel as if she and the sexy detective had formed some kind of bond. That he'd called her the minute he learned anything this morning because he liked her, thought of them as working together to find the truth.

Being nice under these circumstances was manipulative. *And don't forget it.*

Matt could take care of himself. *He'd* ask for

an attorney the second he sensed the detective's real motives. Dad would not only remain clueless, he could easily be pressured into saying things he shouldn't.

So much for the silly thoughts she'd allowed herself last night about Tony Navarro. Foolish for other reasons, too. She hadn't seen a wedding ring, but he could be married, or at least involved with a woman. The way he'd looked at her could have been entirely in her imagination.

"Beth?"

How many times had he tried to recall her to the conversation?

"Thank you for calling," she said and hung up.

She located her telephone directory, a year out of date, but this was Frenchman Lake. Change came slowly. In moments, she scanned the listings for attorneys in the yellow pages. DUI. Personal injury. Tax problems. She flipped the page back, at last seeing a category for criminal law. Her finger paused on William Schaaf, until she saw he was in practice with one of her parents' friends. Even if Dad had never met this partner…no.

She picked another name at random.

A receptionist said she thought Mr. Ochoa might be available. He was and sounded interested in what she told him. "I'd like to help, but I'm due in court in fifteen minutes," he said. "Can we put the interview off until one-thirty?"

Hoping for courage, she promised to tell the detective he had to wait until her father's attorney could make it. Then, panicked, she tore out of the house and exceeded a few speed limits on the way to her father's.

An unmarked police car was already parked at the curb. Beth ran across the lawn and let herself in, following voices coming from the family room, where she found the two men were already seated.

The flash in Detective Navarro's dark eyes told her how unwelcome her intrusion was. He rose to his feet. "I thought I made clear that you can't be here for this interview."

She lifted her chin. "I don't plan to be. However, my father's attorney will be. Mr. Ochoa can't make it until one-thirty, so you'll need to come back then."

Her father was gaping but didn't intervene. He usually did what she told him to.

The knotted muscles in the detective's jaw told her how mad he was. He looked at her father. "Mr. Marshall? Are you willing to speak to me without an attorney present?"

Dad looked at her. "Bethie? Do you think I need a lawyer?"

"Yes," she said firmly. "Talking to an investigator at this point without an attorney present wouldn't be smart." *She* probably hadn't been smart yesterday. She hesitated. "Did he tell you—"

"I did," Detective Navarro said.

Tears formed in her father's brown eyes. "I wondered why we never heard from her, but I never dreamed…" He swallowed. "To think she was *here* all this time."

She put a hand on his shoulder and squeezed. "I know. Let me see the detective out, and then I'll come back."

His head bobbed. She stared a challenge at Detective Navarro, who gave a choppy nod and headed for the front door. He opened it but turned, looming over her.

"He only looks guiltier, insisting on an attorney instead of being willing to talk to me."

Beth huffed. "Does that argument convince many people?"

"I'd think you would want to know who killed your mother."

"I do." She couldn't falter, not now. Not in front of him. "But I know it wasn't Dad, and I won't let you bulldoze him."

"Because that's how I do my job." His pissed gaze held hers long enough to sting before he shook his head. "Good day, Ms. Marshall."

Feeling as if she'd lost something, she had a lump in her throat as she shut the door. Maybe… maybe *this* was the mistake.

But almost immediately, she shook her head. She'd done what was best for her father. Detective Navarro—she couldn't think of him as Tony now—had been nice yesterday. He'd really seemed to feel protective where she was concerned. But even if he had been sincere, it wasn't as if there was anything personal between them. With her mother's identity confirmed, he had gone straight for the obvious, and convenient, suspect: Dad. With a side thought for Matt because he'd lived here, too.

Beth understood, but she *knew* her father.

She couldn't believe a teenage Matt would have done anything that horrible either, but he wouldn't appreciate his sister interfering. Maybe she should call to warn him...but the stuff he'd said yesterday still rankled, as did his willingness to believe the worst about his own father.

Who else, Beth? Use your head, for once. And not to forget his additional digs. *You live in your own damn dream world, just like* he *does. Everybody is* nice. *Well-meaning.*

As if not sharing his cynicism made her stupid.

She'd always sensed his underlying contempt. It had to be tied to the anger at Dad that she didn't fully understand. Matt didn't have much respect for Emily, either. Did he feel that way about all women? Beth had wondered, unable to tell despite watching him closely when he was with Ashley.

Most of the time, she tried to pretend their family was normal. What family didn't have tensions? But she'd been kidding herself, of course. So maybe Matt was right.

You live in your own damn dream world, just like he *does.*

She blew out a breath then turned to go to Dad. It wasn't in her to let him down when he needed her most. Even if he didn't know he needed her.

ANGRY AND FRUSTRATED, Tony drove straight to Wakefield College, taking for granted that Matt would be at work. Would he arrive to find Matt already lawyered up? Remembering Beth's fierce glare, he thought it likely.

The college, on a semester system rather than quarters, didn't hold a summer session, but the admissions department would be busy. Summer was the season for kids between their junior and senior years of high school to tour colleges with their parents.

He had to park a distance away, by the tennis courts, and walk to Memorial Hall, the granite-block edifice with a bell tower that housed the college administrative offices. Like everyone else in town, he'd become accustomed to hearing the hours tolled.

The campus was noticeably deserted, although he saw a cluster of people moving between buildings across the broad lawn that, in another six weeks, would be filled with students reading in the shade of leafy trees or playing Frisbee or soccer in the sunny center.

The daylight basement level of Memorial Hall housed some offices, but probably not Admissions, he decided. No reason for the parents, who wrote the tuition checks, to see the basement, right?

On the first floor, high ceilings and wide halls led in three directions. He immediately saw a sign pointing to the right to admissions and financial aid offices. Inside Admissions, a young woman sitting behind a desk beamed at him. "How may I help you?" Before he could answer, her gaze lowered to his badge and weapon. The smile dimmed.

"Is Matt Marshall in today? I'm Detective Navarro." Tony smiled reassurance. "He knows me."

"Yes, I'll just—" She jumped up and scurried to one of several closed doors with glass insets. After knocking, she cracked it open and talked quickly.

A moment later, she returned to the desk, and Matt appeared in the doorway. "Detective? Come on in."

He wore chinos with knife-sharp creases and a polo shirt the same shade of blue as his eyes. He smiled, undoubtedly for the benefit of the receptionist and an older, rumpled man who stepped out of a second office and raised his eyebrows when he saw Tony.

Matt closed the door behind him and went around to sit behind his desk. "Have a seat."

No attorney.

Tony sat. "I'm sorry to interrupt your day, Mr. Marshall, but—"

"The body is my mother, isn't it?"

Beth hadn't called, then. Because he had asked her not to or because she was mad at her brother after yesterday?

"Yes. I'm sorry. None of this is pleasant."

"Pleasant." Matt cracked a laugh. "I assume you've already told my father."

"And your sister."

"Beth."

"That's right." It was easy to forget about Emily, although he couldn't let himself. "I plan to sit down this afternoon to talk to your father at length, but I'm hoping you can give me some time right now."

"Why not?" Matt made every effort to look relaxed; he pushed back his chair and crossed his right ankle over his left knee.

Tony wasn't fooled. "You were old enough to be observant about the state of your parents' marriage," he began. "Or anything else out of the ordinary happening in your home at the time."

"Out of the ordinary?" Matt looked incredulous. "Like what? Dad and I being best buds? Beth throwing temper tantrums instead of trying to convince everyone we were happy, happy, *happy*?"

Huh. That was a lot of anger to hold onto for so long.

"Even that long ago, you and your father didn't get along."

"No, we didn't. Although I'm not sure he noticed. He lives in his own little world." Color streaked his cheeks as he apparently recalled that Tony had overheard him saying much the same to his sister. "I didn't mean what I said to Beth. I get frustrated with her constant defense of Dad. She refuses to acknowledge how...lacking he is."

"Lacking in what way?" Not that Tony couldn't guess.

"In any way? I figure if he and Mom ever got it on in bed, the initiative had to have been hers. His body must have cooperated—hey, they had to have done it at least three times, right?—but *he* was probably thinking about some philosophical conundrum while he pumped away." He muttered an obscenity, swiped a shaking hand over his face and gave up on the relaxed pose. Both feet on the floor, he rolled his chair close enough to the desk to allow him to brace his arms on the blotter. "That was crude. I'm sorry, but, you know, I wanted a *father*, sort of like my friends had. A guy who'd pitch a baseball, come to games, give me advice. Me, *I* had to depend on my mother." Anger rolled off him in waves, but he managed a shrug. "And then she was gone."

"Sounds like you were lucky to have her as long as you did," Tony remarked mildly.

"Her leaving the way we thought she did was a shock."

"I bet." Tony studied him. A shock? A betrayal was what he really meant. Tony had to wonder again if she hadn't betrayed her kids in a different way while she was still alive, and if Matt hadn't been well aware. "Was there any more conflict in your home than usual right before she disappeared?"

"I'm not the best person to ask. That was my senior year. I tried to be gone as much as possible." His expression was no longer as readable.

"Anything going on with friends of your parents…?" He hung that out there.

"I don't know."

"Do you recall the day she disappeared?"

Matt looked at him as if he was crazy. "You think?"

"Will you tell me what you recall?"

His mouth tightened, but after a minute he said, "It was a school day."

Tony made a mental note to find out if high school attendance records still existed for that year.

"I had football practice after school. When I got home, nobody had started dinner. Beth had had something after school, too, and I think Emily had gone to a friend's. Dad wandered out of his office—Emily and Beth were stuck sharing a bedroom so he could have his little sanctuary—and asked if dinner was about ready." He shook his head, his disgust apparent. "He hadn't even noticed Mom wasn't home."

"But her car must have been in the garage or parked out front."

"She got the garage." He winced at the unintentional meaning. "So I guess Dad might not have noticed. But, yeah, it was weird that she hadn't taken her car."

"Did she work?"

"Part time. Well, except during tax season. She was a CPA," he said, seeing Tony's surprise. "She worked—I don't know—fifteen or twenty hours a week most of the year, filing for extensions for people, stuff like that. February through April were, like, time-and-a-half. Anyway, I thought maybe she hadn't been able to get her car started or something, so I called the tax service she worked for to see if she was still there, but she hadn't been scheduled to work that day. So then we took turns calling everyone we could think of, but no one had heard from her."

I. We. The kids had obviously taken leading

roles in trying to track down their mother. But then, their father had very likely known exactly where she was.

"Beth made dinner," Matt continued tensely. These recollections were understandably vivid. "We kept thinking Mom would walk in the door and be surprised because we were all supposed to know where she'd been, but it didn't happen. Dad waited until morning, then called the police." A shrug said, *You know the rest.*

"When did someone think to check whether any of her possessions were missing?" Tony asked.

"The cop did, when he came to the house. He seemed to think we were idiots for not doing that sooner, but... I guess none of us really thought she'd just walk out. We worried she'd been in an accident or something."

Except her husband had presumably brushed his teeth before going to bed after her inexplicable disappearance. Shaved in their bathroom the following morning, right before he'd called the cops. Under the circumstances, how could he not have noticed the gaps in the clutter on the counter and in the medicine cabinet?

"What was missing?" Tony asked, even though Beth had answered the same question yesterday.

"Her purse, I remember that. It wasn't anywhere. Her cell phone, which would have been in it."

And which, thirteen years ago, would not have had GPS.

"Beth and Dad thought maybe some clothes. Some of her makeup and some things from the medicine cabinet. You know."

Birth control pills. Interesting he didn't want to say that, given his earlier, scathing speculation on his parents' sex life.

"So the responding officer said you'd probably be hearing from your mother."

"Yeah, shows what he knew," Matt said with understandable bitterness.

"You have to understand that most adults who disappear choose to do so. It puts police in a difficult position."

Matt locked gazes with him in a challenge. "But when you're wrong, you're wrong."

"I can't deny it," Tony admitted, then asked, "Did the officer follow up in the next days or weeks? Or did your father contact them when she didn't reappear?"

"I...don't really know." It was the first time Matt had seemed uncertain.

Deciding he'd gotten enough for today, Tony stood. "I've taken up enough of your time in the middle of a working day. Needless to say, I'll be in touch."

Matt rose, too, his body language tense. "Do you know how she died?"

"I'm afraid not yet."

"All right, then." His expression hardened. "I hope you'll go after my father. Who else could have killed her?"

"We do look first at family," Tony conceded but saw no sign that it had occurred to Matt any investigation would look at him, too.

Still, when Tony stepped from the cool interior of Memorial Hall into the heat of the day, he couldn't deny that Matt's question—or was it an accusation?—echoed his own thinking. Indeed, who else could have killed Christine Marshall but her husband?

Matt's vindictiveness disturbed him nonetheless. How could a vague, essentially absent father cause so much anger? Or had there been more to the relationship? Beth, determined to keep her family whole, could have refused to see what was happening.

More to the point, what if Matt's *mother* had turned a blind eye to physical or sexual abuse by his father? Now, that could fuel rage aimed at both parents.

Something to think about.

CHAPTER FOUR

BETH HATED TO leave her anxious father to face
Detective Navarro with no family to support him,
only the attorney. She had immediately liked Phil
Ochoa, a thin, dark-haired man about her age, at
their meeting half an hour ago, but first impressions could be deceptive, couldn't they?

"Is it okay if I wait in my car while Detective
Navarro is here?" Beth asked.

Phil smiled reassuringly. "Sure. We can talk
afterward." After telling her father he'd be right
back, he accompanied her to the front door. On the
doorstep, he glanced back and lowered his voice.
"I see what you meant about him. He doesn't seem
to quite…"

Seeing his struggle, she chose to be blunt, if
not quite as blunt as Matt had been. "Grasp that
he might be in trouble? No. He's a strange mix of
intelligence and—I don't even know how to describe it—disengagement when it comes to everyday life. I think as he ages, he's getting worse."

"Dementia?"

That was one horrifying possibility that hadn't

occurred to her. "Oh, God. Alzheimer's does hit this young, doesn't it?" Given what she did for a living, she'd been amazingly dense.

"I'm afraid so," he said kindly.

But she shook her head. "The thing is, he's been this way as long as I can remember. He just... drifts away from anything he doesn't want to do or think about. It's almost childlike, in some ways. And yet he's written well-reviewed articles for journals and has continued teaching at the college level. I've seen the notes he writes in the margins on student papers and tests, and they can be really pointed." She sighed. "When it comes to remembering to put a casserole in the oven, or noticing that the paint on the house is peeling..."

"You think this was one of the problems he and your mother had."

Beth couldn't see any reason not to be frank with this man. He represented her father. He was here to *defend* Dad.

"I'm sure it was. Even then, I could see it. It had gotten so she was always exasperated, and that can't be healthy for a marriage."

"No," Phil said somberly. "But you don't see him as violent."

"Never. He floats gently through life. I've never seen him mad, or, really, even irritated. I can't picture him ever reacting with a powerful enough emotion to *push* him into violence."

"All right."

They both, at the same time, saw the unmarked police car coming down the street and slowing.

He added, "I will tell you that the detective can't arrest your father with no proof beyond the body being found here in the house. If they didn't find DNA evidence with her body, this is a fishing expedition, no more. In fact, even DNA evidence can be explained away, given their relationship. So don't worry. If it's okay with your dad, who is legally my client, I'll tell you how it goes afterward."

Beth nodded her gratitude. "Thank you."

Tony Navarro strode up the driveway even as she started toward her car. His gaze swept her from head to foot, but she couldn't tell what he was thinking, although she had a suspicion.

He bent his head. "Ms. Marshall."

"Detective." She made her tone as scrupulously polite as his had been. Opening her car door, she heard the two men greet each other by first name before they shook hands with apparent cordiality.

How friendly was their relationship? Before she could get alarmed, she remembered how short the list of criminal attorneys had been in the phone book. A detective was bound to know them all, and vice versa. Frenchman Lake wasn't that big.

Her phone rang as she started the car to take

advantage of the air conditioning rather than swelter. Matt. *Oh, joy.*

Without so much as a *Hi*, he launched into his complaint. "That detective came to the college this morning to talk to me. Howard saw him and wanted to know what it was about."

Howard, she knew, was the director of Financial Aid. She couldn't remember his last name. He was a Very Important Person in her brother's world.

"Did you tell him?"

"What else could I do?" he complained. "You know this is going to be all over town in no time. If I'd lied, he would have found out."

"Why would you lie?" she asked reasonably. "It's not like you're suspected of a crime." Or, at least, he was only a secondary suspect. Did he know that?

"That's what I thought, or I wouldn't have agreed to talk to the guy. But the way he looked at me at the end, I'm not so sure."

Detective Navarro did have a gift for hiding his thoughts. Would he really have stared accusingly at her brother? She reminded herself, with some bitterness, that he also seemed to have a gift for projecting false kindness and caring. So who knew?

"He said he hadn't talked to Dad yet."

"He's interviewing him right now."

"Then where are you?"

"Sitting in my car, outside the house." Staring through the windshield at the closed garage door. Not even wanting to think about the garage, she shifted in the seat enough to look toward the house instead. "I hired an attorney for Dad. He's in there with him."

"*What*? Why would you do that?"

"Because Dad would never think of it."

"Why do you keep bailing him out? I've never gotten it."

"That's what you do," she said simply, although she knew more lay beneath the surface than she had ever acknowledged. "Your parents take care of you growing up, then later, when they need you, you return the favor."

"He's not an old man, Beth. And, anyway, when did he ever take care of any of us?" Anger infused his voice, as it invariably did when they talked about their father. "Do you think he ever changed a diaper? Cleaned up a skinned knee and put on a bandage? Drove you to friends' houses or picked you up after Spanish Club?"

"He did that," she protested, if weakly.

Matt's laugh was hateful. "When Mom insisted? Get real. He was useless as a parent."

"He made a good living. One that paid for your sports equipment, and your first car and college tuition for both of us."

"I'll bet Mom would have made more if she'd worked full time."

"Well, she didn't."

"There wouldn't have been any tuition money if Mom hadn't set it up so part of his income went straight into a separate account."

That was undoubtedly true, but Beth argued anyway. "The money would still have been there. He'd never buy *anything* new if I didn't make him."

"Do you buy his Jockey shorts, too?" he asked nastily.

She stayed prudently silent, except of course that was answer enough. Sometimes when she was here at the house, she'd throw a load into the washer for her father. When she noticed his clothes looking shabby, she bought what she thought he'd like in the same sizes and replaced the ratty socks or chinos or whatever with new.

Because that's what Mom always did.

So? Was that so bad? She'd taken Emily shopping for new clothes, too, and helped Matt with his college applications. And, yes, she'd taken over bill paying, as young as she'd been, except for getting Dad's signature on checks. Including checks for Matt's college tuition.

"Why do you care what I do to help Dad out?" she asked in real puzzlement. "I don't expect you to do a thing."

"Except clean out the damn garage," he sneered.

"Once. When is the last time I asked you to help?"

Silence of a different kind, before Matt burst out, "Who else could have killed Mom? Tell me that! Who else had any reason?"

"What are you talking about? *He* didn't have any reason. Mom was the one who was always mad!"

"Oh, he had reason, and you'd know it if you weren't so good at turning away from anything you don't want to see. Just like *him*."

"Why do you despise him?" She was back to staring at the closed garage. A better question might be *Why do you despise me?*

"Oh, for God's sake—" He broke off. "I have an appointment. I've got to go. Just...let Dad deal with something on his own, for once. Is that too much to ask?"

She heard voices in the background, and her brother was gone.

TONY FELT LIKE a bully by the time he'd finished asking his questions, even though he hadn't exactly used a baton to beat answers out of the guy. In fact, he thought he'd been admirably considerate and soft-spoken. Ochoa hadn't interrupted often, which meant he agreed.

Looking into those eyes, Tony saw the same

bewilderment and distress he had from the beginning. This was like kicking an old, defenseless dog. He pushed himself to his feet and said, "Thank you for your time again, Mr. Marshall. It's my hope we can figure out what happened to your wife."

"I hope you can, too," he said, standing as well. "I don't understand why anybody would have hurt her. And why leave her here in the house?"

"Getting her out of the house unseen would have been a lot riskier," he pointed out. "Did you have neighbors then who would have been home during a working day? Maybe peeking out their front windows?"

John's brow crinkled. "Christine used to say Mrs. Powell must sit at her window with binoculars."

Tony loved neighbors who saw all. "Where does she live?"

"She had the blue house across the street, but she died a few years ago. There must be new people in there now," he added, seeming surprised by the idea.

"All right, Mr. Marshall. I'll be in touch if—" *when* "—I have other questions."

He nodded and seemed grateful when the attorney offered to see Tony out. On the porch, Tony said, "Interesting client you have."

Phil Ochoa smiled crookedly. "He doesn't have

twenty-five barbells poking through every loose bit of flesh on his face, or a shaved head with a swastika tattoo on his scalp. *Interesting* is all relative."

"I'll give you that." Tony saw that Beth was watching them anxiously from her car. "You'll be wanting to reassure his daughter that I didn't use thumbscrews to compel a confession."

Phil laughed. "I'll do that. You know, we should get together for a beer sometime, instead of meeting like this."

"That would make a change, wouldn't it?" Tony nodded and followed the concrete walk to the driveway, where Beth was parked.

By the time he reached her, she'd climbed out of her car and stood waiting, expression wary. His frustration with her had mostly left him. He couldn't even figure out why he'd *thought* she should trust him. They hardly knew each other. Any loyalty she felt was for her father.

Even so, Tony had tangled emotions at seeing her. He couldn't quite dismiss his awareness of her lush body, and he was equally drawn to a face that always seemed open, as if she didn't know how to hide what she was thinking. He felt sure she was a lousy liar. Those big eyes did it for him, too. They were unusually expressive, made up of colors that brightened with amusement or warmth, shadowed when her mood darkened. He didn't like seeing her so worried.

"Your father is safe," he said drily, pausing at an arm's reach from her.

She tipped up her chin in defiance as undisguised as all her other emotions. "Have you eliminated him as a suspect?"

Damn it. "You know I haven't," he said quietly. "Statistics are on my side. We always look at spouses or partners first."

"You're wasting your time."

"Your opinion, Ms. Marshall. And it's my time to waste."

"No, your time is paid for by residents of Frenchman Lake. *I'm* one of them."

He smiled a little. "Granted. Nonetheless, I have to do my job to the best of my ability. I do have training and experience to back up my decisions."

Her chin lowered a fraction. "I know that. But this time, you're wrong."

He had no doubt that Phil Ochoa was starting to wonder what they were talking about. Lingering like this wasn't a good idea. Tony made himself nod and say, "I'll be in touch," then start walking.

Once he'd reached his car at the curb, he looked back to see Beth and Ochoa huddled on the porch, having what appeared to be an intense discussion. Shaking his head, Tony got in behind the wheel, and immediately his phone rang. The caller was his lieutenant.

"You've got your warrant," he said. "Where are you?"

"Right outside the house. I just interviewed the husband."

"If you're ready, I'll have a patrol officer drop it off. Jess and Larry are tied up the rest of the day and probably tomorrow, too, but I can assign a uniform to you. Or we can put padlocks on the garage until someone else is available."

"Half the stuff from the garage is sitting in the middle of the backyard. No way to padlock it." He hesitated. "I'll get started myself, see how it goes. It's not as if we're looking for blood or trace evidence after all these years."

With luminol, they might still be able to see blood, but the head wound, even if that's what had killed her, wouldn't have gushed, and the ME had found no V-mark of a knife wound on the bones. If luminol lit up old blood on the carpet pad beside the bed, say, it could as well be from a woman bleeding when her menstrual cycle began, or cut accidentally at any point in the past three decades. And, while Tony would like to know where Christine had been killed, that wouldn't be proof he could take to a jury that her husband had been the killer. She could have had a lover, or a fight with a tall, angry son. Tony made a mental note to look into other family, too, assuming there was any—brothers, father, an uncle who'd been part of Christine's life.

Tucking his phone away, he was glad things were moving but wished Beth and Phil Ochoa weren't here right now. Either, and especially both, would make executing the warrant more difficult. He didn't like to think how she'd look at him when he rang the doorbell and handed over the warrant.

With some impatience, he told himself to get over this idiocy. Chances were good he'd end up arresting her father for murder. This wouldn't be the first time he'd been attracted to a woman with no possibility of acting on it.

PHIL SAT BACK in his chair and studied Beth's father. "Mr. Marshall, I'm going to ask that you not speak to the police from here on out without me, as your attorney, being present. Do you understand?"

Beth's father frowned. "Yes, yes, of course I understand. But what is it you think I'm going to say that I shouldn't? I had nothing to do with Christine's death. She was my wife."

"Exactly why the detective has to consider you a suspect. Emotions tend to, er, run hot between husbands and wives." He cast a look at Beth that pleaded for backup.

"Think about how common domestic violence is, Dad," she said. "If you'd been furious at Mom—Well, you're the person who could most easily have hurt her and, um, hidden her body. Because you lived here. And you knew when Emily and Matt and I were busy away from the house. You see?"

"But I wasn't furious at her," he protested.

He thought anyone should be able to tell that he wouldn't do something like that, so how could he possibly be a suspect?

Detective Navarro probably thought she was just as naive. And for good reason, except…she knew her father.

Giving up, she laid her hand over his. "I know, Dad. It would really help if you'd think back to the weeks before she disappeared. Was there something going on at work that had her upset? Or with a friend?"

"Wouldn't she be more likely to have told you anything like that?" he asked. "You two talked all the time." His expression brightened. "And Emily, of course. Have you asked her?"

Beth forced a smile. "I will, Dad. But think about it. Something may come to you."

"I'll try," he said, without any hope.

Oddly, she found herself noticing that his hair was thinning as well as receding. More gray laced the brown, too. Had he aged in the past two days? Or had she not paid attention to how stooped his shoulders had become? He'd never been interested in exercise for its own sake. There'd been a time when he had developed a brief interest in native plants, and he'd done some hiking and collecting. The vegetation here on the thin, volcanic soil of eastern Washington was sparse, however, and Beth thought he'd lost interest while she was in elementary school. He lacked the vigor and muscle tone an active man of fifty-nine should still have, that was for sure. Could she persuade him to join a health club or at least start walking for his health?

Bigger issues here.

Phil stirred. "Mr. Marshall, I didn't think to ask whether you divorced your wife for desertion or remained married to her."

Beth blinked. She couldn't imagine, but...

Her father looked astonished. "Of course not! I assumed she'd be back, and then..."

And then, he'd forgotten he'd been married, or that she wasn't there or...?

A few times when Beth was a teenager, one of her friends had asked if she thought her dad would remarry. The idea had made her feel as if she was looking at the world upside down. Did her father ever notice a woman? Or consider asking one out? Did he sometimes think it would be nice to have companionship, if not sex?

Not something she actually wanted to picture.

Nor would she ever have to. Her father was the original egghead. Physical needs were handled absentmindedly, if at all. He often missed meals, too involved in whatever he was thinking or reading about to notice a rumbling stomach. If he'd ever made a romantic gesture, Beth hadn't seen it. Which didn't mean her parents didn't regularly have vigorous sex, but…okay, she *couldn't* picture that.

Her brooding was interrupted by the doorbell.

Phil said, "I wonder…" but didn't finish what he'd started.

Beth jumped up. "I'll find out who it is."

She was a little surprised to realize Phil was trailing her to the living room, dim with drawn drapes. Maybe he was using the excuse to leave?

But the minute she opened the door, she knew he'd guessed who had rung the bell. Tony Navarro, darkly handsome and mostly expressionless. If there was a momentary softening in his eyes when they met hers, she was probably deluding herself to call it regret.

The detective said, "Ms. Marshall. Phil." He handed over some papers. "You'll want to take a look at this."

What on earth? But she'd watched enough crime TV shows to guess. He had brought a warrant to search more than the immediate area around the body. The house?

Phil read swiftly. When he finished and passed the papers to Beth, he didn't appear surprised. "I'm sorry. It looks to be in order."

She turned away to allow herself to concentrate while she skimmed the legalese. "This is for the garage," she said at last. "The stuff we hauled outside, too. And... Mom and Dad's bedroom?" She swung around to stare at Navarro.

"If any evidence was packed away, that's likely where."

"No, actually—" Oh, what difference did it make? "There were a bunch of boxes full of Mom's stuff in the garage."

"Were?" he said sharply.

"Are. I meant to take a couple home, but, you know." *We found our mother's body. Called 9-1-1. You came.* Had he walked her out to her car to be sure she didn't take anything? Had it occurred to him that, while he'd been inside talking to Dad, she could have put some boxes in her trunk? Emily or Matt could have done the same, although not without *her* seeing.

"I'd like to look at the bedroom now," Tony said. "Then speak to you, Ms. Marshall, if you wouldn't mind staying."

Even if Phil agreed to stay, she wouldn't leave her father while the detective was in the house.

Phil frowned at him, then looked at his watch. "Fine," he said shortly.

Beth reluctantly stood back to let Detective Navarro in, uncomfortably aware when he brushed her in passing. Dad had ventured from the kitchen and was now hovering in the living room, his face tight with worry. Maybe he was more aware of his peril than she'd thought.

"Mr. Marshall," Phil said, "the detective has a warrant to search your bedroom, master bathroom and the garage, as well as all the items removed from the garage yesterday."

"My bedroom?"

"In case any of your wife's belongings are stored there," Navarro said stiffly.

"I don't know why they would be." Dad pondered. "I'm not sure what's on the shelf in the closet."

Beth knew exactly what was up there but kept her mouth shut. If Tony—no, Detective Navarro—wanted to look through a box of homemade Mother's Day cards and children's artwork and writings, she might even enjoy watching.

"Beth," Phil said, "if you'll accompany him right now, I need to make a quick phone call to cancel an appointment. Remember, he's restricted to the one room."

"I can do that." She raised her eyebrows at Navarro. "Follow me."

His mouth tightened, but he did as she said. She was aware of his head turning as they went down the hall, but the doors were closed on the linen closet, Matt's bedroom and the one she'd shared with Emily. The front bathroom, which he could see into, was mostly bare, although she presumed Dad used it sometimes. And then there was Dad's office, filled with books on shelves, the floor, his desk, the windowsill and anywhere else he'd found room to pile them. Maybe she'd been too quick when she told Matt that Dad wouldn't have spent the tuition money if it had been readily available. He did buy books. Lots of books. He spent hours a day searching the catalogs of obscure bookstores that sold scholarly and antiquarian books online.

"Do you want to go through Dad's office, too?" she asked, with snide intent. "Maybe you could organize while you're at it."

"I think you need a librarian for that."

Beth sighed, soundlessly she hoped. No, one of these days, she would tackle Dad's books, before the heaps blocked access to his desk and computer. Knowing him, he'd buy another computer and settle in at the kitchen table instead of trying to winnow his collection.

Navarro looked over his shoulder, frowning. "I should have included closets."

"The linen closet? You're kidding."

"Why would I be kidding?"

"Because I took over running the house. Nobody could have hidden anything in there." She stopped and flung open the door. "See?"

Phil came down the hall in time to see the detective standing in front of the linen closet with his hands on his hips.

"Beth, that's not included in the warrant."

"I'm settling his mind," she said tartly.

All three of them gazed into the narrow space divided by shelves holding precisely folded sheets, pillowcases, towels and washcloths. Extra blankets and a chenille bedspread claimed the top shelf, surplus toiletries in a clear rubber tote the floor. It was magazine-worthy. The two men appeared bemused.

Suddenly, Navarro laughed, deepening creases in his cheeks. "Even my mother would be dazzled. You should hire out."

The skin beside Phil's eyes crinkled with amusement. "It is pretty impressive."

Beth flushed, as much from the effect of seeing Tony laugh as from the compliment. "It's easy to keep space neat when no one else ever messes it up."

Tony's smile faded. "You change his bed and do laundry here?"

"Well...sometimes." Weekly.

"I hope your father appreciates you," he said quietly.

Without commenting, she backed away. Passing her again, he entered the bedroom and walked around for a minute, not touching anything.

"Has this carpet been replaced since your mother disappeared?" *Died.*

Beth shook her head. "It's at least fifteen years old." She calculated. "Eighteen. It really needs to go, but we should do it throughout the house at the same time, and everything would have to be moved out. It'll have to be done before the house is sold, but as long as Dad doesn't care..." Becoming aware of the faintly surprised looks on both men's faces, she trailed off, embarrassed at her rambling.

Tony disappeared into the bathroom. She heard cupboard doors, drawers and the medicine cabinet being opened and closed. When he came back out, he wore thin latex gloves on his hands. Without looking at her or Phil, he went methodically through the dresser drawers, lifting clothes and putting them back. He pulled the dresser out an inch or so to see behind it. He got down to look under the bed, checked the drawer on the bedside table then started in on the closet.

Barely glancing at the closet floor—Dad owned only four or five pairs of shoes—Tony moved the clothes on their hangers, slid his hand into suit-coat pockets, rifled through the sweaters on a canvas hanging organizer, then removed one box after another from the long closet shelf.

Phil went in and sat at the foot of the bed. Beth remained planted in the doorway, her arms crossed.

The first rubber tote held extra blankets and pillows. Another held trophies and plaques. Even as a child, she'd been surprised to discover that her father had played lacrosse in college. Mom had been a competitive swimmer and later played golf in occasional ladies' tournaments. Tony lifted a number of these out and studied them before putting them back.

Another box held books for young children. Mom would have stored it on this shelf. Beth supposed her mother would've thought books might not withstand the cold or damp in a garage.

And finally, he came to the one filled with children's drawings and the like. Report cards were in there; she saw the detective take one out and study it, the corner of his mouth lifting. Hers, undoubtedly. She'd never been very good at math.

She could still hear Mom saying, "But if you'd just *try*!"

He dug through this box more carefully. It felt weird, watching him. That was *her* life he was sifting through, hers and Emily's and Matt's, not Dad's. Keeping her mouth shut was hard.

When he at last put the lid back on the box, he lifted his head to look straight at her. He must have seen all the complicated things she felt because he ducked his head in a kind of acknowledgment, or apology. Phil glanced at her speculatively but didn't comment.

Once Tony slid the box onto the shelf, he peeled off the latex gloves. "I'm done in here."

Without a word, Beth turned and walked to the living room. She didn't see her father, even in the kitchen; he almost had to have retreated to the family room. Had he been bothered to know someone was going through his drawers, inspecting his medicine cabinet?

At the front door, Phil said, "I won't hang around while you look through the garage. Unless you want me to, Ms. Marshall?"

She would have laughed, if her mood had been better. "You'd be here for the next two weeks."

"Call if you need me," he said, shook hands with Tony Navarro, then strode to his car, undoubtedly relieved to have escaped.

Tony didn't move. He wasn't watching the attorney's departure; he was looking at her, and his expression puzzled her.

"Do you need the key for the side door?" she asked. "Let me get my purse, and I'll give you mine."

"No—" A hand on her arm stopped her. "Actually, yes, thank you, but there's something else I'm hoping you'll do for me."

Now suspicious, she echoed, "That *I'll* do for you?"

"You must have taken today off work."

"Yes."

He rubbed his jaw. "Is there any chance you could take more time off?"

What on earth? "I could, but why?"

"I could use some help going through the stuff in the garage, and on the lawn." When she gaped, he grimaced. "The truth is, you'd recognize something that doesn't belong, or should be there and isn't. I probably wouldn't."

She shook her head in disbelief. "I'm supposed to use up my vacation days to help you go after my father." Even as she said that, she flashed on that diamond ear stud. If it was a diamond.

He cocked an eyebrow. "Look at it this way. You'll have a chance to point out evidence leading to someone else."

Beth's first thought was that he would be taking the risk that she'd spot evidence pointing at her father…and bury it. Probably why what he was suggesting had to be unusual, if not unprecedented.

And he was right—this offer would make her part of the investigation. What could she do but accept?

CHAPTER FIVE

TONY FELT PROFOUND relief at Beth's agreement to help but suspected Lieutenant Davidson's first impulse would be to scold him, once he learned one of his detectives had brought a family member of the principal suspect into the investigation.

Worry later about justifying this, he decided.

"Can we get started now?" he asked.

"Well… I suppose." She glanced down at herself. "I'm not really dressed for it, but that's no big deal."

"I'll do any dirty work," Tony assured her. Those chinos looked good, lovingly hugging well-rounded hips and long legs. Her pretty three-quarter sleeve cotton blouse, striped in two shades of a mossy green, was probably the kind of thing she wore for work. It would be less professional and more sexy if she'd just undo one more button, he couldn't help thinking, his gaze lingering at the shadowy hint of cleavage he could make out.

"Let me get my purse."

"You don't think the things in the backyard are worth looking at?"

"We'll probably have to, but— Wait a minute."

He stayed at the front door as she snatched her purse from the kitchen table, then paused to say something to her father, who was out of sight in the family room. Tony couldn't hear what was said. When she came back, they went out the front door.

"I know you'll need to go through everything, and Emily and Matt are the ones who looked at a lot of the stuff that's in the backyard, so I'm not sure what's in some of the boxes," she explained. "But—" She came to a halt, looking at the yellow crime scene tape. "Should we duck under the tape, or...?"

"Yeah, let's," he said. "I don't want to take it down yet."

She inserted the key in the side door of the garage and blew out a breath at the same time. "What I started to say is we did come across some boxes full of Mom's things. So I think it makes sense to start there."

"Yes. It does." Damn, could it be this easy? "But if you've already looked through the boxes, why are they in here? I assumed you were shifting them outside as you made decisions."

"We were." The door open, Beth ducked under the tape but then hesitated on the threshold, and he couldn't blame her, considering yesterday's happenings.

He reached past her to flick on the lights, which failed to dispel the gloom. Tony ripped away the newspaper he'd taped over the pane of glass in the door, nudged Beth inside, and went to tear down the papers covering the window over the workbench, too. Unfortunately, the improved light made more visible the missing sheet of wallboard, which Larry and Jess had carried away along with the body. Stains remained evident in the baseboard as well as in the soft wood of one of the bracing two-by-fours.

Beth still hadn't taken a step inside. Her gaze, shadowed by yesterday's horror, was riveted to the missing section of wall. "It's so hard to believe…"

He wadded up the newspapers and tossed them aside. "I know it is," he said as gently as he could. "Bad enough if she'd been a stranger, but finding out your mother had been there all these years…" Maybe not the best thing to say, but the section of wall down to bare studs might as well be an elephant swinging its trunk back and forth.

Beth nodded tightly.

"If you'll point out the boxes, we can take them outside," he suggested.

She drew a deep breath. "It's awfully hot out there. I could plug in a couple of those fans in here."

He let her do so, placed on the far side of the garage. How much the whirring fans actually cooled the stifling air in here was debatable, but they had to be better than nothing.

Beth made a half circle to the workbench, probably so she could approach it from the side that *didn't* abut the opened wall that had served as her mother's coffin for thirteen years.

"There were boxes of baby and children's clothes. Mom must have thought they might have another baby after Emily," she said. "So probably she packed those a long time before she...died." *Disappeared* was what she'd been about to say—had been saying for all of those thirteen years. "I think those boxes are outside. Matt was going to ask his wife if she wanted to look through them, but I don't think he actually took any of them."

Tony nodded. "Let's start with your mother's things."

"All this." She waved, indicating under and on top of the workbench.

"Tell you what," he said, grabbing one at random. "Can you bring those lawn chairs back in here? This is a sitting job."

"Oh. Yes." She looked grateful to have something to do—or for the delay in opening any of these boxes.

When she returned, he said, "You were going to tell me why you left these in here."

She scrunched up her nose. "Because I didn't want to make decisions. Everything else was easy, but these…" Hand on the back of one of the lawn chairs, she stared down at the box. "I think, if she'd been dead—" She flushed, looking up at him. "I mean, if I'd *known* she was dead, and that long ago, I could have faced sorting her clothes. As it was… My feelings about her were so muddled. Thrift store? Garage sale? It felt so…cold. Even Matt was relieved when I suggested we leave these for last."

For another time, she meant. A year, or five years, or ten years from now.

"Did you really believe she was alive?" he asked, curious.

Beth squirmed a little. "Then…yes. Except, I couldn't imagine her abandoning us like that. Matt and Emily and I all went through phases of feeling betrayed and angry. How could she?" She gazed toward the neatly stacked boxes instead of at him. "I suppose, over the years, I started to think something must have happened to her. Because she wouldn't have done that to us. It could have been a car accident, or…or breast cancer or who knows what? Except it never occurred to me that Dad would have been informed, wouldn't he?"

"If they were still married, yes." Tony paused. "Ideally. If she'd moved out of state with a man who didn't tell authorities she was married to someone else, had kids…it might not have happened." He didn't add *But we know she died here, don't we?* The very day she vanished, in fact.

Beth sighed. "Well, this box is the first one I opened that had her things. Except the Christmas ornaments. I told you about those, didn't I?"

"You did." He'd poked through them in the garbage can, to be certain nothing else had been packed with them. "You say *I opened*. Your brother or sister weren't first to look through any of these boxes?"

"No, we sort of divvied up the garage." She turned her head. "We hadn't gotten to the stuff on that wall at all."

"Okay." He pulled two pairs of latex gloves from his pocket and handed one pair to her. "I'd appreciate it if you'd wear these."

Expression dubious, she eased her much smaller hands into them and opened the flaps.

"These weren't taped?"

"No. I assume Dad packed them, if you can call this packing."

Tony would have asked what she meant, except that he could tell right away. *Dumped* was probably a more descriptive word. And what he'd have expected of her father.

Beth had an odd look on her face as she looked at the pink garment at the top. "Matt and I both recognized this blouse right away. It was one of Mom's favorites. It kind of gave us chills."

Putting himself in her shoes, he could imagine. His mother had favorites she wore long past the point when they should have been discarded. Yeah, coming across her ratty red sweater, for instance, would be creepy.

"Do you have any empty boxes?" he asked, suddenly realizing he hadn't planned ahead as well as he should have. "So that we can transfer things as we look at them?"

"Oh. Yes." She jumped up again, bringing one in from outside and locating a second in the garage.

It appeared everything in this box had been pulled off the rod in the closet. They decided to take the clothes off the hangers, which she would add later to a thrift store box outside. He'd look, she'd fold and pack the garments into a different box.

He asked a few questions as they proceeded. Were these clothes that her mother was wearing right before her disappearance, versus older ones she might have pushed to the back of the closet?

Tight-lipped, Beth said, "Right before."

The woman had apparently liked pink, in a variety of shades from pale to deep rose. Envisioning her from the photos he'd now seen, he thought pastels had probably suited a woman who was tiny, blonde, delicately made. She'd had a beautiful smile, although it looked practiced to him. She was in half a dozen pictures on the fireplace mantel in the family room, more in an arrangement on the wall. He'd noticed a certain tilt of her head in virtually every photo. Pretty women learned the angles that showed them to best advantage.

He'd been struck by how those displays left this family frozen in time. Only a few additions had been made, undoubtedly by Beth. Matt, in his high school graduation robes. Emily in hers. Emily in what was probably a prom dress—pink. Matt in college graduation robes, posing in front of Memorial Hall on the Wakefield campus.

Not a single additional picture of Beth. It pissed him off that no one else in her family had noticed.

He'd also found himself wondering whether her mother had helped her see herself as attractive. With a petite mother and a petite sister, both cookie-cutter pretty, blonde and blue-eyed, Beth could easily have felt like the ugly duckling. Ironic, when he was a lot more drawn to her than he could imagine being to her sister, even if she'd been older and had a stronger personality. Still, at least seven inches taller than either her mother or sister, brown-haired to their bright blonde, rounded cheeks instead of sculpted, probably going through stages of being awkward that never happened to either of them… Yeah, he could see it.

She was trying now to hide any distress as she

shook out each dress, or blouse or pair of slacks and folded it as neatly as she had every towel in that linen closet, but tiny flinches or pained sounds gave her away.

He'd have been relieved to reach the bottom of the damn box, except it was only the first.

"I know I should give these to a thrift store," she said finally. "The styles are mostly timeless."

"I'd like you to hold off," he said. The relief in her tiny nod produced an odd, clutching sensation in his chest.

The next box held shoes. These seemed to bother her less, probably because they were more generic. Those she packed into a smaller box, saying, "I'll take these to the thrift store."

Tony didn't bother reminding her to wait. After sliding his fingers inside and then shaking each shoe upside down, he was confident nothing had been hidden with them. Looking at the pile, however, he thought to ask if she remembered any shoes of her mother's that *weren't* here.

She frowned at them, finally saying, "I don't know. She could have had another pair of pumps, or open-toed sandals or… Shoes aren't that memorable."

"No."

"Didn't she have any on?" Beth gestured toward the wall.

"No," he said again, not wanting to say *She wasn't wearing any pants either.*

When he stood to get another box, he spotted a black marker on the workbench. "Do you want to label these?"

"Oh! Yes, that's a good idea."

Tony dragged another large box from beneath the workbench. Through a crack between the folded lid flaps, he saw what seemed to be more women's clothing. So far, this wasn't proving any more informative than the master bedroom inside.

"You and your brother seem to have some tension," he commented, as he lifted out the top of a velour sweat suit—pink, of course. "Emily seemed to stay in the background."

Beth looked up with familiar wariness. He'd love to see a joyful smile on her face.

"Losing Mom was really hard on her," she said carefully. "She and Mom were close, maybe because they were a lot alike. Not just looks but personality and tastes. Although maybe their tastes had to do with their resemblance to each other."

"That seems likely. Pink was obviously your mother's color."

That nose crinkled a little. "When I was little, she tried to put me in pink and purple, too. I felt like a moose when she made me wear some frilly, feminine thing. Once Emily came along, Mom gave up and let me wear whatever I wanted. It was obvious I'd never be girly."

"You don't see yourself as feminine?" he asked, sharp enough to widen her eyes.

"Well, not in the same way." She shrugged, as if indifferent. Which he didn't believe for a minute. "I like myself fine, but I'm certainly not dainty, or the kind of woman men rush to protect."

I would. Tony clenched his teeth to prevent himself making a claim that would be as bad as his earlier temptation to tell her she was beautiful.

Color tinted her cheeks, and her eyes dilated at whatever she saw on his face. "Why are we talking about this?"

"I asked about Emily." Voice rough.

Beth looked away from him. "There's tension. She and Matt bickered all weekend. He didn't want to be here and took offense at just about everything. Emily wanted those Christmas ornaments to remember Mom by, and she was really mad when he dumped them in the garbage, smashing them. And both of us shut her down when she wanted to go through Mom's clothes to see if there was anything she'd wear. It was awful of me to react that way—"

"No." He startled her with his interruption, but he didn't care. "It was natural. I'm more surprised she'd want anything of your mother's, given that you all thought she'd ditched you." Which reminded him that he needed to talk to Emily. Was there any chance she'd seen something to make her suspect that, in fact, her mother was dead?

"She was younger than us enough that I always thought… I don't know…that she wouldn't remember Mom as well? Or…had adjusted better?"

"She was twelve. Not five."

Her pale, clear skin colored easily. "I know, but…" Apparently giving up argument as useless, Beth said, "She has mixed feelings about me, of course. Suddenly, I was in charge instead of just being her sister. I think…she was grateful but also resentful. Which isn't surprising."

"I can see that," he admitted. "My parents were Catholic, which means they had eight kids. I think in most big families like mine, the older kids automatically assume some responsibility for the younger ones, but that didn't mean there isn't resentment."

Her eyebrows flickered. "I'll bet you're not one of the youngest."

Tony grinned. "No, I'm the oldest. How'd you guess?"

"You wouldn't have the job you do if being in charge didn't come naturally for you. Quelling disorder, giving orders."

"*Bossy* is how my sisters describe me."

A dimple he hadn't known she had flashed in one cheek. "You keep saying sisters."

"I have one brother, six sisters."

She laughed and shook her head. "Wow. The one of each I have are trying enough sometimes."

"Count your blessings," he said, more seriously than he'd intended.

Beth studied him for a moment, making him want to twitch. He wasn't used to anyone trying to see deep into him the way he felt sure she was. It was unnerving.

But finally she said, "Matt can be difficult to get along with. He's been angry at Dad for as long as I can remember. Mom was our real parent. Having her walk out— that was hard for him."

Tony couldn't summon any sympathy. Matt had been almost ready to graduate from high school. He hadn't *needed* a mother anymore, not the way his sisters did. He should have dedicated himself to being their support, not thought only of himself.

"I saw he graduated from Wakefield, so he did stick around."

"No, he went to the University of Washington his first two years. He could hardly wait to get away. He found summer jobs elsewhere, too. I was surprised when he transferred to Wakefield his junior year, but he'd decided it was more prestigious than a state school. And...well, I thought he wanted to be here for us."

Thought. Past tense. She must have quickly learned better.

"What about you?" Although he felt sure he knew.

"I went to the community college for two years. So I could live at home. Emily needed me." She averted her gaze. "I finished at Western, in Bellingham, because Emily was a senior by then and not home much. Plus, Matt was back in town, if she needed one of us."

Dad being conspicuously absent from her decisions, Tony wasn't surprised to note.

She gave him a shy look. "What about you?"

Her reciprocal curiosity pleased him. "Portland State. Just far enough away. And, yes, I grew up here, too."

A smile played with the corners of her mouth. "You and Matt, huh?"

He groaned. "And yet, here I am."

She didn't ask further but eyed him with that same open curiosity.

"My father died," he said. "He was a foreman for one of the vineyards. Tractor rolled on him. Several of my sisters and my brother were still at home. My mother needed me."

Something wistful flitted over her face. "It seems we have something in common."

"Yeah." He had to clear his throat. "I guess we do." He couldn't make himself look away from her, and it seemed she had the same problem.

It had to be a minute before she shook herself. "Shouldn't we keep working?"

"We should." He stood to drag another box from beneath the workbench.

AFTER THE LINGERIE and another box of clothing that must have been taken from her mother's dresser—jeans, T-shirts, long underwear, sweat shirts and the like—Tony suggested they call it quits until the next day. Not letting him see how relieved she was, Beth agreed.

"Are you planning to stay?" he asked.

"Stay? Oh, talk to my father, you mean." Make dinner for him? "I'll go in and check on him, but... I think I need a break."

"Understandable." He rubbed the back of his neck. "Did you get lunch?"

"Sort of. I fed Dad."

"And pretended to nibble?"

She made a face at him.

"Are you hungry enough for an early dinner? I'm starved. I worked through lunch."

However casual he made it sound, the suggestion startled Beth. Maybe he'd have offered the same to anyone he was working with. Or was only being polite, or was concerned about her or—

Apparently she'd been too slow to answer. Lifting the tape for her, Tony said brusquely, "If you'd rather just get home, that's fine."

"No, I—" Oh, what was wrong with her? But she knew. "It's just…aren't we, well, not enemies, but adversaries? You were mad at me this morning."

"I was, but not for any defensible reason."

What did that mean? What reason for his annoyance was *in*defensible?

"I was being an idiot, okay?" He locked the door and handed her the keys. "Let's make it nine tomorrow morning, if that's okay?"

"Sure. I suppose I should warn Dad…"

"He doesn't teach summer quarter?"

"Actually, he does have a couple of classes. An evening one, I think, and… I can't remember." She stopped when she reached the concrete walkway leading from the driveway to the front porch.

Tony nodded at her and kept going toward the street.

"If…if you meant it," she said to his back.

He stopped and turned slowly.

"I'd better meet you somewhere. After I say goodbye to Dad." She gestured toward the house.

"What sounds good?" he asked. Cautious, she thought.

"Pretty much anything."

"That's no help."

"Mexican?"

He nodded. "Okay. You know Tia's?"

"On Birch? Sure."

"I'll see you there."

She kept going, wondering if she was crazy to go out for a meal with him. What would they find to talk about besides the investigation? Or did he intend to delve more into her memories?

A quick call and she could cancel—but she didn't want to.

Fifteen minutes later, she parked in a nearly deserted lot beside a stucco building painted an eye-catching sunset orange. Tia's wasn't situated close to either college, or downtown with the high-end restaurants, boutiques and tasting rooms. Locals ate here, she'd discovered. One of Beth's co-workers had recommended it.

Entering, she paused to let her eyes adjust to the dim interior. The cool air felt wonderful, since the air conditioning in her car hadn't really kicked in with the drive being so short. She saw Tony leaning against the front counter, talking with a dark-skinned woman whose hair was liberally streaked with silver. He was teasing her, and she swatted him playfully.

Beth joined them. "*Hola. Siento haberle hecho esperar.*"

His surprised expression gave her great pleasure. "You speak Spanish."

"I'm not entirely fluent, but I get by. I use it a lot on my job."

"That makes sense. Beth Marshall, meet my aunt Paloma."

"You're Tia?"

The woman grinned. "*Sí*. Tony—" she poked him with an elbow "—wouldn't dare take a pretty girl anywhere else to eat." She studied Beth. "I've seen you. You come here often." Her nod held satisfaction. "*Muy bien*."

Beth smiled. "I love your food."

"*Gracias*. Now sit, sit. I'll bring you a menu."

Tony obviously didn't need one.

Once they were alone in a booth, Beth said, "I can't believe she's your aunt."

"I stumble over family everywhere around here." He sounded rueful. "One of my brothers-in-law is my car mechanic. One of my sisters is a nurse in the ER. An uncle has an auto body shop. A cousin owns a golf shop. I can get you a good deal on flooring if you want to replace that carpet, since another brother-in-law owns Best Flooring."

"Oh, my. I don't know whether I should commiserate or envy you."

"Some of both," he said wryly. "Aunt Paloma is actually one of my favorite relatives."

"Because she feeds you."

He laughed. "Maybe. Although Mamá feeds me, too, when I give her the chance."

"Wasn't it…sort of lonely, away from family?"

"Again…yes, and no. While you were at Western, didn't you feel as if you'd been freed?"

She wanted to lie and say of course not. But this was a rare chance to talk to someone also constrained by family. "I did," she admitted. "It's not like I was exhilarated. More…"

His expressive eyebrows rose. "Relieved?"

She nodded. "It always seems strange to me that most people my age aren't close at all to their families. Maybe one reason I went into the work I do is to help make it possible for families to keep their elderly near instead of dumping them in nursing homes." Okay, that sounded awful. "Don't get me wrong—that's the best decision in lots of cases. Sometimes, they need a level of care they can't get any other way. Some elderly have insurance that covers a nursing home or memory-care facility, but not home care. And I don't know about you, but if I end up senile in my eighties, I wouldn't *want* my kids to devote their lives to taking care of me. I had a great-aunt who spent something like twenty years caring for her invalid mother, and got a break when she married and had kids before—guess what?—she spent the next thirty years or so nursing her husband. That's too much."

His expression now was the furthest thing from *cop*. He had a way of looking at her that was outside her experience, so gentle and understanding, she wanted to lean on him and let him make everything right for her. It was actually a little bit scary, since she wasn't very good at trust.

"You've been taking care of your family for a long time, Beth."

"That's different." Hearing his aunt's approach, she exclaimed, "Oh! I'd better make up my mind."

She'd intended to go for her usual burrito until she heard Tony order the *pan con bistec*, which he said was Cuban. He asked for fried plantains on the side instead of shoestring potatoes. In the end, he talked her into trying the classic *ropa vieja*, which was shredded beef stewed in tomatoes and spices.

Before she could ask about the Cuban specialties included on the menu, he picked up the thread of their previous conversation. "I grew up in a culture where we depend on family. It's comforting in a way," he continued, "but it increasingly clashes with modern life in this country. Should our eighteen-year-olds turn down opportunities that would take them too far away? When they love their classes or have exciting jobs, are they selfish *not* to race home when summoned to be useful to a sister going through a difficult pregnancy or to parents who are getting so they need help?"

How much had he had to give up to return to Frenchman Lake because his mother needed him? He hadn't mentioned relationships, but the strain of distance would certainly snap those. "Doesn't everyone face those dilemmas?" she said.

What an odd conversation to be having with a man she'd known for only a couple days, it occurred to her.

"I think it's a little different for a lot of people. Two working parents. Grandparents who don't live close by, cousins you see on Thanksgiving, if then. You aren't going against the norm if you move to the east coast for a job, bring your own kids to visit their grandparents once a year, fly home only when a parent is having major surgery or dying. That's all anybody expects."

"So what's healthier for the individual?" she challenged him.

He only shook his head, something that might be weariness ghosting across his face. "Don't know." He looked up and smiled past her, just as Beth heard footsteps. "Tia Paloma, you shouldn't wait on us, too."

"Hardly anyone here right now," his aunt assured him. "Hot plates," she warned automatically, as she set them on the table. "Anyway, what should I do? Send your cousin Ana to take care of you? She's too busy on her phone to remember to refill your drinks." She shook her head. "That girl."

Tony grinned at her. "We're all young once."

"Young, *sí*. Head stuffed with cotton candy?" She rolled her eyes. "No."

Tony laughed as his aunt hustled away. "Ana is sixteen, glad to have a job but wishing it wasn't with her aunt for a boss."

"She's not Paloma's daughter, then."

"Nope. I have four sets of aunts and uncles here in Frenchman Lake, and another uncle in Walla Walla. You see what I mean?"

Walla Walla was barely a forty-five minute drive.

She offered him a twisted smile. "There was a time I'd have given anything to have an aunt and uncle right here in town."

Of course, he understood immediately. "Someone who would have helped you, instead of depended on you."

Beth nodded. "I'm not sure anyone can ever truly see the needs and struggles and joys of a family from the outside."

"But that's what you do all day, isn't it?" He sounded unnervingly thoughtful.

She met his eyes. "Isn't that what *you* do every day, too?"

His eyebrows knit. "I...hadn't looked at it that way." But then he smiled crookedly. "You're right."

She returned his smile in a way she hadn't yet dared. "Music to my ears."

His laughter was music to hers.

CHAPTER SIX

TONY AUTOMATICALLY ASSESSED three men entering the restaurant. Ana was leading them to a booth a distance from Tony and Beth's, when one of the men glanced their way.

"Beth!" Lean and athletic, hair graying and face darkly tanned, he broke away from the others.

Tony set down the sandwich he'd just picked up. The man, who appeared to be about her father's age, looked first at Beth, then, with curiosity, at Tony.

"What's this I hear about you finding your mother's body?"

Beth set down her fork.

Irritated, Tony thought, *Thank you, that's just what we want to talk about over our meal.*

"Dr. Schuh. Oh, um, this is Tony Navarro. Tony, Alan Schuh. Dr. Schuh was our pediatrician."

"And friend," the man said firmly. "My wife and I got to be good friends with Beth's parents," he told Tony, who smiled noncommittally.

"We did find Mom's remains," she admitted, voice constrained. "It's been very difficult."

"Where did you hear about it?" Tony asked before she could continue. He saw the other two men looking their way.

"I ran into Howard Farrar."

"The admissions director at Wakefield," Beth murmured to Tony.

"Ah. We didn't meet, but I saw him."

Schuh's gaze moved between them but settled again on Beth. "Are you all right? Sounds like Matt was pretty shaken."

"We all were, but…it's a relief, in a way, to know what happened. That she didn't leave us."

"But murdered! And it had to be murder, didn't it?"

Tony decided it was time to intervene. "I'm the detective leading this investigation. I'd be interested in speaking to you when you have time."

"Me? Good lord, why?"

Tony didn't read too much into the doctor's alarm. He got that reaction a lot.

"I'd like to hear about Christine from different perspectives. She may have said something to you or your wife that will be relevant."

"Oh. Well."

Tony whipped out a pen and small notebook. "If you'll give me your number, we can set something up later."

Schuh gave work and personal numbers, then

beat a retreat after telling Beth to give him a call if she needed anything. Anything at all.

The two of them remained silent for a moment. Then she sighed. "Howard has a big mouth."

"You know him?"

She wrinkled her nose in the way he thought was cute. "Only secondhand. Matt talks about him constantly, worries about what he thinks, brags about his approval."

"Not surprising."

"No." She sighed. "Maybe I should say, *Matt* has a big mouth."

Tony laughed and reached for his sandwich again. "You might well say that."

"He could at least have asked his boss not to gossip. I hate the idea that everyone is going to be talking about us in no time." She tipped her head toward the three men, who were talking animatedly but in low voices with an occasional stolen look their way. "What do you want to bet Dr. Schuh is spreading the news this very instant?"

"I wouldn't bet against it. Do you know either of the others?"

"I don't think so."

"I'm afraid this was inevitable." Although he could have wished otherwise for Beth's sake. "Did you tell your co-workers why you were taking time off?"

"No. They probably think I'm doing something fun."

None of this was fun. "I'm sorry," he said quietly.

She met his eyes. "Thank you. But this part isn't anything you could control."

"No."

She started eating her *ropa vieja* with apparent pleasure, which led her to ask her questions about the Cuban food on the menu. Tony told her that his father's side of the family had come from Cuba.

"My grandparents," he explained. "My dad was a little boy then. Tia Paloma is one of his sisters, born here." He paused. "I'm told Navarro is a Basque name."

"And your mother's side?"

Hearing genuine interest, he said, "Mexico. Tia Paloma didn't think a Cuban restaurant would make it here, so she started with only a few Cuban items among the Mexican. Over the years, she's added more, until the menu is close to fifty-fifty."

"I guess I'm just timid, sticking to the familiar," she said with a sigh.

"Most of us like the familiar," he consoled her. "Why else am I here so often?"

Her laugh, free of strain, rewarded him.

Replete, they sipped coffee. Tony was glad they were sharing the restaurant with so few customers. In something like another hour, the dinner crowd would start filtering in. Not that he and Beth had discussed anything he didn't want overheard; in fact, they'd managed to avoid any talk about the investigation or her family, except briefly after the pediatrician had intruded.

She wanted to pay her share of the bill, but Tia Paloma never brought one. When she came by the table, Beth tried to persuade Tony's aunt to take her money but failed.

"No, no!" Tia Paloma waved her hands vehemently. "Tony is family. You're his friend. No, impossible."

"We're not really friends. We're…sort of working together."

His aunt backed away, lapsing into a spate of Spanish, saying that if Beth came for lunch alone the next day, she could pay, but not when she was with Tony.

Beth laughed and gave up. "Then, *gracias*. I have a new favorite dish."

Aunt Paloma retreated in satisfaction, winking at him over her shoulder.

"I think… I might go home," Beth said, sliding out of the booth. "I'd intended to grocery shop but, now that I've had dinner, I can wait until tomorrow."

He hesitated but decided to be honest. Again. *He* was developing a big mouth where Beth was concerned. "I'm going to try to catch your sister."

"By surprise?"

"I'd rather," he said, "but I'm not totally set on it, or I wouldn't have told you." He watched her absorb that.

"I won't warn her."

They started for the front, which necessitated passing by only a few tables from Dr. Schuh and his friends. Without thinking, Tony laid a hand on Beth's back, ostensibly to steer her. Good God, was he making some kind of claim? Why? Because he hadn't liked the man's insistence that she call him if she needed anything?

She's supposed to call you? a small voice taunted.

Yes, damn it!

Way too early to say anything like that. Especially since he wasn't a hundred percent sure she shared his interest. Whether consciously or unconsciously, she might be trying to soften him, make him more reluctant to pursue her father.

Is it working?

He answered the question confidently. No. He couldn't let anything he felt for her divert him from the investigation. Or forget how it could end. How many times had he arrested a suspect and removed him from his home, while dodging blows or trying to shut his ears to pleas from distraught family members?

Feeling chilled even as they exited the air-conditioned restaurant into the heat of the day, he knew he shouldn't have let their relationship get so personal. If—when—he arrested her father, all Beth would have to do was look at him, pain and accusation in her eyes, to deliver a hammer blow.

Of course, he wouldn't have kissed her anyway, not in the bright sunlight after such a casual meal, and especially not given the potential conflicts. But when he said "I'll see you in the morning," he must have sounded remote because her expression closed, too. Her "Thank you for suggesting this" was said in the pleasant tone she saved for strangers.

Watching her maneuver out of her parking spot without so much as glancing his way, Tony swore aloud.

BETH HAD NO idea what had gone wrong, but Tony—or should she go back to Detective Navarro?—was every bit as cool the next morning when she let them into the garage again. Which was just fine. Good, in fact. Better that she didn't suffer any romantic delusions.

She wordlessly accepted a new pair of latex gloves and lifted a box from the workbench.

"Wait. Let me—"

"I have it," she said, setting it on the concrete floor.

His forehead creased. "You don't have to do any heavy lifting."

"You're kidding, right?" She sat in the same lawn chair as yesterday.

He scowled at her. "Why would I be kidding?"

Tart was okay, acid wasn't, she counseled herself. "Who do you think handled these boxes in the first place? Who do you think cleared this garage?"

Tony sat, too, but carefully, as if testing again the sturdiness of the chair, with its aluminum frame and webbing. It splayed a little but held firm. "I assumed you had your brother here for the bigger stuff," he said.

"I did call him for anything really heavy," Beth admitted, wishing she hadn't started this, "but there wasn't much."

Mouth tight, he opened the flaps of the box. They both peered in.

"What is this?" he asked.

She couldn't not talk to him, she supposed. "I didn't really go through this one either on Sunday. It's kind of miscellaneous. Maybe stuff Mom packed."

After poking around a little, Tony lifted out a gold-trimmed porcelain tray, which really should have been wrapped, as delicate as it was.

The glimmer of memory she'd had when she first opened the box solidified. "Wait. That was on the dresser. Mom would drop her earrings and watch and what have you on it. Dad his change. You know."

"Did your mother switch it out for something else?"

Slowly, Beth shook her head. "I don't think so. I...didn't notice when it disappeared." She gazed at the back of a picture frame lying face down. "Dad must have not wanted to look at things that reminded him of her."

"Strange reaction for a man who claims to have believed she'd be back."

She skewered him with a look. Or tried to, anyway. "I doubt he packed up her stuff the day after she disappeared. It could have been months later."

To his credit, Tony said, "You're right." But then he added, "Wouldn't you have noticed?"

Beth reached for whatever was in a frame and wasn't surprised to recognize it immediately, too. "Mom did this," she whispered. It was crewelwork, a riot of pink and white and pale yellow roses against a cream backdrop. "It was a kit. The kind where the fabric was printed with the colors you were supposed to use. It still took forever, with the stitches so tiny."

He studied it. "One of my sisters does things like that. She's given me a couple."

Beth blinked. "You have framed crewelwork like this in your house?"

"In my house, yes." He grimaced. "Somewhere. On the walls, no."

Yesterday, she would have laughed. Today, she only said, "I need to grab some of that newspaper to wrap these things. I'll bet Emily would like to have them." Before he could open his mouth, she added, "Later. I know."

Another frame held her parents' wedding photo. She stared at it for the longest time, seeing how happy they both looked, her mother beautiful, her father handsome. This had always been on the dresser, too, never with the other pictures in the family room.

She felt Tony's gaze but couldn't let herself look up to see his expression. If it was gentle, sympathetic, she might break down whether she believed his kindness insincere or not.

The box held several porcelain figurines, two chipped, a pair of embroidered pink satin pillows, and a pink china lamp base. Emily would probably love to have all of these.

For the first time, Beth wondered how her father felt about pink. Nothing in this box, except maybe the porcelain tray, seemed to belong in a man's bedroom. Maybe he hadn't dumped it all in this box because he was angry and hurt; maybe instead he'd thought, *At last I can get rid of this pink crap.* Would he tell her if she asked?

"Anything here that doesn't look familiar?"

Tony asked. "Or that you know wasn't in your parents' bedroom?"

She shook her head and nestled the lamp base in a bed of crumpled newspaper. Once Tony closed the flaps, she labeled the box with the black marker and let him slide it into the same place she'd taken it from.

He returned with another. This one was filled with albums of family photos as well as loose ones that hadn't made it into an album.

"Did your parents take a lot of pictures?" Tony asked.

"More when we were little, I think. I don't remember Mom getting the camera out so much once we were teenagers." Amusement lifted the corners of her mouth. "We probably weren't as photogenic. Or she was so annoyed at one or all of us, she didn't feel like memorializing us."

He chuckled but then rubbed his chin thoughtfully. "Would she have taken pictures of their friends?"

"Like Dr. Schuh and his wife? I don't remember." There were an awful lot of photographs in that box, she realized. "Do we have to go through them?"

He looked about as enthusiastic as she felt. "Maybe. Let's set it aside for now. I'm hoping you can tell me who your parents' friends were." He frowned. "Although, I meant to ask. This Dr.

Schuh and his wife. Have they stayed friends with your dad?"

She drew a complete blank. "I have no idea. I should, shouldn't I? But…things were so unsettled after Mom vanished. Nothing would have been the same. And really, what social life they had would have been at Mom's instigation. I mean, if the Schuhs invited him over for dinner, he'd have gone, but would it have occurred to him that he was supposed to reciprocate?" She couldn't imagine. "I suspect most friends tried to be supportive and finally drifted away."

"Yeah, it's a little hard to picture—" He gave her a chagrined glance. "Sorry."

"No, that's okay."

There were only a couple more boxes that she'd identified as probably Mom's stuff. There might be others that Matt or Emily hadn't mentioned—especially Emily, who might have thought she could spirit something away without either her sister or brother noticing. Heavens—she might very well have done that. They'd all gone back and forth so often, Beth wouldn't have noticed Emily slipping out to her car.

Should she say something to Tony? She sneaked a look at him just as he set down the next box. He'd worn cargo pants today—the gloves had come out of a pocket on his right thigh—and a navy blue T-shirt. Seeing muscles flexing in his arms, she forgot why she'd looked at him in the first place. He wasn't muscle-bound, like guys who spent too much time at the gym. He was... just right. Sexy.

And suddenly her face felt hot. *Please don't let him notice.*

Of course, he said, "You okay?" His voice was a little raspier than usual.

She didn't raise her gaze from the latest box. "I'm fine. You know, I forgot to plug in the fans. Are you getting hot?"

He cleared his throat. "Let's hold off."

How many million times had he said that?

Beth groaned when she saw the jewelry box. Tony lifted his eyebrows.

"I should have taken that home. It's such a mess, though." She raised the lid. "Everything is tangled up. Do you know how hard it is to unknot delicate chains?"

Tony poked at the top tray. "That's a really big diamond."

"If it is a diamond. I noticed it. I didn't look to see if the other earring is there."

"I don't know. A couple of my sisters have diamond engagement rings. This looks real to me." His dark eyes met hers. "You don't sound as if you remember it. Them."

"I...don't." Beth frowned. "I was only fifteen, though. And not girly."

One side of his mouth twitched. "Right. You didn't like pink, and you didn't like jewelry?"

"I *hated* pink," she said with more heat than she'd intended. "Jewelry... I like it okay now—" she touched a fingertip to the small gold post in one of her lobes "—but then, I was at an awkward age, and I sort of kept my head down and hoped not to be noticed." *Oh, good—tell him how pathetic you were.* She added hastily, "I'm sure Mom never said anything about having diamond earrings, which you'd think she would have. If only to say something like *Now remember, girls, these are worth quite a bit.*"

"Yeah," he agreed, "you'd think she would've." He picked up the diamond—or fake diamond—stud and lifted it to the light. "Would she buy something like this on her own?"

"I don't know," Beth had to say, again. "Emily might have a better idea. Mom and I weren't talking that much then." Belatedly, it occurred to her that was a stupid thing to tell the police detective investigating her mom's murder. Had he considered *her* a suspect? She'd been big enough to overpower her mother...

"What are you thinking?" Lines in his forehead had deepened. "I don't like your expression."

"Just..." She drew a deep breath. "I must be on your suspect list, too. That hadn't occurred to me."

"You're not," he said shortly.

"Why not? Fifteen-year-olds are capable of doing terrible things."

"They are. You?" He shook his head. "You take care of people. You'd never knowingly hurt someone."

She should have been reassured, but for some reason that stung. "I'm not a saint, you know."

He gave an odd, gruff laugh. "You're the only person I know who'd take offense at being described as *caring*."

"It's just…" Why *had* that bothered her? "I'm more than that. I get mad, I dislike some people, and, yes, there are times I resent feeling responsible for everyone else!"

"I know all that, Beth." He reached across the space between their lawn chairs and gripped her hand.

She looked at his hand, so much larger than hers, the fingers thicker, his skin darker. His touch felt good—warm and secure. Beth felt a tiny, worrisome stir of arousal.

"Do you?" she said bitterly, wrenching her hand free. "That'd be a first."

Oh, what was wrong with her? Pity parties were meant to be private. And this was stupid, anyway. She loved her family and *chose* to take care of them. Sure, it would be nice if, just once, someone tried to take care of *her*, but, honestly, she'd be so confused she'd be bound to turn it around in no time.

"Beth, I see more than you think I do," he said quietly.

She shook her head. "Forget it, okay? Let's do what we're here for."

Watching her, he didn't move for a minute. Finally, he shook his head and began to dig through the belts and scarves at the bottom of the box before lifting an odd lumpy item out. "What…? Oh, it's one of those things filled with rice or beans that you can warm in the microwave."

"Do you suppose they rot eventually?" she said dubiously.

He turned it. "I don't see any blood on it. As far as I'm concerned, we can throw it away."

When she pointed, he carried it across the garage and dropped it in a cardboard carton labeled Toss.

When he came back, Tony said, "Let's look through the jewelry box and not worry about untangling chains or tarnish. Okay?"

She nodded. He located a large plastic bin and dragged it over to use as a table. Beth set the jewelry box on it, took out the tray and put it aside, but Tony didn't make a move.

Seeing her surprised glance, he said, "None of the jewelry will mean anything to me. This job is yours. Tell me if anything that she often wore is missing or there's something that surprises you."

Beth nodded. She picked out the lump of chains that looked like a heap of snakes. Most, from the way they'd blackened, appeared to be sterling silver; a couple might be gold. Pendants...oh! She remembered that tiny bird. And the pearl, which was attached to one of the gold chains.

"I think... Dad bought her that. Their first Christmas together?"

She kept going. Lots of earrings. It would take work to pair them up again. Most were costume jewelry, nice enough that Emily might like them or they could be donated to the thrift store. *The pearl necklace... I might keep*, she thought, *now that I know she didn't choose to leave us.*

In the bottom, amidst a jumble of bangle bracelets, a silver charm bracelet and bead necklaces, she found the other diamond earring. The setting and post could have been silver, except they hadn't tarnished at all.

She squinted at the back, looking for a stamp. "I think this is white gold, or even platinum."

"We need to have a jeweler look at them," he said, taking the one from her and fishing for its mate. "Once we know more, I can ask your father about them."

Beth dug deeper, setting the cheaper stuff out of the way in pursuit of a glint she'd seen. It was a pendant, an even larger diamond set in a swirl of that same shining silver. Except...not silver. The matching, impossibly delicate chain was almost weightless draped over her hand.

Beth couldn't take her eyes off it. "This looks really expensive."

Tony's lawn chair squeaked as he moved. "Yeah, it does."

"Mom did make a good income. She might have rewarded herself after a good year. Or...or she and Dad agreed to pick out their own Christmas presents." Except Dad didn't own anything comparable, unless you added up an awful lot of books.

"Then why don't you remember her wearing these?" Tony asked, his gaze on the necklace, too.

"I told you." Her quick response was...defensive? "I might not have noticed."

"Your brother or sister might," he said, soothing.

She bit her lip, hard enough to sting, before she nodded.

He accepted the necklace from her and allowed it to slither through his fingers to lie beside the obviously matching earrings. "Have you at least glanced at everything?"

"Yes."

"What should be there but isn't?"

Trying to think, Beth frowned. "Nothing. Except...did you find her rings?"

"Plural?"

"Engagement ring and wedding band?"

"Neither were with her body." He looked and sounded energized. "So what happened to them?"

"Dad might know. If she left them on the dresser—or, wait, the computer desk would have made more sense—he might have put them away. Her *I'm leaving you* note would have been more convincing if it looked like she'd taken her rings off, wouldn't it?"

"It would." He sat back, frowning a little and gazing ahead as if not seeing anything in the garage. "But, if so, why wouldn't he have said she had? Why would he let you all think she would be coming home?"

"Because…he wanted to let us hold onto hope for a while?"

Tony looked at her, his eyebrows a little crooked.

"I guess that doesn't sound like Dad, does it?" And he was right. Nothing like that would ever occur to her father. "Do you think whoever killed Mom thought she'd be harder to identify without the rings?"

"Even then, DNA was commonly known," he pointed out. "And comparing dental work, which is what we did."

"If Dad killed her, he'd have made sure she 'left' the rings, and that we all saw them. They would have supported his story."

"They would have," Tony agreed, some reluctance in his voice. "Although your dad doesn't strike me as a great planner."

A spike of anger had her dumping jewelry back in the polished wooden box. "You're convinced that he's the killer, aren't you?"

"He's still likeliest, Beth."

She shook her head, glaring at him. "Do you always go for the easy answer?"

Some stiffening of his shoulders and a narrowing of those dark eyes were all that gave away his reaction to her jab. "Do I try to turn every crime into a convoluted mystery, when it isn't? No. Am I as impartial and thorough as I can be? Yes. Why else am I here with you?"

The backs of her eyes burned, but she wouldn't let him see that much vulnerability. "Good question."

He scooted the plastic tote with the diamond jewelry atop to one side, letting her pack the jewelry box away while he brought the next cardboard box, narrow and tall. The last of those Mom's things that she'd set aside.

"This one is all prints or artwork, I think," she said, stripping everything she felt from her voice.

Once again, he let her remove them one by one. Most were framed prints, not very interesting. A few looked vaguely familiar; all ran to being pretty or cute. Beth had a niggling memory that this box had once sat on the top shelf of the linen closet. Maybe Mom had traded these out for variety?

The portfolio, however, she didn't remember seeing before yesterday. Open, she saw that it contained unframed prints, most matted. Curious, Beth pulled them all out.

The first couple seemed to be original watercolors, better quality than the framed stuff. The view in one was across a cove of Frenchman Lake at the curving lines of wine grape vines following the contours of the hills that sheltered the lake. The other was a close-up of a vine, heavy with grapes.

The third she didn't even see because her gaze was caught by what had lain beneath it. A colored-pencil drawing of a seductively smiling, nude woman, hair spread on a pillow, legs wantonly apart. Beth was vaguely aware that Tony had leaned forward, expression arrested. She couldn't take her eyes from this beautiful, obscene drawing.

"That's—How can it be?" Her stomach lurched, and she clapped a hand to her mouth. "Dear God. That's my mother!"

CHAPTER SEVEN

THE INSTANT BETH uncovered the drawing, Tony knew he was looking at Christine Marshall. A Christine very different than she'd appeared in the photographs he'd seen.

For Beth's sake, he wanted to whisk the damn thing out of sight. Still, he'd half hoped for a surprise to turn up—although he couldn't have predicted this one—and he had a job to do.

"Are you sure it's your mother?" he asked, with some urgency.

Her head bobbed. Her hand remained over her mouth. He hoped her stomach wasn't going to revolt.

"The face could be hers, the body entirely imaginary," he suggested.

She shook her head so vehemently that strands escaped the elastic at her nape.

He resumed studying the drawing. Okay, this woman was obviously petite, slender, even delicate. Small-breasted, slim-hipped. In fact, she was built a lot like Beth's sister.

Beth's hand dropped to her lap, although her

eyes never left the drawing. "We used to go swimming a lot. We showered and changed in the dressing room. I was shy and stayed wrapped in a towel as much as I could, but Mom was confident enough not to be self-conscious."

Another way of saying her mother was proud of her body. Rightly, he couldn't help thinking, given that she'd been forty-two when she disappeared. *And* that she'd borne three children.

"See?" In a tone lacking all animation, Beth, pointed to a faint line that could have been a shadow, or a crease. "She had a C-section when Emily was born."

"Damn," he murmured. "Who drew this?"

"I don't know." She looked sick. "Dad can hardly draw a stick figure, in case you were wondering."

He actually hadn't been, even though husbands had been known to commission this kind of drawing or painting of their wives. John Marshall? Tony's imagination didn't stretch that far.

This drawing was both skilled and sensual. It caught the beckoning position of spread arms and legs as well as the heavy-lidded eyes and a teasing smile. If the artist hadn't also been her lover, Tony would swallow his badge, pointy edges and all.

"The style doesn't look familiar?"

"I—" Beth started to take her head, but stopped. "I don't know," she said haltingly. "I mean, I don't remember seeing anything like this. Why would I have?"

He watched her for a minute, seeing doubt she didn't want to acknowledge. Tony thought there was a good chance that, somewhere, sometime, she'd seen a drawing by this same artist. His experience said that pushing her now wouldn't help. The memory had to make its own labyrinthine way to the surface.

"We'd better make sure there isn't another one," he said.

Appearing somewhere between numb and horrified, Beth shifted the erotic drawing to one side with a nudge that suggested she didn't really want to touch it. He couldn't blame her. Even as he studied the next piece of art, he imagined himself helpfully organizing contents of his mother's garage or closet and finding something like this... Good God! He repressed a shudder and made himself concentrate.

He was looking at a watercolor of a basalt rimrock, a natural formation in this volcanic country that resembled the remnants of an ancient castle wall. It was beautifully done, surely by the same artist as the other watercolors.

Next came a watercolor of a sunset over ocean waves that looked amateurish.

That was it.

All five pieces of art were laid out in front of

him. Three different artists, he'd swear. The ocean painting verged on generic and lacked a signature. The rimrock—he'd buy that one, if he saw it for sale. He liked the sculptural lines of the vineyard above the lake, but vineyards didn't do much for him. Those three watercolors were signed, but the scrawl was unreadable.

He supposed it was conceivable an artist that talented could draw human figures in an entirely different style. Hard to see, though. The lines of the drawing were precise rather than fluid, despite the woman's erotic sprawl. He pictured the artist—a man? Tony presumed so, but couldn't be sure—sketching an outline, then coloring within the lines, in a way. Concentrating on each tiny detail.

The four watercolors were matted, likely by the artists. The erotic drawing hadn't been. Christine couldn't have framed and hung it in her house, that was for sure.

He glanced at Beth, who had hunched forward.

"What are you thinking?" he asked.

"That I can't believe my mother let anyone draw this."

Let? Her mother had posed for the artist. Nothing involuntary about it.

"Beth, did you ever have any reason to suspect she had a lover?"

She shot him an outraged look. "No!" But he'd

swear she'd pulled into a tighter ball, like a woman expecting a blow—or sheltering a secret.

Part of his job was to push and push until whomever he was interviewing broke. Look for the tells, like her current posture, and use them. But he flat could not make himself do that, not to her, not now. She was still part of his job, but she'd triggered completely *un*professional feelings in him. And, damn, he'd have to watch that.

In this case… Thinking back to her brother's hostility toward his mother as well as his father, Tony doubted he'd have to get his answers from Beth. Matt knew about the lover, sure as hell, and was hot-tempered enough to spill as soon as he was asked the right question.

"Okay," Tony said. "Let's slide all these into the portfolio, trying not to touch them anymore than we already have."

"But…we're wearing gloves." Beth looked up at him and wriggled her fingers.

"Yeah, but we don't want to smear an underlying fingerprint."

"The artist would have had to touch this, wouldn't he?"

Oh, yeah. Unfortunately, the texture of the paper was rough enough to make Tony wonder how well a print could be lifted, but he had hope. Not that a fingerprint was likely to do much good until he had a suspect, however. What were the odds Christine's lover had committed a previous crime and therefore was in the system?

He glanced at his watch, calculated and said, "Are you able to go on?"

"On?" Beth followed his gaze to the piles on the far side of the garage, the ones no one had gone through yet. Her sturdy agreement came as no surprise.

THEY WORKED FOR several more hours, finding nothing of interest to Tony. Beth had to go back to making decisions: keep, recycle, throw away or thrift store.

She came across a tent packed in a long, narrow bag, as well as several sleeping bags. She didn't remember ever going camping, but Matt might. The sleeping bags they'd taken for overnights at friends' houses and when friends slept over at their house. Provisionally, she decided to keep those and get rid of the tent.

Two boxes proved to contain back issues of academic journals: *The Harvard Review of Philosophy* and *Philosopher's Imprint*. Beth had a suspicion her mother had gotten tired of the overflow and packed these up without Dad's knowledge. She was tempted to either drop them into the recycling or haul them over to the Wakefield library to see if they'd like some extra back issues, but her conscience overcame her. She'd ask him what he wanted to do, even knowing he'd be delighted to recover them and add them to the heaps in the house.

She'd intended for some time to get someone to turn either her or Matt's old bedroom into a real library to supplement the built-ins in the family room and the bookcases in Dad's office. More wall-to-wall shelves, with the books truly organized, would at least get them off the floor. Until her father added too many more.

Frowning at the periodicals, Tony said, "Your father doesn't seem like a home improvement guy."

She gave a small laugh. "That's safe to say. What are you thinking?"

"The piece of wallboard." He nodded over his shoulder. "How someone could haul it in here unnoticed."

"Oh. I think it might have been here."

He stared at her.

"Mom and Dad tried a do-it-yourself job putting shelving in his office. Maybe a year or two before she disappeared? She was getting mad at the piles of books everywhere. I think she'd thought the bookcases in the family room would solve the problem."

"Doesn't sound like she knew him very well."

Beth's smile was sad. "Apparently not. Anyway, they put up those wall-hung tracks, and used some kind of special screws or thingies that are supposed to prevent the whole thing from tearing out of the drywall."

"Books are heavy."

"They started collapsing almost right away, leaving holes in the walls." She hesitated. "Mom was not happy. They had to hire someone to re-place the drywall and spackle it. Then, instead of custom built-ins, they just bought tall, wood book-cases. I…have this vague memory of a piece of wallboard left over. It was lying on its side over there." She gestured.

"So our killer was an opportunist."

"You mean, he knew the wallboard was there."

"Yeah. It's been bugging me. Bringing the new sheet in and breaking up the old one and getting it out unseen wouldn't have been any easier than carrying a body out unnoticed."

She shivered. When Tony apologized, she shook her head. "Believe me, I've been envision-ing all of it already."

She went on to the next box in hopes of distract-ing herself. This one held children's board games, puzzles and toys, as did the next one, confirming her suspicion that her mother had pack rat tenden-cies, too. When she said so, Tony laughed.

"I think my mother does—or did—too. Every time one of my sisters has another kid, Mamá comes up with more baby clothes, or a plastic rattle or a creaky old stroller."

"She might be shopping thrift and consignment stores," Beth suggested. "Wanting to help her kids without them knowing she's spending money."

His gaze sharpened. "I never thought of that. Huh. It sounds like her. I always wondered because wouldn't you think eight of us would wear everything out?"

She enjoyed his chagrin. "Yep."

"Well, crap. Do I tell my sisters?"

What an unexpected conversation to be having with the detective investigating her mother's murder. She said, "Unless your mother is struggling financially, I'd vote no." As if *she* had any vote in his decisions.

He didn't seem to notice her embarrassment. "Mamá isn't rich, but she's okay. We'd take care of her even if she runs through her savings and Social Security. You're right. I'll keep my mouth shut. I'll bet she enjoys the shopping."

"Most women do."

He lifted his eyebrows. "But not you?"

"Not especially. If I need something to wear… well, it's just something everyone has to do. I guess if I ever have children, it might be fun." To distract herself, she reached for something enveloped in black trash bags, secured with masking tape that was peeling. When she tugged up one edge enough to peer in, she said, "Oh, ugh."

Tony took a look, too. "That's the saddest looking Christmas tree I've ever seen."

"Well, assembled..." She gave it up. It would still look tattered and fake. "I hated not having a real tree. I can't remember when we quit using this one." She stood and dragged it to sit next to the big box labeled Toss. Returning, she said, "I would really like to think I didn't inherit the frugal gene. At least, not taken too far."

Grimacing, he said, "The Depression did this to our grandparents' generation. Well, not my paternal grandparents. They weren't able to bring much at all when they came to America. Mamá's parents, now, they fussed over every penny any of their kids or grandkids spent."

"I do understand that." She waved at the remaining accumulation. "*This*, on the other hand..."

"Maybe you should buy your father an automatic garage door opener for Christmas. No, his birthday. It's in September, right? If he started parking in here, he might quit thinking of this as a storage unit."

September? Christmas? On a tiny burst of hope, she asked, "Does that mean you don't think Dad will be in prison by then?"

"It takes a long time to bring someone to trial these days." He hesitated. "I'm not making you any promises. There's the possibility your father stumbled on this drawing. Surely even he would have been enraged. In any marriage, this would be a fire starter."

"He'd have been upset, sure. Enraged…isn't him." *Oh, Dad, I hope you never saw this. Never have to see it.*

Tony bent his head, as if acknowledging her point without necessarily agreeing. But he continued, "I will say I'm ready to pursue the possibility of an unknown man who had a relationship with your mother. Someone with money and some training as an artist."

Snide was tempting. *It's about time.* Or, *Really? You actually opened your mind enough to see that I'm right?* But she refrained, of course. Partly because *nice* was so ingrained, she had to struggle to express anger or any other negative emotion, and partly because she didn't want to give him reason to shut her out.

"Thank you," she said, sounding meek.

He shot her an odd look, opened his mouth… and changed his mind. "Let's get on with this."

More junk. Christmas decorations showing their age—she pushed that box aside to go through more carefully, to be sure she didn't throw away a beloved nativity scene or some such thing. Clothes that had to have been her father's, maybe when he'd been a student. Looking at them dubiously,

Beth saw how high-waisted the pants were by to-day's standards. If they were in better shape, she'd call them vintage. As they were? Toss.

Women's clothing, very 1980s at a guess. Stirrup pants, waistlines again high on all the pants she lifted out. Dresses in bold prints that, even on a woman as petite as her mother, must have been really short. Blouses had *big* shoulder pads. There was a lot of tan and brown and orange. Except for the pink leg warmers and a pink and purple velour sweat suit. Oh, and glittery jellies. Beth had had a pair when she was a kid, although they'd already been a larger size than these. Mom wore a five, and frequently complained that her foot was sliding around in them. She'd been known to buy kids' shoes to get a better fit.

As far as this box went, Mom had only saved things in good condition, which meant they could go to at least a thrift store if not consignment. All too well, Beth could see her mother in a pink leotard, tights and leg warmers, with her blonde hair teased into some kind of cute side ponytail. She almost shuddered. She should count her blessings that fashion had moved on by the time she cared what she looked like. This stuff would have been fine for someone who was slim and cute. Not so much for tall and too well-rounded.

"You get this expression sometimes," Tony growled. "You hunch your shoulders. I don't like it."

"What?" she said in surprise, although she squared her shoulders because—he was right. "I was thinking how cute Mom would have been in some of these outfits." She had a belated thought. "Or Emily would." She really should let her go through this box. It wasn't as if seeing Emily in any of these clothes would bother her or Matt.

"Sure you were," he said, sounding almost mad. "What you were really thinking was that they wouldn't have been cute on *you*."

"How did you—" She stopped, but not in time. Heat in her cheeks told her that.

"You must have had boyfriends."

"Of course I have!" Some. A few. Just…never one who hadn't either disappointed her or drifted away, less than passionately committed.

He glowered at her. "Then you can't tell me no man has told you how sexy you are!"

The excessive heat drained from her face, leaving it…cold. "I…don't think anyone has ever put it that way."

"How did they put it?" His jaw muscles appeared to be knotted as tight as fists.

Of course, she couldn't bring to mind a single compliment any man had ever paid her. There *had* been some, just… It took her a minute to come up with an answer. *I didn't believe them.* Why would she, when she'd always felt like a moose? Plain, overweight. Feet too big. Hazel eyes instead of sparkling blue. Hair that was mostly brown. Freckles across a nose that, okay, wasn't too big but also wasn't slender, tipped up, classic or cute.

The cold invaded her stomach. How could she not have realized how completely her self-image had been formed by the time she was twelve or thirteen? By her mother and the darling little sister following her?

"I...don't remember," she said softly.

Something changed on Tony's face. She hoped that wasn't pity she saw.

He stood, muttering something she thought might be, "I swore I wouldn't." He held out a hand anyway. "C'mere."

Beth hesitated.

He waggled his fingers, his expression the furthest thing from pitying now. His mouth had softened, while the skin stretching over his cheekbones seemed more taut than it had been. His dark eyes burned.

Heat curled low in her belly and between her legs, replacing the chill. Slowly she rose, timid but wanting this. She laid her hands in his and let him pull her toward him.

When they were barely inches apart, he released one of her hands so he could raise his to her face. He cupped her cheek, his thumb wandering, playing with her lower lip, while he devoured her with his eyes.

"I've wanted you since the minute I set eyes on you. Your sister would never appeal to me. You have a woman's body." He spread her fingers and placed her hand on his chest, then squeezed her hip. "Curves. Long legs. You have the most beautiful eyes I've ever seen. Some men like tiny women with boyish bodies. Plenty of us are a hell of a lot more drawn to a woman who looks just like you." His voice had been falling, until now it was barely a husky whisper. "Are you hearing me?"

She nodded, although the way her pulse had accelerated, she was lucky she *could* hear. Feeling shy, she lifted her other hand to his chest, too. Beneath one palm, his heart beat hard and fast. Her fingers flexed for the pleasure of being able to touch.

"I shouldn't do this," he murmured, "but, damn." He dipped his head and skimmed his lips over hers.

So soft, so tempting. A little sound rose from her throat as she sought his mouth again. Another brush, a nibble. Her hands slid upward, found the strong muscles that ran from his neck to his shoulders. He teased her with another fleeting kiss, but this time the tip of his tongue slid damply across the seam of her lips.

Beth moaned and rose onto tiptoe. One of his arms came around her, hard, flattening her against his body, and she flung hers around his neck. This kiss was deep, hungry. His tongue explored her mouth, demanding a response. Her awareness narrowed to *him*—his tall, muscular body, his scent, the texture of his thick, silky hair beneath her fingers, the heat and taste of his mouth. The ridge against her belly made her want to rub herself against him. In fact, that's exactly what she was doing, his grip on her hip guiding her movements.

Beth had never felt like this, unashamedly aroused, no voice in her head whispering doubts. The experience was so heady she hardly noticed when he began to ease back. His lips traced the line of her jaw; his tongue touched the exquisitely sensitive spot beneath her earlobe. A groan vibrated in his chest. He lifted his head and opened a couple of inches between them, although he was still gently kneading her hip—no, really, her butt—while the fingers of his other hand remained tangled in her hair.

Dazed, she stared up at him. Didn't he want to keep kissing her?

No. Obviously he didn't.

He discovered how fat my butt is. I did something wrong. Embarrassing. Maybe he never *had* really wanted her. This was just…manipulation. A way to gain her cooperation.

"Knock it off."

"What?"

He gently bumped his forehead against hers, then kissed her nose. "Those freckles…"

What…? She gave her head a small, bewildered shake.

"Beth, I can't think of anything I want more right now than to unroll one of those sleeping bags, lay you down on it and make love to you."

Startled, she studied his face to see if he meant it.

At last, he took his hand from her hip and moved it to her waist. The other hand, too, so he could hold her close to him but also keep her from plastering herself back against him.

Because he doesn't really want—

"There are two things stopping me. Besides the fact that a sleeping bag wouldn't keep the concrete from being really hard."

They could use *both* sleeping bags. Of course, she didn't say that aloud.

"One," he continued, "is that I like my job. You're not a suspect, I meant that, but you're not just a witness, either. Two, what if I still have to arrest your father? Or—"

He didn't finish, but she could fill in the blank. *Your brother.* A suspicion as ridiculous, in a different way, as believing her father could kill anyone.

"You'd hate my guts," Tony finished, gruff now. "It would be worse for both of us if we'd had sex."

He'd downgraded it from *making love*, Beth couldn't help noticing. At least he'd given her a chance to regain some semblance of dignity. She stepped back, and his hands dropped from her waist.

"You've made your point," she said, annoyed that her voice sounded a little husky. "Maybe you should have thought it out before you started this."

"I did, but I get irritated when you shrink into yourself the way you do. I can tell every time your confidence takes a hit even if I don't know *why*." He was all but glaring at her now.

"How can you tell?"

"Body language." He waved a hand at her. "Expression. Your eyes give you away. I don't know. I just can."

"That's...that's ridiculous."

"We both know it's not."

"Well, quit!" Beth made sure he couldn't see any of her self-doubt now. "I'm not some pathetic woman who needs you to buck up her self-esteem. As if one kiss from you is a magical cure." She wished. As therapy, it had actually worked really well while he was applying it. Long term, all he'd managed to do was intensify her lack of confidence in her physical appeal.

Except, he'd undeniably been aroused.

He was a man, and she'd been rubbing against him like...like a cat in heat. She cringed at the thought.

He snapped an obscenity. "There you go again!"

Beth lifted her chin pugnaciously. "You have no idea what I was thinking."

He leaned forward, hands planted on his hips. "Oh, yes I do."

They glared at each other until he made a rough sound, bent his head and rubbed the back of his neck.

"I have to get out of here."

"Fine."

He drew a couple of deep breaths, presumably meant to be calming, then looked at her again. "Can we resume this after lunch? Or are you too mad at me?"

"We have to finish. I'm doing this for my father's sake, and I won't back off."

Somehow, he cleared all expression from his face. She'd seen him do it before, but this time it really bothered her. He was wiping away the importance of this scene—the kiss *and* the argument. Getting back to business.

Well, if he could do it, so could she. She nodded at the portfolio. "Are you taking the jewelry and that?"

He followed her gaze. "I am. There's no surface large enough on the pendant or earrings to hold a fingerprint, but I'd like an appraisal. We need to look for fingerprints on the drawing, and maybe the portfolio itself." He hesitated. "With your permission, I'll take some of her things so we can lift her fingerprints."

"And Dad's," she said slowly.

"Probably. He's likely to have touched anything that was in their bedroom at some point, and certainly when he packed them up. I'll have to ask him for prints, so we can eliminate his."

Sure. Elimination. That's what was on *Detective* Navarro's mind. What he'd said made sense, though. Dad's fingerprints would be everywhere. Except on the drawing, and probably the other art. He might have glanced in the portfolio before he threw it in the box with the various framed prints Mom had kept. But pull anything out and look? Not Dad.

"Fingerprinting is messy," Tony said. "I can't guarantee some of the artwork won't be ruined."

Beth absorbed that. *The drawing* was what he really he meant. Repulsion gave her goosebumps. "I don't care. I never want to see it again."

"Good." He scooped up the jewelry and looked around. "You have anything I can put this in?"

"Oh." What had she done with— There they were. She fished a sandwich bag from a box. "Here."

"Excellent." Looking satisfied, he dropped the

jewelry in and zipped the top closed. "I need to give you a receipt for all of this."

She shook her head. "I don't care."

"Not optional. I'll have to get one out of the car."

Beth followed him out, turning off the light and locking up as she went. At his unmarked police car, he rummaged in the glove compartment and produced a pad of carbon copy receipts. He took only a moment to scrawl in her name, his, the date and the items he was taking, then rip off the top copy for her.

"Why don't we make it two o'clock?" he said.

She shrugged. "Sure. Although, you know, I could finish going through the stuff along that wall. It all seems to have been there forever."

Tony shook his head. "I need to be there."

Because she could hide something that might point a finger at her father. Wow. He'd been right—kissing had been a really bad idea. Trust seemed like a bare minimum before she locked lips with a guy.

"I don't like that expression, either. I wasn't suggesting—"

"You were, but I understand." Clutching the slip of paper, she stepped back. "Goodbye, Detective Navarro."

He looked frustrated and slammed the car door.

She'd pulled out her keys and reached her own car by the time he pulled away from the curb.

If Dad had been here, she'd have felt obligated to go in and make lunch for him, but as it was, she'd eat out. Somewhere Tony Navarro would never think of going.

And fat butt or not, she wasn't having a salad.

In the spirit of defiance, she decided on a drippy chicken teriyaki sandwich. As soon as she'd ordered at the café, she called Matt, but he didn't answer. Her news didn't seem like the kind of thing that should be left on voice mail, she decided. This evening was soon enough.

Emily answered right away. "I am *so* bored. My appointment didn't show. But I have to stick around because I have a two o'clock."

"I'm glad I caught you." Beth hesitated, but her sister and brother had a right to hear this. "I... that is, Detective Navarro and I found a couple of things in the boxes of Mom's stuff."

"Like what?" Of course, Emily was intrigued.

"A pair of earrings and a necklace that look expensive. I think they might be real diamonds."

"Really? You never wear jewelry, so can I—"

Beth unclenched her jaw. "You're missing the point. I don't remember ever seeing these before. Where did she get them?"

"The only diamond I remember was her engagement ring."

"It gets worse. We also found a drawing of Mom naked."

"*Mom*?"

"It's obvious she was having an affair." Beth felt brutal saying this. Of all of them, Emily clung mostly closely to the memory of their mother. "And that her lover was also an artist."

"Mom?" Emily said again, sounding lost this time.

"It's definitely Mom, who obviously posed for the, um, portrait."

"That doesn't make sense."

Unfortunately, it did. "Somebody killed Mom, and I know it wasn't Dad. Who do you think did it?"

Silence.

"I feel like I recognize the artist's work. As if somewhere I saw something else he drew. Do you remember anyone we knew who did pencil sketches? Really good ones?"

"No! And what makes you think Mom posed? This guy could have *imagined* what she looked like."

"Did he *imagine* the scar from her C-section?"

"I can't talk to you anymore!" her sister cried.

Her phone disconnected, Beth slowly set it down just as her lunch arrived. Typical Emily, who had to be force-fed any dose of harsh reality. Producing a smile for the waitress, Beth draped the napkin on her lap, then looked at the heap of fries and the—yes—drippy sandwich. She should have gone for a salad after all.

CHAPTER EIGHT

THE FACT THAT he'd been stupid enough to kiss her—and then had to *stop*—would have given Tony plenty of brooding material. The argument that followed made him sick. Lunch held no appeal.

Jeweler first, then, he decided. It would be a quick distraction.

He'd dealt before with the independent jeweler downtown. Given that this was the lunch hour, he was relieved as soon as he walked in to see the owner behind the glass counter, his nearly bald head bent as he studied something in his hand through a loupe. The store was deserted, too, which was good. Tony was almost to the back before Steven Thurman looked up.

His smile seemed genuine. "Detective Navarro. Dare I hope you're in search of an engagement ring for a beautiful lady?"

The image of a beautiful lady popped up right before Tony's mind's eye, and his fingers twitched at the memory of her luscious curves. Damn it. He'd never kissed a woman when he was on the job. Never even *thought* of kissing one...until he set eyes on Beth Marshall.

"Afraid not," he said, also smiling, if crookedly. "I promise I won't go anywhere else when—" *if* "—the time comes. Today's business."

"Something for me to look at?"

"Yep." Tony pulled the sandwich bag from his pocket and set it on the glass counter.

It happened that the store's diamond jewelry was displayed in the case right beneath. He saw immediately that the pendant and earrings were as fine, or finer, than anything Thurman's Jewelry had for sale.

"Ah," Thurman murmured. He produced a small, soft cloth, on which he shook out the pieces. "What do you need to know?"

"Well, first, *are* those diamonds? And a rough value, if you can give me that."

It wouldn't be the first time the jeweler had provided this service, which he never charged for. He considered helping the police to be his civic duty, he had insisted, the first time Tony had come in.

Where Tony had felt clumsy picking up anything as delicate as these pieces, Thurman's touch was deft. He chose the pendant first, turning it over and peering through the loupe.

"The setting is platinum, as I suspected." He flipped the pendant over, studying the stone at length through the monocular loupe which, he had once explained to Tony, offered a 10x magnification.

"It's the standard for grading diamond clarity," he had said absently.

Now, he made humming noises as he set aside the pendant and peered intently at each earring. At last, he put them on the cloth and looked at Tony. "If you want a thorough appraisal, I have a fellow who stops by on a regular schedule. He'll be here next week—"

"That's not necessary. Yet," he amended. "The, er, owner will likely need that eventually. As I said, a rough idea of quality and value is all I need for my purposes."

"These are very fine, as I imagine you've guessed. We grade diamonds by color, cut and clarity, as well as size. These are remarkably colorless— which is positive, for a diamond."

Which meant nothing to Tony, but he nodded.

"Clarity, also excellent, although I thought I saw a tiny inclusion in this diamond." He nudged it with his finger. "Round cut." He paused. "I believe the earrings are two carats each, the pendant three carats. The earrings alone would sell in a retail store for a minimum of ten thousand dollars, perhaps significantly higher. The pendant, perhaps the same. And those are conservative estimates."

Tony came close to gaping. Christine Marshall's

lover—and Tony had no doubt she'd had one—
had spent upwards of *twenty thousand dollars* on
some pretty jewelry for her? What was she supposed to do with them, when she couldn't wear
them around her husband? Or had she slipped
them out of the house and put them on before she
got to work, like a middle-school girl wearing
clothes her mother wouldn't allow? Well, Christine had certainly worn them when she was with
her lover.

"Thank you," he said, tucking his shock out
of sight.

"Let me put these in boxes to protect them."
The jeweler disappeared in back and returned
with two black velvet boxes. He gently stowed
the pendant and earrings, hesitated, then put both
boxes into the sandwich bag and handed it over.
"Tell the owner we charge ninety dollars for a full
appraisal, which is fairly standard. I might be interested in buying these myself, should he or she
decide to sell."

"I'll pass that on," Tony agreed. "For the moment, these are evidence in a criminal investigation."

"So I assumed."

"Any chance you sold these yourself? It might
have been ten to fifteen years back."

"No, I'd recognize these pieces. I carry comparable quality now, but less so that long ago. You

might try jewelers in Walla Walla. Although the odds of them remembering…" He shrugged.

He didn't have to say that the pendant and earrings could as well have been purchased in Seattle, Spokane or online.

Thanking him again, Tony tucked the jewelry into a pocket of his pants, buttoned it carefully, then walked out to his car. Straight to the station next, he decided; he didn't want to be responsible for pricey diamonds any longer than he had to be.

During the short drive, he thought about Christine. If she'd been in love with another man, why hadn't she left her husband? Because of the kids? Or because the lover had had his own impediment—say, a wife? If he had been married, he'd have to have been plenty wealthy to drop that kind of money on another woman without his wife noticing.

When Tony was a kid, growing up in this eastern Washington town, not many people had much money at all. The wheat farmers, who lived out of town, were about it. He'd had a few friends whose parents or grandparents took the whole family to Hawaii at Christmas or Disneyland for spring break. By the time he graduated from high school, the wheat farmers were either selling their land to be planted in wine grapes or planting those vines themselves. Huge, ostentatious houses sprouted atop ridges, while downtown businesses retreated to side streets, leaving the picturesque main street to boutiques, tasting rooms and restaurants, all geared to tourists. Handsome old homes were turned into bed and breakfast inns.

Drawn by the mystique of high-end wines, some residents and probably most visitors apparently had money in a way he didn't and never would. His mind turned to the woman he shouldn't have kissed. He didn't even wonder whether Beth hungered for money or the things it could buy; this was a woman who'd chosen to work with the elderly and their anxious families. Salaries in social services tended to be modest.

Matt, now, he had a streak of ambition, if Tony read him right.

This might be a good time to catch him. Would his sister have already called him? It would be interesting to find out.

MATT HADN'T BEEN enthusiastic when Tony called and asked to speak to him, but he'd agreed, suggesting a bench in the shade near the duck pond on the Wakefield campus. Tony offered to bring iced coffee, which required a small detour.

Beth's brother was there ahead of him, probably from eagerness to prevent his boss from seeing him interviewed by a cop again.

"This isn't as iced as it was," Tony said, handing over Matt Marshall's drink of choice.

"Thanks. It'll be good, anyway. It's damned hot today."

Summer around here was hot every day.

Tony sat a couple feet from the other man, took a long swallow of his blessedly cold and caffeinated drink and looked at the few ducks swimming desultorily in circles. None even bothered scrambling out of the water in hopes of crumbs.

Tony decided to get right to the point. "I've found evidence to suggest that your mother had an affair."

Matt snorted. "Like we didn't all know that."

All? "You're saying Emily and Beth knew, too?"

Matt pressed the chilled cup to his forehead and closed his eyes. "Emily... I don't know. Beth did. She asked me something once that made me sure."

The feeling of betrayal dismayed Tony. She'd described them as adversaries. Had he really let himself trust her to this extent? All he knew was that an uncomfortable lump seemed to be wedged in his chest.

"Your father?" he asked.

"Oh, Dad." The laugh was as much a sneer as anything. "He could have walked in on her naked in bed with the guy, and all he'd have done was look puzzled and say, 'Have I met your friend?'"

"You don't think he'd have cared."

Matt shifted, straightening his legs, then tucking his feet beneath the bench. Even so, his shoulders looked stiff when he said finally, "He'd have cared. It's just that he wouldn't notice any clues more subtle than seeing his wife with her legs spread for another man. A strange cologne on his sheets? I doubt he'd even ask. Mom flustered and rosy-cheeked and stinking of sex while asking solicitously about Dad's day so he wouldn't notice the sound of the back door closing?" Tendons stood out in Matt's hand and forearms. "Why would she bother? She could have introduced her bed buddy and said brightly, 'Look who stopped by.' Dad wouldn't have thought a thing about it."

Had he pulled that scenario out of a hat? Tony didn't think so. He asked, "Did she introduce her lover to you?"

Matt scowled. "No! What makes you think that?"

"But I get the feeling you do know who he was."

"No." He set his coffee on the bench beside him and bent forward, elbows on his knees, hands yanking at his hair. "If I'd known… God. What could *I* have done?"

Clearly, he had felt helpless and angry, a volcano ready to blow. Was the anger directed more at his mother—or at the man tearing apart Matt's family?

"Has Beth called you today?" Tony asked abruptly.

"Beth?" Matt turned his head enough to look at Tony. "No. Why would she?"

"She and I have been going through the boxes of your mother's things that were packed away in the garage."

Matt straightened, his hair now wildly disheveled. "You mean her clothes?"

"And other things." He told Beth's brother about the diamond jewelry and the drawing.

Both shock and revulsion in his blue eyes, Matt stuttered, "Mom...naked?"

"Yes. It's...clearly erotic in intent."

He shook his head, not in disbelief so much as shock, if Tony was any judge. "You think my father found it."

"That's one possibility."

"Jesus. I always thought—"

"What?"

"—that he did walk in on them. Even so... Damn." He ran a shaky hand over his face. "It's hard to picture him..." Once again, he trailed off.

"Killing?"

"Well...on purpose."

Tony swallowed some coffee. The head wound could conceivably have resulted from an accident of some sort. They'd wrestled and she'd fallen, striking her head on a corner of the dresser. Except the dent looked more rounded than that. A baseball bat, maybe a heavy-duty flashlight, seemed like better guesses.

"You all but accused your father of killing her, the last time we talked," he said.

Matt hunched into himself, a little like his sister did too often. "I didn't mean it, not really. Dad's... well, you've gotten an idea what he's like."

Tony nodded.

"I've been angry at him as long as I can remember. I needed a father. Instead, it was like having a ghost drifting around the house, vaguely surprised when the living people noticed his presence. When I figured out that Mom was screwing around on him, I got even madder. At her, but mostly at him. It was *his* fault. Why *would* she stick around? And then this was going on right underneath his nose, and he either didn't notice or pretended not to because that would ruffle his existence. I wanted him to *hurt*." Rage shook his voice. "To *feel* something." He swore again, and let his head fall back. "I thought I'd gotten over this crap. Ashley keeps telling me—" He applied the brakes so hard, he all but skidded, taking a wary, sidelong look at Tony.

"Telling you?" he asked mildly.

Matt let out a long sigh. "She points out that he could have been a lot worse. He didn't use his fists, he didn't belittle us. He's a gentle man who connects poorly to other people."

Ashley's words, Tony assumed.

"We're…about to start a family. I know I should get past this, before I become a father."

Tony surprised himself by saying, "You have a good start. You know what he *didn't* give you that you needed."

"Uh…yeah?"

"You might make a list someday. What qualities of his do you want to own? Which ones don't you?"

"None." He gave his hair another tug. "Of course that's not true. I'm a reader, like he is. I've chosen to work in academia. He did faithfully bring home a paycheck, and, as Beth poked me with the other day, he paid my way through college." He frowned, possibly in thought. "I don't see Dad cheating on Mom."

"All positives."

"Shit."

Tony gave him a moment to brood, then asked, "If you never saw the man, how did you know your mother was having an affair?"

Matt described a series of small things that an adult male would have recognized sooner than he had at seventeen. Coming home unexpectedly, to have his mother pop out of her bedroom and head him off was one. She'd barred him from opening her bedroom door once, after he'd been sure he heard a man's voice in there and became suspicious. Low-voiced phone conversations with too many smiles and giggles. Lies about where she'd been and what she'd done. A new, more youthful hairstyle, a lot heavier makeup than she'd been accustomed to wear. Hang-ups when Matt answered the phone after getting home from school earlier than usual.

"Did you ever ask her outright?"

"I did the day I heard the voice in the bedroom, and she refused to let me look so I could *know* no one was in there. She got all outraged, but it felt like cover to me."

"Did you hang around to see who came out?"

He shook his head. "I'd come home during lunch period because I'd forgotten to bring my clean PE clothes. I couldn't stay."

"Ah. Did you ever search to see if you could find proof?"

"You mean, dig through her drawers or something?" Matt looked surprised. "What would I have looked *for*? Like, condoms? But how would I know she and Dad weren't using them?"

"You might have found the drawing," Tony pointed out.

Matt went still. "Where was it?"

"In a stiff paper portfolio with some other unframed art. It was in a box that also held some framed prints that Beth thinks might have been displayed in the house at some point."

"I saw that box on Sunday when Beth was taking a look in it." He sounded wooden. "Even if I'd noticed it back then, I wouldn't have thought of looking through it. My mother's taste in art leaned toward cute and pink." He rose to his feet. "I did not see the drawing. I did not kill my mother. I wouldn't—" He swallowed, as if at the taste of bile. "This is the last time we talk without my lawyer being present."

"Matt, my job is to explore all possibilities, however unlikely. This was…a passing thought."

"It's a shitty one. And that's all I have to say." He turned and strode away, never looking back.

Tony drained the rest of his coffee. It had gotten so he was more surprised by generosity than he was by utter selfishness. Had his cynicism made him unlikable? Probably. Was that how Beth saw him? But, if so, why had she responded so passionately?

And, God, how had he lost control to the point of doing something so stupid?

Thoughts dark, he sat unmoving longer than he should have. He roused only when his phone rang. Mamá. No doubt to remind him he'd been shirking his family duties this week.

TONY REAPPEARED A LITTLE after two, seeming withdrawn, even troubled, which scared Beth. He had little to say and mostly watched as she went through one box after another—although he did insist on bringing them to her and taking them away according to her direction. It would be one thing if she were as tiny as Emily— Wait. Had she *really* just thought that?

Yes, and it had slid through her mind with such comfortable familiarity, Beth had to recognize what a mess she was beneath her steady facade.

After something like an hour, she ignored the carton he'd just set at her feet.

"Is something wrong?" More wrong?

He turned to her with a brooding look. "I went by the jeweler's."

Apprehensive, she asked, "What did they say?"

"Top quality diamonds set in platinum. Retail value altogether, in the neighborhood of twenty thousand dollars."

Her mouth fell open. "Oh, dear lord," she finally said.

"Not the quarter of a million dollars' worth draped on an actress walking the red carpet for the Oscars, but a lot of money for most people around here."

Momentarily distracted, she blurted, "How do you know that? About the Oscar ceremonies?"

He shrugged. "Sometimes a sister or a niece will stick one of those celebrity magazines under my nose."

"Mom and Dad never would have spent that

kind of money on jewelry. And they didn't have the kind of friends who did either."

"I didn't think so." The watchful dark eyes never left her face. "Did your parents have the money? Was it a question of priorities?"

"It's true they could have bought nicer things if they hadn't had three kids. Mom insisted on starting a savings account for each of us as soon as we were born."

"How do you know it was her?"

"I...assumed. I mean, she was the practical one. Except..."

"Except?" Tony prompted.

"Dad was different when we were little. He was more engaged. We did stuff as a family. I imagine it was usually at Mom's instigation, but he seemed to have fun when we went to the county fair or swimming at the lake. He had his head in the clouds, but... I think it was when Mom started to get so aggravated at him that he withdrew. Once Mom left—died—then he was even worse. It was as if she was his link. You know?"

He made a noncommittal noise before saying, "Matt holds a lot of anger. He seems to think your father wasn't present in the ways he needed."

Remembering the explosive conversations with her brother last weekend, Beth nodded. "The thing is, Matt was big into sports. Dad never understood the appeal. The only organized sport he played was lacrosse, so he couldn't coach Little League teams or anything like that, not the way some of the other fathers did. It might have been different if Matt's interests were—" She groped for an idea that might have united her brother and father, but came up short.

Tony's eyebrows drew together. "Cars? Art? Computers?"

Beth sighed. "Dad might have gotten interested in chess, or math problems, or...or if Matt wanted to learn to speak Russian."

"Intellectual pursuits."

She nodded.

"What about you and Emily?"

"Emily had Mom."

Understanding and, damn it, that compassion softened his face. "Are you saying you didn't?"

"No, it wasn't— Well, it was, but—"

A rumble of amusement helped untangle her. "Is it that hard to say?"

Beth scrunched her nose at him. "I loved my mother, and I'm sure she never intended to make me feel inadequate, but she did. Dad didn't. I was more of a reader than Emily or Matt, too. More introspective, I guess."

"More like your father."

She had to nod. "I understand him better than they did, which I suppose is why I have more patience with him."

"Hmm." Tony studied her for a minute. "Any new thoughts about the drawing?"

She shook her head. "Nothing." Which wasn't a lie, except she was still conscious of *something*. It was like catching movement out of the corner of her eye, but whenever she really looked, there was nothing there.

"I talked to Matt again today," Tony said suddenly. "Maybe an hour ago."

"Really?" she said in surprise. "He hasn't called me."

"Would he?"

"Well… I'd have thought so."

"Have you had your phone with you?"

"Yes…" Her head turned. Where *was* her purse? And…when had she last used her phone? "It must be in the car." Gee, darn. She'd missed Matt's latest furious tirade. She might delete any message from him unheard.

"Ah. Well, he's not happy with me. I asked him some hard questions."

She eyed him. "Like what?"

"I wondered if *he* might have found the drawing, back then. Confronted your mother."

"And killed her?" she said incredulously. She'd known in one way that Tony had Matt on his radar, but she hadn't realized how seriously he took the possibility.

"If it helps, I think it unlikely." The ghost of a

smile crinkled the skin beside his eyes. "Matt's face is almost as expressive as yours, for one thing."

"As *mine*? What are you talking about?"

"You'll never make a good liar," he said gently.

"*Humph.*" And if that wasn't childish.

"That was a compliment, by the way."

Wonderful to think she was completely transparent to this man. Did that mean he was well aware of all her conflicting, and way too strong, feelings about him?

Probably.

"Telling me you can read my every thought is not a compliment," she grumbled.

"You know I can't do that. It's more…what you're feeling that shows."

"Great."

"Beth…" He sounded unusually tentative, for a man whose confidence seemed deep-rooted.

She looked up in surprise.

"Matt said something that bothered me. He… seemed to believe you knew your mother was having an affair."

"What? I didn't!"

If he relaxed, it was subtly, but Beth realized she was getting better at reading him, too. Which he'd hate.

"He said you'd asked him something once that made him think you knew."

"Asked him…" A few times since finding Mom's body, Beth had had odd flickers of remembrance that slipped away before she could catch them. But this particular memory didn't dodge out of sight. She stared right at it. "Wait. Oh, no. I'd forgotten…" She wanted to curl into a ball.

But his hand had closed over hers, immensely comforting, as was the deep timbre of his voice. "What, Beth? Things frightening to you then can't be so bad now."

No. Her mother had been murdered, and her body squished behind a new sheet of wallboard in the garage, to stay there hidden all these years. Not much rated, compared to that.

"No. You're right. Um, I got sick one day. My English teacher—" now, why did she remember what class she'd been in? "—gave me a pass to go to the office and call home, but Mom didn't answer. I didn't want to be stuck with the nurse, so I claimed I felt better and…just left. I knew I'd be in trouble later, but I didn't care. I threw up partway home, right in someone's flower bed. I tried to cover it with bark, but…"

The humor in Tony's eyes would have made her laugh at her young self, if the rest of this memory wasn't so hateful. "What a dumb thing to have been so humiliated about." She huffed out a breath. "Well, I made it home—it was only about a mile—and then realized that, without my key,

I couldn't get in with Mom gone. Except her car was there. The door wasn't even locked, so I went in and called, 'Mom!' I heard this weird *thud*. She…she half opened her bedroom door, and I could tell she didn't have any clothes on, except she was sort of clutching her bra to her front. She said she was just getting out of the shower. She told me to hop into bed, and she'd be there as soon as she finished getting dressed. So that's what I did." She fell silent, realizing how incredibly naive she'd been for a teenager. Mom hadn't even looked *damp*. "I suppose she pushed him off the bed so she could head me off. I didn't really suspect, except later I got to thinking."

"What did you ask Matt?"

"Just…whether he'd noticed Mom being kind of strange lately. And he made me tell him what I was talking about."

"She took some serious chances." As he thought, Tony rubbed his jaw in that way he had. "With three kids and a husband who must have had lots of breaks during the day. Professors don't teach more than, what, three or four classes a quarter?"

"If that. Even if he only had a couple of classes in a day, Dad didn't usually come home between, though. I mean, he had office hours, too, and he could write or plan his next lectures there as easily as at home." She grimaced. "Probably better. Given the three kids."

Tony chuckled. "Okay. Still."

Beth bit her lip. "You're thinking that it would have made more sense for them to have sex at his place. Unless…"

"Unless he was married, too. That's my guess."

She nodded unhappily. That made sense.

"What kind of clients did your mother have at work? Do you know? Did she handle businesses or individuals?"

"I think both. I know she did Dr. Schuh's clinic—he was in with a family doctor and a nurse practitioner—as well as his and his wife's personal taxes. So there might have been others like that."

"*Was* in? Did you not continue going there?"

"No, even Emily was old enough to start seeing our family doctor, whose office is by the hospital."

"Back to your mother's clients. Doctors, lawyers, other professionals, not to mention the wheat farmers or early vineyard owners, all would have had more money than your parents did. Would that have appealed to her?"

It made Beth really uncomfortable to dissect her mother this way, but it wasn't as if she could ever know. Or…deserved her children's loyalty? Hadn't she been betraying them as much as she was her husband, in a way? As it turned out, the betrayal had killed her and left all of her kids damaged, too.

"Maybe," she said finally. "Dad didn't care about money at all. Mom never would have overspent. You have to understand that. She was really meticulous paying bills and keeping records."

"You've looked?"

"I took over the bill paying after she disappeared."

Tony shook his head. "A fifteen-year-old girl. Of course you did."

"It wouldn't have made sense for Matt to do it, given how close he was to leaving home," she protested.

Sounding irritated, he said, "Maybe your father skated on his responsibilities because first your mother and then you *let* him. Did you ever think of that?"

She looked away. "I…sometimes."

He clasped her hand again and squeezed. "I'm sorry, Beth. I shouldn't have said that. I didn't mean that to sound like I'm criticizing you. You *were* a kid, doing your best to keep your family going. Obviously, you did just fine. They were lucky to have you."

Beth focused on his hand, strong, so much bigger than hers, and chose not to say anything. Only she knew how much resentment Emily and Matt felt. That didn't suggest she'd done such a fabulous job, did it?

Then she lifted her gaze to his. "You give really mixed messages, you know."

His jaw muscles flexed. "You know as well as I do why that is."

She wished she could believe she was so amazingly irresistible. *Not* believing made it a lot easier to pull her hand free and say, "Well, stop."

CHAPTER NINE

HE'D DESERVED BETH'S ACERBITY, Tony reflected. And probably more.

At the station, he sat with his chair back, his feet stacked on his desk, and brooded.

After leaving her at the house, he'd stopped at her mother's old tax and accounting firm, where he had spoken with one of the partners. Trish Senyitko hadn't known Christine well at all; they had only overlapped for about a year. Keith Reistad would remember her best, but he wasn't in right then.

And she had declined to provide a list of Christine's clients. He would need a warrant for that, she had said, with a definite chill.

He'd just gotten off the phone with Lucy Jimenez, an assistant DA, who had submitted the warrant request to a judge.

He still needed to talk to any neighbors of the Marshalls who had lived there thirteen years ago. Once he did that, though, the cat would be out of the bag. The gossip, the questions, wouldn't be pleasant for any of the Marshalls.

Tony frowned. He should head out to the community college and talk to John's colleagues who had been there long enough to have met Christine at faculty functions, too.

Another thing to ask Beth: names of her parents' friends. Not that the lover was necessarily one of them. But, if nothing else, Christine might have confided in a female friend.

Tony was a lot happier to have an excuse to call Beth than he should have been.

You give really mixed messages, you know.

Trouble was, his *feelings* weren't mixed at all. If it hadn't been for the job, he'd have been after her from the minute they'd met.

He glanced up to see Troyer escorting someone to his desk for an interview. Another detective in the department, Jack Moore, had fallen in love with a woman who was a suspect in a teenage girl's disappearance. At the time, Tony had been too busy to pay much attention, but he knew nobody had come down on Jack.

Beth wasn't even a suspect. The problem was that her loyalties lay with her father and brother, both of whom *were* suspects.

Uh huh. What if you end up arresting her father? Remember that little glitch in your campaign?

No, he hadn't forgotten, but his instincts told him John Marshall hadn't killed his wife, that

Beth was right; her father simply wasn't capable of that level of rage and violence.

Who could object if he took her out to dinner and they didn't talk about the investigation?

Except he did have those questions he needed to ask.

Wait until tomorrow.

A glance at his computer told him five o'clock had come and gone. He'd probably wasted a good ten minutes waffling here, on top of the earlier, useful things he had accomplished. She might have stayed to make dinner for her dad.

Didn't mean she had to stay and eat with him.

Tony did some internal swearing, reached for his desk phone…and put it back down. He needed to go somewhere else to make this call. He had to draw a line between on the job and off the job. He grunted. Too bad he'd already irrevocably blurred that line.

He ended up at the rear of the building, looking at the parking lot. Smokers sometimes gathered out here, but he was alone right now. Another hesitation, another go-around with his conscience, or at least his sense of self-preservation, and he mumbled a foul word and hit the green dial button. Maybe Beth would be less of a distraction if they actually got something going.

The unanswered rings had him bowing his head. Why would she want to talk to him again, considering they'd spent all day together and ended on a lousy note? Four rings. Five. Should he leave a message, or call it quits for tonight, at least?

"Hello?" She sounded breathless. "Detective?"

Detective. She kept promoting, then demoting, him.

"Can you make it *Tony*?"

The silence could only be wary. Finally, "Why are you calling?"

He leaned against the stucco wall. "Will you have dinner with me?" he asked baldly.

Another pause. "You know, if you have questions, you can just ask them."

He squeezed the bridge of his nose between his forefinger and thumb until cartilage creaked. "I do have some more. But... I was hoping we could take the evening off."

More silence. This was one reason he much preferred face-to-face conversations.

"What about your job?" she asked. "What about me flipping out when you arrest my father? Or won't I be mad, as long as we stop shy of getting between the sheets?"

He winced. "You're not a suspect. We can... take it slow." *Begging, are you?*

"I should say no."

"Please don't." Yep, begging was about right. He heard the soft whoosh of air. "All right. I'd like to have dinner with you. But, Tony? If this is some kind of trick, or you back off again, that's it."

"Understood. Uh…can I pick you up?"

Her "Fine "sounded terse. "I'm home now."

They agreed on a time and to do something casual, and he ended the call on an astonishing burst of exhilaration.

WHEN THE DOORBELL RANG, Beth jumped six inches. Stupid. She'd been *expecting* him. And given that they'd had lunch together—was it only yesterday?—she didn't know why she was so nervous.

Except she did. She'd spent the past couple of days pining for him like some lovelorn teenager, when she wasn't worried sick about Dad. This was undoubtedly a bad idea, but she was going to do it anyway.

Tony stood on her doorstep, his appearance unchanged from when they'd parted this afternoon. Black boots, chinos and a tan polo shirt. "Sorry," he said, glancing down at himself. "Something came up. I didn't have a chance to go home and change."

"That's okay." She eyed his badge and weapon. "Do you wear a gun on all your dates?"

His grin was wicked and sexy enough to bring her to meltdown. "Turns some women on, you know."

She rolled her eyes. "I bet." There probably

were cop groupies, even in a town this size. "Let me grab my purse."

When she came back, he nodded at her skirt. "Pretty."

"Oh." Of course she was blushing. "Thank you. I was grungy from working in the garage."

"While I sat and watched," he said ruefully.

A moment later, they walked to the shiny red pickup truck he'd driven on Sunday, when he had admitted to coming straight from home, interrupted in the middle of mowing his lawn.

"Where do you live?" she blurted. "I mean, obviously you have a house, since you were mowing, instead of an apartment, or…" She waved toward her townhouse, which had a minimal yard cared for by a landscape service hired by her landlord.

He opened the door for her. "Only about a mile from your dad's. I own a pretty ordinary rambler."

Once she'd boosted herself inside the truck's cab and reached for the seatbelt, he closed her door and went around to get in behind the wheel. Before reaching for his seatbelt, he unclipped the badge and holster from his belt. "Just for you." As he set it them in the glove compartment and locked it, he asked, "Anything special you'd like? I was thinking of pizza, but I can be talked into something else."

Pizza sounded good to her, too, and it turned out they both liked the same place, which made her wonder if they'd happened to walk past each other there. If so, he hadn't caught her eye, and she obviously hadn't caught his.

The interior of the restaurant felt pleasantly cool. After some discussion, she and Tony decided to share a Margherita pizza, made here with fresh local tomatoes and basil leaves. They both filled their plates at the salad bar, got drinks and chose a booth.

"My stomach is growling," she admitted. "I wasn't very hungry at lunchtime." She took her first bite.

"I wasn't either," he said quietly. "I'm sorry."

"It's okay. I understood, you know."

She was glad he didn't comment.

The quiet felt peaceful as they both made inroads on their salads. She was the first to break it.

"Matt left a couple of grumpy messages on my phone. Which I deleted after listening to him complain about me not answering when he calls."

"Great tactic to make sure you can hardly wait for his next call."

She laughed. "Exactly."

"Sounds like my mother, except she wields guilt expertly enough to get results."

Intrigued, Beth said, "Really? Does she have a hold over you?"

"You mean, a deep, dark secret? No, thank God. But she raised us to live up to certain standards, and along the way I think we all internalized heavy-duty guilt as our punishment for falling short."

She set down her fork and studied him. "What kind of standards?"

"God and family come first. I'm not sure in what order," he said wryly. "This has not been a good week. She chewed me out Sunday for missing church—"

"Because of my call?" Speaking of guilt.

"No, the morning service had come and gone long before dispatch called me. I overslept, probably because I didn't feel like going."

"And why was that?"

He rolled his shoulders, his discomfiture plain. But he'd started this, not her. And…she wanted to know him. He'd hinted before at his mixed feelings about his family.

"I work long hours. Sometimes, I want to be alone. Or with a friend, or a woman—" he reached for her hand, seemingly not even noticing he'd done it "—not surrounded by thirty-five family members with eight conversations flying by, half of them including a *Tony, will you do this?* or *Tony, Mamá said you could help me.*" He shook his head. "I love them all, and I really don't mind helping out. I just wish the demands weren't so never ending."

"You do have an awful lot of family." All she

had to do was mentally multiply what she had by ten to make her shudder.

He grimaced.

"If you moved a little farther away…"

"With my father gone, I can't do that."

"But she has all your sisters and their husbands. If they're married?"

"Four are. The youngest is still in high school, and Isabel is in college." His smile appeared. "The University of Washington. Mamá wanted her to stay closer, but Isabel is the smartest of all of us. She's determined to be a doctor, and that's the best place for her. Wakefield or Whitman College would have been great, but we couldn't afford that kind of tuition. Anyway, I thought she needed to go away."

Beth said, "I think it's good for everyone to have at least a taste of independence." She frowned. "What about your brother?"

"Also in college, at Central."

Another state school, this one in Ellensburg, on the eastern side of the mountains, like Frenchman Lake, but a two- or three-hour drive away.

"Two of my married sisters are pregnant right now," Tony continued. "Beatrix, who is closest in age to me, already has two kids. Eloisa has a three-year-old on top of being pregnant. My brothers-in-law are all good guys, but they work full time, at least, and all but one have their own families in the area."

"Sometimes," Beth said softly, ashamed but needing to say this anyway, "I wish I didn't have any family. I know I don't mean it. Think how lonely that would be. But for a week or two, or a month or two…"

He smiled again, squeezed her hand, then let it go so he could resume eating. "Maybe a year or two," he suggested.

Beth giggled.

The pizza was fabulous, and they talked more as they ate, but less seriously. When she asked, he agreed that his given name was Antonio, as she'd suspected. They compared favorite and least favorite movies, TV shows, books, social media habits. Beth found his political views an interesting mix and teased that he must get paralyzed when it came time to make a decision about every vote. He didn't disagree.

She didn't want to hurry the evening—she'd have been happy to sit here talking to him for hours—but excitement hummed in the background. He was going to kiss her again. She knew he was.

If he was hoping for an invitation into her bedroom, he'd be out of luck. She'd never done that on a first or second date anyway, but in this case, Tony's apology hadn't entirely restored her trust in his sincerity. And also…she couldn't forget, and doubted he had either, all the complications in this relationship. With him, she'd have to be very, very sure this wasn't only fast-acting but short-lived lust.

Then there was Dad, who needed her. Protecting him was something she had internalized as much as Tony had the guilt his mother used to keep him on a leash.

Family, she thought with frustration, except she had a surprising, wistful moment, wondering how it would be to have her own. The little girl and boy in her fleeting fantasy had warm brown eyes and their daddy's black hair.

And then she wondered if Tony would want children at all after growing up the oldest of eight and still responsible for many of them.

Second date, remember?

"Ready to go?" he said suddenly, as if he'd run out of patience with their conversation.

Embarrassed, Beth realized she couldn't remember what they had been talking about. Which made her wonder what he'd seen on her face as her thoughts wandered.

"Yes, of course."

Once she slid out of the booth, he laid a hand on her back, as he had at his aunt's restaurant. Proprietary. Beth had never realized her lower back was so sensitive.

Unfortunately for her mood, on the drive home, she remembered him saying he had more questions. And, of course, they still had all those boxes sitting on the lawn to go through. Those didn't worry her. The questions did.

Maybe it would be better to get those over with before he kissed her. In case she'd regret another kiss, once she heard what he wanted to know.

When he pulled into a visitor space behind the row of townhouses, Beth took a fortifying breath. "I'm wondering if you'd like to come in for a cup of coffee and to ask me those questions you have stored up."

TONY ALMOST GROANED. He'd been thinking about long, luxurious kisses, maybe some cuddling, while she'd apparently latched onto his casual comment as if it were barbed wire biting into her flesh.

"Coffee, yes. But I thought we'd agreed to take the night off."

"I'm a worrier." And, yes, anxiety showed in her eyes. "In case you haven't noticed. Avoidance just makes me more anxious."

"Beth, I'm looking for information. I promise, this isn't anything that will upset you."

"Then why not do it now?" she asked stubbornly.

There was the line he should have drawn, but

continuing to argue was clearly useless. Shaking his head, he said, "Now it is. Ah…do you mind if I bring my gun in? I don't like leaving it out here."

"Why didn't you say so at the pizza parlor?"

He smiled. "I picked a booth that let me keep an eye on my truck."

Fortunately, Beth laughed. "No, I don't mind. Having both of us worried at the same time couldn't be good."

After snapping the holster back at his belt, he also grabbed the spiral notebook he kept in the glove compartment, locked up and followed her to the back door.

This row of townhouses were new and looked classy, at least from the outside; he'd noticed them but hadn't ever had cause to enter any of them. No security system, he saw, as Beth let them in, but she probably didn't need one. Neighbors were only a wall away, and her designated parking spot was directly behind her unit. The lighting at the back of the building wasn't great, but the neighborhood tended to be low-crime.

The inside was a lot fancier than his house. Hardwood floors, gleaming granite countertops in the kitchen, coved ceilings. He might have been intimidated if her furniture had been as expensive looking, but it wasn't. He guessed she'd picked up some of the wood pieces at thrift stores or garage sales and refinished them. Pillows on the sofa had been sewn from quilt blocks.

Seeing what he was looking at, she said, "I look for old quilts that are really tattered, so I don't have to feel guilty cutting them up. I make pillows and table runners from the parts I can salvage."

"I like them." He did. The gently faded fabrics gave the room a comfortable air, helped by warm woods, a couple of bookcases and what looked like an old Persian rug, a little ragged in places. "Nice place," he added.

"The rent is more than I should be spending." She dropped her purse and keys on the go-through to the kitchen. "My last apartment was out by the mall, and there were suddenly a lot of break-ins. The final straw was when I came home one day to find my window jimmied and my TV and iPod gone."

"I think we caught that guy. Didn't you get a call?"

"Yes, and thank goodness my TV was one of them found in his garage. That's it." She nodded toward the modestly sized flat-screen television hung on the wall. "My iPod didn't show up. Which wasn't that big a deal, but... Oh, you must hear this all the time."

"You felt violated," he said flatly. "Your home should be the place you feel safe. Those are pretty crummy apartments, Beth."

"They weren't so bad when I first moved in."

One of his sisters and her husband had lived out there for a couple of years, moving once their baby was born. Tony had been relieved, although he, better than most, knew no place was completely secure.

Beth poured them both coffee and brought it to the living room. When she kicked off her sandals and curled her feet under her at one end of the sofa, Tony took his cue and sat at the other end. Then she looked inquiring.

"All I wanted to know was the names of your parents' friends," he explained. "I'd like to talk to some of them." Maybe all, it just depended.

"Oh. Well, sure." She made a face. "I've heard from several of them."

"They called you?" Idle curiosity, or fear of what had been found?

"People are nosy, you know."

A grin tugged at his mouth. "I do know that. I'm even nosier than most."

She laughed, looking relaxed and happy, which made him happy. In a contradiction, his desire to keep her that way set him on edge. He was already worrying about the well-being of too many people.

"Tomorrow, I'll grab Mom and Dad's address book," she said. "That would have phone numbers, and everyone I forget to mention. In fact, you can take the book, as long as you promise to give it back. I don't think Dad uses it often."

"That would be a big help. I'd still like your impressions." He held his pen poised above the notebook.

So she started with Debra Abernathy, who'd been divorced two or three times already when Beth had last seen her and had been good friends with Christine. "No kids," Beth added.

Had Christine envied her several-times divorced friend because she had the freedom to date new men?

Beth came up with a list of couples that her parents had socialized with on occasion, commenting on each briefly.

"I only vaguely remember the Hartleys. I think that's their name," she said about the last. "I don't think Dad liked them that much."

"Closest friends?" he asked.

"As a couple…probably the Longleys, the Oberholtzers and the Schuhs. Maybe the Sagers, although mostly Mom and Dad went there because Mrs. Sager threw parties for every occasion."

Mrs. Sager, she told him, managed the Verizon store at the mall. Beth wasn't sure about Mr. Her mother had been a little disparaging about Gail Schuh because she'd never worked.

"Didn't you tell me the Schuhs are divorced now?"

"Yes, but I don't know when they split up or if she's still around here."

Tim Oberholtzer was a banker, his wife a florist. Teresa Longley was a middle school counselor; Beth hadn't liked being assigned to her because she felt sure Teresa would report anything she did wrong to Christine. "Matt liked her," she added, "but I don't think she and Mom were friends when he was at the middle school." Michael Longley was an attorney, a partner in a firm Tony had had dealings with. He particularly disliked one of the partners who handled criminal defense but didn't recall meeting Longley. Beth thought her mother had met Michael through work, so maybe he specialized in tax law. Beth wasn't sure about his wife.

She named a few more female friends, but didn't know them well. "Mom got together with them when we were in school," she said with a shrug. "But she'd talk about them. You know."

"What about your father?"

"He's friends with one of the philosophy professors at Wakefield. I think Dad still has dinner at his house sometimes. Jong Lee. Dad emails regularly with a bunch of people in his field, too."

"Anybody else to add?"

"Nobody I can think of right now. I can ask Matt and Emily, if you'd like."

He hesitated over that but couldn't think of any drawback. "Sure, that would be good."

"I might have forgotten someone. I don't think any of their friends had kids close to my age, so my interest in them was pretty limited."

Tony smiled at that. "I wish I could say the same about my parents' friends."

Her laugh was a light ripple he could almost, but not quite, call a giggle. "If they all had eight kids, it stands to reason most of them would have one close to your age."

He sighed. "Fortunately, they didn't all. This generation, we all have friends—and a couple of my sisters have husbands—who aren't Latino or even Catholic. I can't say that about my parents."

She nodded. "The times are changing."

Tony held up the notebook, then tossed it on the coffee table. "This will give me a good start. Now will you come over here?" He lifted an arm invitingly.

She said "Sure," but looked a little shy, which had him speculating about her sexual experience.

He for damn sure wanted his sisters to remain virgins at least until they were in serious relationships *and* in their twenties, which undoubtedly made him a hypocrite. And, okay, he did judge women who hopped in and out of bed with too many men. It was hard to shake your upbringing. Otherwise, he assumed a woman Beth's age would have had relationships. He surely had. If she'd had many, or they had been very successful, he'd expect her to be more self-confident, though.

Since they hadn't reached a stage where he could ask, however, he let his curiosity go. And she wasn't too shy to scoot across two cushions and slip into the circle of his arm. She even leaned against him with gratifying trust, her head settling against his shoulder.

He tucked her closer and bent to rub his chin on top of her head and breathe in her scent. He wanted to kiss her, but felt surprisingly content just holding her, warm and cushiony.

"I can hear your heartbeat," Beth murmured.

"Will it put you to sleep?"

She lifted her head to look at him. "I'm definitely not sleepy."

"No." He had to clear his throat. "Me either." He nuzzled her cheek, found his way to her earlobe, where he lingered to nibble, then moved to the tender skin at her temple. He paused to look at her, eyes closed, lashes fanned on her cheeks, her lips parted and cheeks pink. His heart gave something closer to a clunk than a beat. He took in the dusting of freckles that helped give her an innocent, girl-next-door beauty belied by her sinfully sexy body.

After an inarticulate sound, he kissed her. She let him in immediately, her tongue meeting his eagerly. His body surged. Desperate for more contact, he half lifted her to straddle his thighs. For a moment, Beth looked startled, but when he squeezed her waist with one hand while slipping the other around the back of her neck and drawing her down, she smiled. The curve of her lips had his curving, too, even as he deepened this kiss, taking, demanding.

She strained against him, her urgency the equal of his. She made little sounds—gasps and whimpers—that drove him crazy. His free hand dipped under the hem of her knit shirt and flattened on the smoothest skin he'd ever felt. Muscles in her belly tightened as he stroked upward until he reached his goal and was able to cup her breast through a bra that felt like satin. Damn, he wanted to tear it off, but even with his brain fogged with desire, he knew he didn't dare. Still, he kneaded her and rubbed his palm over the tight nubbin in the center.

Her hips rocked, until she was riding his erection. Tony shifted his attention to her other breast, not wanting to neglect it. Fingernails bit into his neck, an erotic sensation. She moaned.

"Damn," he muttered, claiming her mouth with shattering thoroughness. Her hips moved, and he shoved himself up to meet her. They'd started a dance that he didn't want to stop.

Somewhere, somehow, he found the self-control

to ease out of the kiss. He persuaded his hands to soothe instead of incite. He strung kisses along her jaw, down her throat. She let her head fall back as he licked the small hollow at the base, tasting her.

And then she gave a shaky laugh. He lifted his head and met her heavy-lidded eyes.

"So much for me standing firm." Her voice was husky enough to feel like another touch on some especially sensitive part of his body. "I think my body overrode my brain."

"It's supposed to work that way."

"Is it?" Her gaze became searching, her expression grave. "That's never happened to me before."

"Good." Oh, hell, there was the primitive part of him. "I didn't want to stop, you know."

She gave a tiny wriggle that wrenched a groan from him. "I noticed."

"Laugh, will you?" He grazed one of her breasts with his knuckles. When her back arched, he smiled, then sobered. "I don't want you to ever regret getting naked with me. We need to wait until you're sure you won't."

"Me?" She arched her eyebrows. "What about you?"

His first instinct was to deny any doubt, but that wouldn't have been completely honest. Sex he wouldn't regret. Hurting her he would. Beth wasn't a woman he could take lightly. This quickly, he could imagine loving her, even thinking about making a life with her. And *that* scared the crap out of him.

He kissed the tip of her nose, smiling. "Until *we're* both sure we won't regret it."

"Deal." She sighed and climbed off his lap, leaving him aching and wishing— But she was right. It was too soon.

He patted her butt. "Walk me to the door." At least he could sneak in another kiss before he left.

CHAPTER TEN

PARKING HIS UNMARKED police car, Tony studied the elegant stucco building in front of him. Painted a muted gold, accented with a wrought iron gate, it housed the law firm of Longley, Parsons & Schaaf. Complete with an arched opening leading into a small courtyard with a fountain, it had the look of a Spanish mission.

One of the three reserved parking spots was empty. In the other two were a Cadillac Escalade and a silver Lexus. He'd done some research before leaving the station and knew Longley drove the Escalade. Gleaming black, shiny gold trim, massive. Tony kind of doubted the attorney ever intended to haul anything in it.

With regret—yep, there was that word—Tony had instructed Beth to go ahead digging through the boxes in the backyard. He had sent an officer to help her and to be present if she found anything of interest. He'd decided he had greater priorities—and that he had to trust her.

He had also asked which of her parents' friends

had called her after hearing she'd found her mother's body.

"Debra Abernathy, which isn't any surprise," she'd said promptly. "The others were Michael Longley and Tim Oberholtzer. Mr. Oberholtzer said he'd talked to Dad but hadn't gotten a good idea of what was really happening and was worried about Dad. Mr. Longley sounded deeply concerned about how this was affecting all of us."

Hearing her puzzlement at that, Tony moved Michael Longley to the top of his interview list. He had called the law firm the minute they opened this morning and been told that Longley would fit him in at ten o'clock.

Tony wore dress slacks and shoes and even a tie today, although given how hot the day already was, he couldn't make himself put on the suit coat. He'd have done it for court, but not for anything less. Still, he liked to look as professional as the people he was interviewing, and he planned to tackle an attorney and a banker this morning.

A slick-looking young man in a spiffy gray-on-gray suit led him into the back, passing conference rooms and offices without names. Michael Longley's had his in gilt letters on a frosted glass pane in the door.

The man behind the desk rose to his feet and said, "Thank you, Jeff," in clear dismissal. Then he came around the desk—cherry wood, at a guess, and as shiny as the Escalade—and held out a hand. "Detective Navarro."

Tony and he shook, the assessment mutual. "Mr. Longley."

Longley looked to be in his fifties, dark hair shot with silver, but he was handsome, lean and athletic, just as Alan Schuh was, and maybe five foot ten. Deeply tanned—did these guys spend a lot of time on the golf course?—so that his skin was as dark as Tony's, sharpening the effect of his gray eyes. Spending that much time in the sun or a tanning booth didn't seem smart, but he looked good and had an air that probably worked especially well with female clients and jurors.

He gestured Tony to a cluster of upholstered chairs around a coffee table on one side of the large office. "Please, have a seat."

Doing so, Tony said, "Thank you for seeing me so promptly, Mr. Longley. As you may have guessed, I'm here because of Christine Marshall's murder."

He nodded, his face set in serious lines. "I assumed that, but I'm not sure how you think I can help."

"I understand that she met you on the job. I was surprised that tax law isn't your specialty."

"Frenchman Lake isn't a large town," he said, leaning back comfortably and steepling his fingers. "As a result, none of us can afford to narrow our focus too much. Will Schaaf comes the closest, with his interest in criminal law, but even he also handles some malpractice and personal injury."

Schaaf was the asshole Tony had faced in court a couple times. He nodded to express his interest.

"Russ Parsons does divorce and family law, as well as, oh, this and that. My bailiwick is wills, trusts and estates, including real estate law, some business, partnership and incorporation law, that kind of thing. Except for longtime clients, we stay away from bankruptcy, DUIs, Social Security." He said the last with a hint of disdain that was hard to justify considering how vicious divorces and child custody battles often were. And then there was the criminal law part of the practice.

"So anything to do with money comes your way," Tony said.

"Well…it's considerably more complex than that, but I suppose if we're to simplify, the answer would be yes."

Tony wondered if Longley patronized his clients the same way. "I can see why Christine's business would intersect with yours."

"That's right. We had several clients in common."

"And your firm? Did her firm handle your taxes?"

His tone cooled. "As a matter of fact, they did and still do. However, Christine chose to work part time and confined herself to clients whose returns were more straightforward than ours."

Tony read this to mean people who actually expected to *pay* the taxes they owed.

"I see. Had you known her husband before this...friendship developed?"

The light gray eyes narrowed a fraction. "No, we found ourselves occasionally meeting for coffee and the like and decided to introduce our respective spouses."

"In your case, Teresa."

"You *have* done your research." And he wasn't thrilled.

"A necessary part of my job. In this case, Ms. Marshall—Beth—recalled having your wife as her school counselor."

He smiled. "Oh, yes. As it happens, Teresa and I divorced nearly ten years ago. I believe she's in the Tri-Cities now."

"And have you remarried, Mr. Longley?"

His posture became less relaxed. "How is this relevant?"

"I doubt it is. I'm principally curious how your ex-wife felt about your...friendship with Christine." The pause had been brief, but Longley heard it.

He sat up and gripped the arms of his chair. "Does throwing out vague accusations work well for you, Detective?"

Tony let himself smile. "Quite often it does, in fact. I didn't mean that as an accusation, however. It's just that male-female friendships are still somewhat unusual and subject to misunderstandings."

"Again, I don't understand what this has to do with her murder."

Tony leaned forward, injecting some of his intensity into his voice. "Someone killed Christine Marshall. That someone likely knew her well and was familiar with the house. We're not talking about a stranger happening to find her home alone."

"I suppose I assumed—" He broke off in a pretense of not wanting to finish what he'd already implied.

"Assumed?"

"Well, don't you look first at family members, in this kind of circumstance?"

"We do, of course, but we also look at friends, co-workers, clients."

"You're suggesting...what?" Longley donned outrage as easily as he did other emotions. "That she stumbled on some illegal or immoral action I'd taken practicing law, so I had to silence her? Or do you assume that we had a fiery affair that ended badly?"

"She was a beautiful woman."

Facial muscles tight, the attorney said, "She was

attractive. I meet many attractive women, Detective. I haven't killed one yet."

He hadn't denied having sex with some of them, Tony couldn't help noticing.

"And did you have an affair with Christine?"

Longley shot to his feet. "I did not, and I resent your implication. I've given you all the time I can afford."

Tony nodded and took his time getting up. He even smiled. "I'll be in touch if I have further questions, Mr. Longley." He was at the door before he stopped and turned back. "Oh, you might want to check any records you still have for the day she disappeared. Being such good friends with the Marshalls, I'm sure you remember it. I'd be glad to cross you off my list if you can provide proof that you were traveling or in court all day, for example."

The attorney's glare felt like a laser sight on Tony's back as he left.

BETH FOLDED THE flaps on the last cardboard box and sagged. She had wilted hours ago, but hauling every box into the shade or even into the garage hadn't made sense. So she'd plastered on the sunscreen, worn a straw hat she'd had forever and endured.

Poor Officer Webley looked as relieved as she felt. Patches of sweat darkened his uniform under his arms and across his back. He'd fetched a towel from the trunk of his car and used it throughout the day to wipe sweat from his face.

"Nothing here," she said.

It was hard not to notice that the top of his head was very sunburned. The officer looked to be in his twenties, and maybe he hadn't wanted to draw attention to his bald patch by applying sunscreen. She had seen him pat it with the towel a few times when he thought she wasn't looking.

"I vote we both get out of the sun," she said. "Thank you for your help, Officer."

"Is there anything I can do…?"

"Nope. I'm going to pop in the house and talk to my dad, then go home and take a cool shower."

He worked up a weak grin. "The shower sounds good to me."

He went out the gate between the garage and house, and Beth let herself in through the French doors.

Her father sat in his recliner, looking toward the photos on the mantel and doing absolutely nothing. Beth couldn't remember ever seeing him without a book or journal at hand.

"Dad?"

He blinked and looked at her. "Are you done?"

"Yes. Nothing. Officer Webley is gone."

"I hope you were careful with the sunscreen."

Startled, she studied him anew. The comment was out of the ordinary for him.

"I tried," she said. "It's hard when rivers of sweat are washing the stuff off as fast as you put it on."

"You're so white-skinned. I remember how easily you burned as a child."

He'd noticed?

"I still do." She went into the kitchen and grabbed a bottle of water out of the fridge. "Do you want anything?"

"No, thank you."

Sitting on the sofa, she guzzled half the bottle, then pressed it to her hot forehead. After a minute, she lowered the bottle. "What were you thinking about?" she asked.

"I was...remembering," he said slowly. His face had lines she'd never seen. "I'm not quite as oblivious as you think I am, Beth. I knew your mother was planning to leave me. I didn't know what I could do to stop her. If she wasn't happy, it didn't seem right to prevent her from going. What I never believed was that she would leave you kids."

"No. Thinking she had...that was hard."

He nodded. Still looking pained and a decade older than he had the last time she saw him, he said, "I don't think I've ever said thank you. I know how much you did. I shouldn't have let you.

I suppose I was selfish to accept what you offered. I should have found a way—" His Adam's apple bobbed.

"Oh, Dad." She jumped up and went to him, half sitting on the recliner arm and bending to give him a hug. "I love you. I'd have been selfish *not* to help. I don't regret a thing."

He scrutinized her in a penetrating way, as if really seeing her for the first time. "I hope that's true." He tried to smile, although his eyes had a sheen. "I do love you, Beth. All of you, of course, although I know Matt wouldn't believe me if I told him."

Even Dad wouldn't believe her if she said *Nonsense! Of course Matt loves you!* Beth didn't know that he did. She'd discovered recently how tired she was of her brother's resentment. "So, you weren't a baseball coach," she said.

Dad tried another smile that wobbled. "To think she was dead all that time, her body right here. I felt so angry, so disappointed in her, and she never deserved any of it."

And Dad didn't deserve to be left beating himself up when his wife had done things to make him so mad and disappointed.

Beth barely hesitated. "You need to know that Detective Navarro has found some evidence that makes him believe Mom was having an affair."

His gaze seemed to turn inward. "I...suspected

that, too," he said softly. "I wasn't entirely honest with the detective."

"I had no idea."

"I'm glad," he said simply. They were both quiet for a minute. Finally, he said, "Do you know what he's found?"

"I found a pair of diamond earrings and a matching pendant in her jewelry box. I didn't recognize them and, when Detective Navarro took them to a jeweler, he valued the set at around twenty thousand dollars."

"Twenty thousand?" Her father stared at her in shock. "But…where did she…?" His shoulders slumped. "I should have known that she wanted things like that. I could have done more to—"

Beth hugged him again. "Dad, no woman needs anything like that. How she could accept that jewelry—" Her voice shaking, Beth couldn't finish. She hadn't realized how much anger she held.

Her father patted her thigh. "She loved you. Don't doubt that."

"I'll…try not to." She hesitated. "Dad, were any of your or Mom's friends artistic?"

He looked startled. "Why on earth—?"

"Oh, an unframed drawing and a couple of watercolors I found. I thought someone you knew might have done them, and that's why Mom kept them."

His forehead creased, giving her the sense he had taken her question seriously, but after a moment he shook his head. "Not that I can recall. Your mother did enjoy art fairs, you know."

"I haven't forgotten, since I went with her to a few." She forced a smile, even if she was still choked with anger. "You know, it's getting toward dinner time. Shall I—"

He tried to smile. "Thank you for offering, but I'm not at all hungry. I'll get myself something later. You should go home. Or—I never think to ask whether you're dating anyone. You'd bring him over to meet me if you became serious about a man, wouldn't you?"

Her stomach knotted. He'd already met the man she was dating. And she could not bring herself to say *I'm actually seeing someone now. Um, it's Detective Navarro.* So she lied.

"There's nobody serious at the moment." Well, that wasn't really a lie. "And of course I'd bring him to meet you." She kissed his cheek and rose to her feet. "If you're sure..."

"I'm sure."

"Then I'm going home."

He actually started to push himself to his feet before she shook her head. "Don't get up. Call if you need anything, okay?"

In her car, she started the engine but left the door open until the air conditioning kicked in.

Bending forward, she bumped her head on the steering wheel a couple times. Hard.

Dad still didn't know about that awful drawing.

She'd lied twice to her father. Once straight out, and once by omission. Beth was queasy with guilt when she finally backed out.

Of course, that's when her phone rang.

DEBRA ABERNATHY HAD agreed to meet Tony after she got off work. She'd suggested Starbucks.

He'd learned that she was an insurance agent and that, coincidentally, she lived in a townhouse on Beth's block. Had both women changed so much, they didn't recognize each other?

Having arrived first, he sat down with a tall iced coffee with milk and watched the people in line and new customers arriving. He focused immediately on a woman who resembled the driver's license photo of Debra Abernathy, despite hair that was an eye-popping shade of red instead of her previous blond. No, probably she hadn't really been blonde either, he realized.

Once she had her drink, he stood so she could see his badge, and she immediately headed for his booth at the back. "Detective Navarro?"

"And you must be Ms. Abernathy."

"That's right." She slid in, facing him.

Her face was unlined, making him suspect a facelift. It was harder to defeat the sagging skin

JANICE KAY JOHNSON 223

on her neck. Her hands gave away her age, too, with some liver spotting and knobby knuckles. Nonetheless, she was a striking woman. He wondered what marriage she was on now or whether she was between.

"I can't believe her kids found Christine," she said. "That's awful. And I know they're adults now, but still."

"They were pretty shaken up," he agreed. "They probably guessed right away that the remains had to be hers."

He let her ramble for a few minutes, interested in how much she knew.

"I called Emily after talking to you this afternoon. She was hysterical about some naked picture of Christine."

Oh, hell. Either Matt or Beth had been sure to tell their sister about the drawing, but Tony doubted she had any discretion whatsoever. Who else had she told?

"That was one of the things I'd hoped to talk to you about," he admitted.

"Did she *pose*?" Ms. Abernathy leaned forward, expression fierce. "Or did some piece of shit photograph her on the sly?"

"She posed. And it isn't a photo. It's a quite skillful drawing."

The woman gaped. "A drawing?"

"One of my questions for you is—did Christine

Marshall ever mention a friend of hers who was an artist? Probably not professionally," he added, "although I can't be sure, but certainly talented."

"That was a long time ago." Her eyes lost focus as she looked back. "I remember her being really flattered by a portrait," Ms. Abernathy said after a minute, "but I took it to be one of those quick sketches artists make. You know, a few lines, smudged a little, but it really does look like you?"

"Do you recall who the artist was?"

She shook her head. "I don't know if she told me or not. If it comes to me, I'll call you. You think *he* might have killed her?"

"It's one possibility."

She sipped her coffee, also iced, and brooded. "I knew she had a lover. I was actually glad for her." Her gaze held a challenge now. "I don't suppose you can understand that."

Oh, he understood. He just didn't approve. Given his family's faith, marriage was for life. A man or woman feeling trapped might be tempted into infidelity. But Christine Marshall had had the option of telling her husband she wasn't happy and leaving him before she slept with another man. Why hadn't she done that?

Again, he arrowed in on the same possibility: the man was also married and not ready to trade in one wife for another. When they were being targeted by a serial cheater, women often failed to recognize what he was. Pushing him for more than he intended to give could be humiliating. For Christine, it might have been dangerous.

"I understand you were close friends," he said.

"Who told you that?"

"Beth."

"Oh." Her face softened. "She was such a sweetheart. Always worried about everyone else."

So Beth hadn't changed. And, damn, he wished they'd planned to get together this evening. He hadn't wanted to come on too strong, but the need was strident enough for him to decide to call her once he was alone. If nothing else, he'd hear her voice.

"I find it difficult to believe Mrs. Marshall wouldn't have told you who she was seeing," he said, keeping his tone mild. She'd be more likely to open up if this didn't turn confrontational.

"Well, she didn't. Wouldn't. I had the feeling..." She hesitated. "I supposed that the man was someone I knew. I wondered if she thought I'd disapprove."

"Perhaps because he was married?"

"If I was friends with his wife, maybe." She made a little humming sound as she thought. "I was annoyed, I admit. I'd recently been through a divorce and was seeing a new man, and I told her everything. I think Chris was in love with him, whoever he was. She had that glow. Maybe she was hugging her happiness tight or was secretly afraid that people knowing would threaten her dream future."

"Could he have made her promise not to tell anyone?"

"Yes." Ms. Abernathy seemed struck by his suggestion. "God. That's what it was like."

"Any hints?"

Again, she appeared to cast her mind back but finally shook her head. "He was handsome, successful, wealthy, or at least that was my impression. As far as she was concerned, he walked on water." She frowned. "If it's true he bought her some big diamonds, maybe he really was successful and wealthy."

"Several men in her circle of friends seem to meet that description," Tony said. "Tim Oberholtzer, Michael Longley, Alan Schuh."

Ms. Abernathy wrinkled her nose. "I suppose any of them would qualify compared to a man who taught at the community college."

Was she even aware how derisive she sounded? If John Marshall had taught at Wakefield, a nationally known college, would he then have qualified as a worthy husband?

What would it feel like to have your wife constantly urging you to strive for something bigger, better, even though you were happy in the job you had? In his case, maybe being a detective in a town as modest as Frenchman Lake wouldn't be good enough. Why wouldn't he want to work for Seattle PD, since that would give his wife more bragging material? Or shouldn't he at least rise in the hierarchy, take the sergeant's exam as soon as possible, become a lieutenant, even a captain? So what if he liked investigations and wasn't eager to be stuck behind a desk doing administrative work?

No wonder if John had taken to tuning out his wife.

Tony continued with his questions, but didn't learn anything more of value. She'd only been acquainted with the three men and their wives through Christine. Two of three had later gotten divorces, but she hadn't heard any gossip. She gave him a few more names to check out, a useful reminder that he shouldn't narrow his investigation too quickly. In this town, Christine could easily have met someone like a vineyard owner at a tasting party. And then there were those clients, many of whom neither her husband or children would have had any reason to meet.

He thanked Ms. Abernathy for coming, gave her his card in case she thought of anything new, and they parted on the sidewalk.

STILL SITTING IN her car in front of Dad's house, Beth said into the phone, "You're the one who hung up on me."

"I was upset!"

When wasn't Emily? Easy answer: *when she got her way.*

Eager to segue away from the topic of Emily's volatile state of mind, Beth said, "I'm glad you called because I forgot to ask you not to tell anyone else about the drawing. It's not the kind of thing we want the rest of the world to know about."

"Well, you're too late," her little sister said spitefully. "Mom *deserves* to be humiliated."

"Mom is past humiliation. Matt and Dad aren't."

"Matt's just so full of himself, who cares? And Dad... Dad won't even notice if people are talking about him."

Now she sounded like Matt. She wouldn't like it if Beth pointed that out, though.

"You're wrong," Beth said quietly. "Please tell me you didn't let everyone know that I have a feeling I've seen another drawing the man did. Or that I'm trying to remember who it was."

The sulky silence was answer enough. Beth gritted her teeth. "I have another call coming in that I need to take."

"You just don't want to talk to *me.*"

"Right now, I don't." Beth cut her off, wishing she hadn't answered in the first place.

So why was it that Emily saw right through her when she was lying, but Dad didn't?

Should she tell Tony that Emily had been blabbing? He hadn't asked them to keep quiet about the drawing, not really. Of course, he might have assumed he didn't have to, counting on their desire to keep their family's turmoil private. This uneasy feeling—okay, fear—was probably silly. It wasn't as if she actually *did* know anything that would help identify her mother's killer.

Beth sighed and drove home.

The phone rang again as she was stepping out of the shower. She grabbed the towel with one hand and the phone with the other. Her heart sped up when she saw Tony's name.

"Hi." She bent over so her hair dripped on the bath mat and dried her body with the free hand.

"Hey." His voice was its usual sexy rumble. "You sound out of breath. Is this a bad time?"

"No, I'm just getting out of the shower."

There was a long, long silence. "Damn," he said at last. "I wish you hadn't told me that."

The day's stresses melted away, and she smiled in a way that probably looked silly, but who cared? "If I sound a little funny, it's because I'm toweling myself dry while juggling a phone."

He groaned. "Can I come over? Right now? You could get back in the shower and start over once I'm there."

Beth laughed. "Not a chance."

"Not even for the coming over part?"

Beth hesitated. "I could put something together for dinner, if you'd like."

"That's an offer I'll take," he said, sounding satisfied. "I'm on my way. No hurry getting dressed. I've always wanted to see a woman come to the door wrapped in a towel."

She blew a raspberry.

CHAPTER ELEVEN

TONY WASN'T KIDDING about being on his way. Beth was still hastily French braiding her wet hair when she heard the knock. She finished braiding on the way to the back door.

He looked as sexy as ever but also tired, she thought. Peering past him, she said, "You nabbed the visitor's spot. You're lucky. The guy two doors down has friends over at least every other day. He blasts his music." She grinned. "Hey, if he tries it tonight, I'll send you over."

He gave a huff that was almost a laugh. "Breaking up parties is a patrol officer's job. Lots of fun."

"I'll bet." She started for the kitchen, Tony behind her.

"Has anyone ever told you what amazing legs you have?"

This was the first time she'd worn shorts around him. She was barefoot, too.

"Thank you." She came to a stop in the kitchen, turning in time to catch him eyeing her in a way that made her blood heat.

So much for the cold shower.

"I can make a creamy sauce with stewed tomatoes that's good over pasta," she said. "It's quick and easy."

"Good. Can I help?"

"No, why don't you sit and talk to me?" She stood on tiptoe to reach the cans of stewed tomatoes and evaporated milk. "Oh, did you hear from Officer Webley? Poor man."

"I did, and why *poor man*?"

"He's sunburned."

Tony tipped his head and scrutinized her. "Your face is a little pink, too."

Because she was skimpily dressed and he was here. Instead of sitting at the kitchen table, he'd settled on a tall kitchen stool, close enough she could see the individual bristles on his jaw.

"It was awfully hot out there. And boring."

"So I gather."

"I didn't disagree with a single decision either Matt or Emily made about that stuff." Pulling a fat yellow bell pepper from the refrigerator, she asked, "What about your day?"

"I irritated a lot of people and can't say I learned anything useful." He blew out a sigh. "Did you know Emily is telling people about the drawing?"

"Yes. She called just after I left Dad's. I don't even know why, when she was so sullen. She said Mom deserved to be humiliated and, when I pointed out that she was kind of past that, Emily went off about what a stuffed shirt Matt is, and saying Dad wouldn't notice even if people are talking about him. I kind of hung up on her."

"Good."

"Do you hang up on your sisters or mother?"

He grimaced. "I should."

Beth laughed, even though she didn't actually feel like it. With the sauce simmering, she put hot water for the pasta on to boil, then turned to face him.

"Tony, Emily hasn't just told people about the drawing." Seeing the way his expression changed, she went on. "She told them I'd seen another drawing by the guy and am trying to remember who he is."

He swore. "I cannot believe— No, I can. Is she malicious or just stupid?"

Defending Emily came automatically, even though Beth had wondered the same thing. Except she'd wondered instead whether her little sister was that dumb—or hated her.

"Would you like it if I said something like that about one of your sisters?"

Tony made a disbelieving sound. "If she shoved me onto a busy freeway? Yeah, I think I'd wonder about her motives."

Beth turned hastily to stir her sauce and added the evaporated milk she'd already measured out. "I...couldn't tell if she even thought about what she'd done. It was like…" Frowning, Beth tried to pin down her impression. "She's mad at everyone. Maybe…maybe she intended to challenge Mom's killer, to say 'You'll be caught. You'll pay for what you did.'"

She didn't hear him move. The first she knew, his big hands closed on her shoulders, and he gently turned her around. The compassion on his face was almost more than she could stand.

"Are you not friends at all?"

"We are." Or so Beth had believed. Or deceived herself. "She's…moody. She always was, really. She clung to me after Mom left, until teenage hormones hit a year later. Then she needed me desperately one minute, screamed 'You can't tell me what to do!' the next. I guess some of that has lingered." She found herself searching Tony's face for understanding. "Did I tell you how she blew up at Matt last weekend for throwing away those Christmas ornaments? I thought she really wanted them to bring back a time when she was happier. Now, I don't know. She resented us telling her she couldn't have Mom's clothes, too. Maybe she's a spoiled brat who didn't want to be denied anything she wanted. But if that's so…it had to be *me* who spoiled her."

The warmth in his dark eyes didn't abate. "Oh, sweetheart…not true. She *had* parents until she was twelve. What's more, you were a child when you took responsibility for her. You did your best, and I'm betting it was pretty damn good. Anyway, from what you say, she resents Matt, too, and what did *he* do to her?"

"I don't know," she had to admit. "Dad…well, Matt and he had the rockiest relationship, but I guess Emily wanted his attention more than I realized."

"She'd lost her mother. You'd all lost your mother." His smooth voice had hardened. "How could he not see how much you all needed him?"

"I don't know." How often had she said that lately? "Dad and I talked today. Let me cook, and I'll tell you about it."

"Okay." There was his gentle side again. "Is there anything I can do?"

He poured drinks and got out silverware and napkins, while she poured the boiling water and pasta into a colander, then transferred the pasta to one bowl and sauce to another.

When she brought them to the table, going back to the refrigerator for grated parmesan, Tony said, "Why don't we hold off on the serious stuff until we're done eating?"

"Are you trying to tell me my sister makes you queasy?" she said, in mock challenge.

Tony laughed, but his eyes looked serious when he said, "I don't like it when she upsets you."

Stunned, Beth was conscious of warmth

spreading from her chest outward until even her fingers and toes tingled. It was like nothing else she'd ever felt.

Because no one has ever worried first about me, she realized. *Or...worried about me at all.* No, she came to everyone else's rescue. Wasn't that her entire purpose in life? Well, friends cared, but that was different. They didn't focus on her the way he was doing now.

"What are you thinking?" Tony had paused in the act of sprinkling parmesan on his pasta.

"I..." She shook her head, then smiled tremulously. "Thank you."

He watched her for a moment, as if unconvinced, but finally nodded.

They ate for a couple minutes without either speaking. Beth finally said, "Will you tell me why you went into law enforcement?"

He smiled. "You mean, what tragedy pointed me that way? Wasn't one."

"Something must have."

"Actually, I went pretty wild when I was sixteen, seventeen. I was the oldest, and my parents expected a lot of me. It wasn't only that I wanted to party like my friends did, instead of babysitting my little sisters and brother. It was the lectures about how I was their role model. I felt pressure to be perfect. So, being a typical American teenager..."

"You rebelled." Beth found herself smiling. "I'm having trouble picturing you drunk and disorderly, but okay."

"I turned into a shit. Got arrested a couple of times. I was with some buddies when they stole a car."

"Really?"

"Oh, yeah. That's when I got lucky. The cop who stopped us singled me out. He volunteered at the Boys and Girls Club. In my rebel mind, *not* a cool place—" Tony's amusement showed "—but he talked me into playing some pickup basketball games there, hanging out with him. I wasn't his only project, but I felt like I mattered to him. He told stories about being cop, and I soaked it all up. My parents were grateful but uneasy, too."

"Was he Latino?"

"No, and that was part of it, I'm sure. Mostly, Mom and Dad and a lot of other people they knew had butted heads with the police. There was a good-size population of illegal immigrants around, and they were scared to death of cops. So they were both dismayed and proud of me for graduating with a degree in criminology and then from the police academy. My father asked if I'd pull some brown-skinned farm worker over just because he had a taillight out, and I said yes, but that I'd only warn him to get it fixed, not insist on seeing his birth certificate."

"Has it been an issue? I mean, are you expected to look for immigration violations?"

He shook his head. "Not so far. In fact, we try to stay hands-off. It's more important to us that people who witnessed a crime be willing to talk to us than be afraid we'll get them deported."

"That makes sense." She'd had that impression. "Your police friend. Is he still around?"

"Retired, but yeah. I'll take you to meet him someday." He resumed eating, not seeming aware of the implications of that promise.

Her sense of warmth and hope deepened. "Does he have a family?"

Tony shook his head. "He and his wife hadn't had kids, and she'd died of cancer a few years before I met him. That's probably why he started volunteering the amount of time he did."

"You were lucky that he believed in you."

His eyebrows rose. "You mean, that he bullied me into taking a hard look at my options?"

Beth laughed. "Either/or."

"I don't know what would have happened to me if he hadn't come along. I don't like imagining."

"You don't really think…"

"If I'd been arrested for stealing a car when I was seventeen, I could have been tried as an adult. Or sent to juvenile detention until I aged out. Would I have emerged a reformed, optimistic young man? I really doubt it. No, he caught me just in time."

That…sobered her. Trying to see a hard-bitten ex-con instead of the Detective Navarro she knew was a challenge, but he was right. Not much separated tough young men or women who took one path from those who took another.

He pushed his empty plate away. "Okay," he said, in a different voice. "Now I want to know what the *hell* you were thinking to tell your sister something that could put *you* at risk if it got out!"

"Don't yell at me." Was her lower lip poking out the way Emily's did when anyone lectured her?

"Beth."

Hearing the warning, she said, "I didn't think of it that way. I was telling her what's going on, that's all. It didn't occur to me that she'd pass on every detail of what I said, and especially not to Mom and Dad's old friends. It's not like she'd ever talked to any of them. Who knew they'd call her? And…" Her throat clogged. "Mom was killed an awfully long time ago." Even more meekly, she asked, "You don't really think I'm in danger, do you?"

Tony scowled at her. "Probably not, but— Damn it, Beth, I wish you'd kept that to yourself."

"It's so frustrating not to be able to remember!" she cried. "Maybe there isn't anything *to* remember. We all get that déjà vu feeling out of the blue."

"We do," he said on a sigh, "but this is different. You knew these people. You could have seen her lover showing your mother another drawing, or she left one out and you saw it. You were in and out of the pediatrician's office. Could some of his own art have hung on the wall in the waiting room or even his office? What about the others? Did you ever go with your mom to the law firm or get invited into the bank manager's office?"

Frustrated, she only shook her head. "I don't think so. You need to show the drawing to Dad. If any of their friends—or supposed friends—was that artistic, wouldn't the subject have come up?"

"Yeah." Tony seemed to brood for a moment. "You're right. Maybe I've underestimated him."

"I think I did, too." Beth told him some of what her father had said when they had talked earlier. "I think he was ashamed of himself."

"He should be," Tony said bluntly. "And I know you don't like it when I criticize any of your family members, but he used you. He's still using you."

She swallowed. "Or I enabled him."

"Don't turn this around so you can blame yourself. Go on out to the mall, Beth. Loiter near a group of teenage girls. Take a really hard look. You were a kid just like them, at least until you had to become the adult in your family."

Her chin rose. "How's the pressure your parents put on you any different?"

He didn't move, maybe didn't even breathe. "In one way it wasn't," he said finally. "The difference was I always knew if I let down one of my sisters or brother, it wasn't a big deal. My parents were there *being* parents. My attitude would have been different if I'd really been needed. If Dad had died earlier—" He shook his head. "You had to step up because nobody else would."

"You can't have it both ways. Haven't you been telling me Dad would have had to be the parent if I hadn't made it easy for him to keep on the way he had been?"

"No," he said quietly. "Enabling, that's your idea. He may be dysfunctional in some ways, but he just told you he *was* aware of what was happening, and he chose to let you make sacrifices to make his life easier."

She opened her mouth—and closed it. Because he was right. In one way, she'd been touched to have her father let her know that he did appreciate what she'd done. What she hadn't entirely recognized was her resentment.

It was funny because at the time she hadn't felt any. She'd been scared, desperate to hold her family together, to make everything as much like it had been as she could. But sometime in the intervening years, she'd brewed her own bubbling pot of anger.

"I don't like being angry!" she burst out.

"I know. Hey, come here."

His rueful smile caused a meltdown. She pushed back her chair and went around the table to be met with open arms. Tony helped her settle on his lap and cuddled her close. He had the most amazingly comforting shoulder. Except comfort wasn't all she felt. The view of his strong neck and jaw, the shadow of stubble, lips that looked so soft, had heat curling inside her. She suddenly wanted to kiss his throat, maybe even lick that copper-brown skin, discover his taste. Feel the roughness of his cheek under her own lips.

"Tony?" she whispered.

He bent his head to see her face. "Hmm?"

"No. Never mind."

"Now you have to tell me what you were going to say." His long fingers slipped into her hair.

"I was being silly. I guess I wanted...reassurance."

The groove in his cheek deepened with a smile. "You need to hear that I think you're the sexiest woman alive? Again?"

Beth snorted. "I won't believe you at all if you lay it on that thick."

"You can probably tell how I react every time

I touch you," he said, his voice an octave deeper than usual.

She had noticed the hard ridge against her hip. She wanted to stroke her hand over it. Even the idea gave her a cramping sensation between her thighs. She clenched them tighter to contain it.

"Yes."

"But that's not what you were talking about, was it?"

She shook her head against his shoulder.

He didn't respond for a minute, although his arms tightened. "This guy would be a fool to go after you. It would be like waving his hand in the air and saying, 'I did it.'" He paused. "I do wish your sister hadn't painted a target on your back, though. It makes me not want to take my eyes off you."

Beth straightened, bracing herself with a hand flattened on his chest. "You're supposed to be re-assuring me, remember?"

"I'm…feeling a little distracted." His eyes darkened, if such a thing was possible. "Maybe kissing you will help."

She tipped her face up in silent answer. *Please.*

He took her mouth, but gently. Brushing his lips over hers, waiting until she strained upward before doing it again. Sucking her lower lip into his mouth had her gasping. She gripped the back of his neck and held on, returning each caress, each nip. When he stroked his tongue into her mouth, she dug her fingers into the hard muscles on his chest.

The kiss became hungry, making her feel as if she'd needed him forever. His urgency *was* reassurance, if not what she'd asked for. He truly wanted her. Nobody had ever kissed her like this, as if he couldn't get enough, as if touching her could push him to his limits.

He lifted his head, looking at her with such intensity Beth heard herself make a small, broken sound. Then she seized her opportunity and kissed his neck. His skin was salty and something else that tasted inexplicably male. She nibbled and kissed her way up to the scratchy jaw that had so tempted her. All the while, his eyes blazed down at her.

One of his hands squeezed her waist. The other closed over her breast, lifting, shaping. His hips pushed up, and he groaned.

"Beth?"

"Umm?" She rubbed her cheek against his, loving the contrast in textures.

"If this isn't going anywhere, I think I need to stop."

She went utterly still, disappointment flooding her. "You don't want…?"

DON'T WANT? Did she really not get it?

"I want," he said harshly. "Too much." Even

as he spoke, his thumb played with the hard nub of her nipple. He couldn't seem to make himself take his hand from her breast. "I'm sorry. I usually have better self-control than this."

"Oh. I want you, too."

His muscles locked. She was going to explain again that this was too soon, and Tony knew it was for her. But, damn, he was on the edge. Having her full hip pressing against his cock, her lips on his skin, her nipples hard, had him feeling like a sixteen-year-old boy who'd put his hand on a woman's breast for the first time. Self-control was not in that boy's capability.

The fingers on his neck stroked, then kneaded. She had strong hands. One more thing to turn him on.

"I'm not on birth control," she said shyly.

"I have a condom in my wallet." He wished he had two. Once wouldn't be enough. When he got home—

"Do you…always carry them?"

Tony shook his head, his mouth brushing her hair. "Only when I'm in a relationship." He smiled crookedly. "Or hoping. I don't do bar pickups."

"Do you do bars?"

The sexual tension hadn't eased, but he was able to laugh. "No. A lot of cops I know do— Edgar's, near the police station, is a favorite. Me, I've broken up too many brawls, seen the results of drunk driving too many times, investigated too many deaths in tavern parking lots to find them very appealing."

"I should send you home, but I don't want to."

His brain was hazy enough that it took him a second to untangle that. "You mean—"

Beth nodded, and he surged to his feet with her in his arms. "This chair is a little too hard for what I have in mind."

"You're a detective. Can you find my bedroom?" she teased.

Laughing again, he strode toward the short hall. He felt sure this was a one-bedroom unit and was proved right. Bathroom on the left, bedroom on the right. He barely had an impression of the room, beyond creamy white walls, art and textiles adding color and a bed that had to be full size, with an antique spool bed frame and a fuzzy, butter-yellow spread. Too short for him, but they'd manage.

To slow himself, he resisted the temptation to drop her on the mattress and come down on top of her. Instead, he lowered her to her feet, her body sliding along his. The pleasure of feeling every soft curve had him gritting his teeth.

He framed her face with his hands and asked gutturally, "You're sure?"

Beth bobbed her head, her gaze shy but eager, too.

"God, I want you." Despite his determination to

be gentle, this kiss went ballistic from the beginning. It was as much her fault as his. She pushed herself up, her tongue tangling with his, her body rubbing against him. Desperate, he wrenched his mouth away long enough to strip her knit shirt over her head. He bent her back and sucked her breast through her bra, but enough brain cells were functioning for him to realize belatedly that it had a front clasp. One flick and it fell open.

Her breasts were glorious, luscious swells of creamy flesh topped with generously sized areolae and taut nipples. He licked one nipple, then had to have her flat on the bed.

Beth squeaked when he lifted her but, when he zeroed in on her breasts, she blocked him with both hands. "Shirt off."

Oh, yeah. Fortunately, he was wearing a polo shirt, which he could rip right off, but he also had to remove his holstered gun and badge. He tossed them on the bedside table along with his belt and phone, pulled out his wallet and removed the condom, then let the wallet fall.

She looked as fascinated with his chest as he was with hers. He teased and suckled until her hips rocked. Her hands moved the whole while, tangling with his chest hair, teasing his flat nipples, squeezing muscle.

Tony didn't even remember disposing of the rest of their clothing. Naked, she was the most beautiful thing he'd ever seen, a man's dream come true. Slim and yet rounded in all the right places. Long legs. He tore himself away from her breasts and her mouth to explore those legs, kissing the arched bottom of her feet until her toes curled, running his mouth up smooth calves, tickling the tender flesh behind her knees. The skin on the inside of her thighs was so silky, his fingers and mouth lingered, until he was drawn upward to nuzzle the moist curls.

She gripped his hair and gasped. He lifted his head to see her alarm, which made him smile even as he continued stringing kisses upward. Had no man ever put his mouth on her that intimately? That primitive side of him was pleased. Next time, he told himself. Once this wasn't so new. Hipbones, belly with a tiny bit of give, ribs that felt delicate beneath more smooth skin.

While he sank into a luxuriant kiss, he slipped his fingers between her folds, finding her wet and so responsive, his need intensified. He twisted away to don the condom, then went back to kissing her as she clutched at him.

Her legs fell open at the slightest nudge. The blood roared in his ears as he eased his way inside her. Once he was deeply seated, he hesitated.

"Don't stop," she whispered.

Blind with need, he pulled out and drove deep again, and again. She planted both feet on the mattress so she could grip him with her thighs and push up to meet his every thrust.

Her throaty cries and the feel of her fingernails biting into his back ripped away any tattered remnants of self-control. He was lost, their bodies rocking, him on the brink. He hooked an arm around one of her thighs, pulling it higher—and she began to spasm around him. He let himself go, slammed by a release so powerful, his mind shut down.

When the stunning pleasure finally ebbed, he couldn't even manage to roll to one side.

TEARS PRICKED BETH'S EYES as she wrapped her arms around the hot, male body pressing her deep into the mattress. Wonder and tenderness filled her. *So that's what it's supposed to be like.* She loved having Tony sprawled atop her, somehow vulnerable in a way she'd never seen him. His weight felt so good, she held on tight when he groaned and tried to move. "Don't."

"I'm crushing you." His voice was deep, creating a vibration against her breasts.

"No."

He rolled anyway, but took her with him, so that she remained snug against his body. "That was amazing," he murmured, as he rubbed his cheek on her head.

"Yes." She'd call it an understatement, at least

where she was concerned. Extraordinary for her might be average sex for him.

A faint buzzing came from the bedside table. He lifted his head, reached over her for the phone and touched the screen to open a text. After reading it, he said a word she was sure he wouldn't use in front of his mother and let his head fall back on the pillow.

"Your job?"

"No." His chest rose and fell on a long sigh. "My sister. Eloisa. Her husband's out of town. My mother says Eloisa isn't answering her phone. She's been so nauseated she's losing weight instead of gaining, and her little boy is too young to know to answer her phone if mommy has collapsed."

"Oh. You'd better go." She only hoped he wasn't making up an excuse to extract himself from her bed.

"Yeah. Let me try her. She may just be dodging Mamá." One ring followed another, nobody picking up. "Damn." He kissed her cheek and sat up, making a grumbly sound. "I'm sorry, Beth. I don't want to leave."

She managed what she thought was a credible smile. "I hope your sister is okay."

"Me, too." He found his knit boxer shorts and pulled them on, followed by his pants and shirt.

Feeling ridiculously shy, considering his hands

and mouth had explored so much of her body, she slipped out of bed and started getting dressed, too. Out of the corner of her eye, she was very aware of Tony putting on his socks and shoes before feeding his belt through the loops on his pants. The badge he shoved in a pocket, but he snapped his holster back on. She hadn't had very many men in her bed, and watching him do such everyday things gave her unexpected joy.

Unless he was running out on her.

She slipped on flip-flops, perfectly adequate to walk him out. She'd kick even those off once he was gone. She liked going barefoot at home.

On the way to the back door, he said, "I should help you clean up."

"Don't be silly. It won't take a minute."

The cool night air felt good, so she stepped out on the concrete landing with him. A three-quarter moon hung high in the sky. It would have been a romantic night to go for a walk or a drive. But, no. Tony gave her a hasty kiss, said, "I'll call you in the morning," and loped toward his pickup truck.

She watched as he backed out, wondering if he so much as glanced back through the rearview mirror as he drove away down the alley. Probably not; he had to be more worried about his sister than he'd let her see.

He had turned the corner and gone out of sight when a crunch on gravel close by made her pulse leap. Beth spun toward the sound, except one of the flimsy flip-flops didn't pivot. Tangled with it, she was stumbling when she saw the tall, dark shape swinging a baseball bat at her head.

CHAPTER TWELVE

BETH SCREAMED AS she fell forward, a whip of wind lifting her hair when the bat passed above her head. Even as she crashed painfully to her hands and knees, she kept screaming. She wanted to scrabble away, but this monster out of the darkness had to be readying another swing. So instead, she flung herself at him.

The crack of bone and searing pain sent her down again, her fingertips barely grazing his pants. This time, she rolled but bumped up against her own concrete stoop almost immediately.

Back porchlights came on and voices called out. Running footsteps approached, and her attacker bolted. She saw his back as he crossed the alley at an angle, almost beneath a streetlight.

Then a young man was crouching at her side. "Jesus. Are you all right?" He raised his voice. "Has anyone called 9-1-1?"

"I did," a woman answered. "What happened?"

"Call again. Make sure they know we need an ambulance."

Beth had never felt pain like this. It was all she

could do to keep herself from whimpering. "Arm," she whispered.

At his tentative touch, she cried out.

"You're bleeding."

Was she?

He dropped to his knees beside her and talked to her, telling her she'd be fine, he'd broken a leg once and it hurt like hell but once it was casted, it quit hurting. She could have people sign her cast, he told her.

She realized at some point that she was gripping his hand, and then that he was the guy who played his music too loud but right now was being so kind she'd never mind again.

A patrol car reached them first, and she told the officer she'd been assaulted by a man swinging a baseball bat. "He ran away. That way." She managed to point. "Tell Detective Navarro. Just here."

He went to his car and talked on his radio. An ambulance finally pulled up. She must have passed out when the two EMTs lifted her onto a gurney because the next thing she knew, she was being unloaded at the hospital.

Someone asked who they could call for her. She wanted Tony, but what if his sister had collapsed? Besides, they'd be contacting him anyway. She gave them Matt's name and phone number, then endured as a nurse washed grit from her raw hands and knees with a stinging solution.

No, she had no known allergies to medications.

At last the doctor gave her a shot that didn't kill the pain but made it seem so distant, it might not be hers. Now drifting, she closed her eyes.

THE FLICKER OF light he saw through the front blinds didn't soothe Tony's worry. When her husband wasn't home, Eloisa kept the TV on all the time.

"I don't feel so alone," she'd told Tony.

Guilt took a bite as he hammered on the door. He should have stopped by a couple times in the past two days, made sure she was all right. He knew Eloisa never told Carlos about her fears.

"He has to work," she said. "He deserves to go out with his friends sometimes." Seeing Tony's expression, she shook her head. "Carlos is a good man."

He'd seemed okay to Tony, but he knew that if he had a wife, he wouldn't like finding out she'd been hiding something like this from him.

This was her second pregnancy, and she'd suffered in the first four months of the first as much as she was this time. He hoped they had the sense to limit the size of their family, Catholic edicts or not.

Swearing, he started down the porch steps. He'd go around back, look in the slider before he broke a window to go in—

The door opened behind him. "Tony? Is that you?" his sister said timidly.

He swung around. "Why the hell didn't you answer the door sooner? You scared the shit out of me!"

"I was asleep!" she exclaimed, indignant. "Why are you here?"

Yeah, she was dressed, but barefoot, and her hair was sticking out in strange ways. A petite woman like their mother, Eloisa looked frail now, only a small bump showing her pregnancy. At four months, he thought, she should be ripening, not losing what muscle and fat usually padded her slight body.

"Because you haven't been answering your phone, and Mamá was worried."

"I love you all, but sometimes I hate being babied." She backed up. "Come in."

Finally able to smile, he ruffled her hair on the way in.

She snorted and stomped to the kitchen. "I suppose you want coffee."

No, he wanted to go back to Beth's and slide into bed with her. Except he didn't have another condom, he reminded himself, before looking speculatively at his sister. Did she and Carlos ever use them? Might he find some in the bathroom?

Forget it. He could make a quick stop at a convenience store.

Uneasiness stirred. It would be smarter to go home. If he went to Beth's, he might fall asleep after making love with her again. Stay the night, which could give her the wrong impression.

"Jaime asleep?" he asked his sister.

"Of course he is." She planted a hand on her hip and glared at him. "You think I take naps while my little boy gets into trouble?"

Laughing, Tony swept her into a hug. "No, I think you get into trouble because you won't accept help. How much food have you been able to keep down today?"

"Enough. Mamá wants to force feed me. She's seen me puke, but she's convinced if she wills me to eat, it'll stay down. She's wrong."

"She aggravates me, too," he said, calming her with a hand on her shoulder. "But she loves us. You know that."

Eloisa heaved a sigh. "I know. Tonight I didn't want to talk. I didn't realize she'd call the cops."

Tony grinned. "If not for her cataracts, she'd have come herself."

She frowned at him, her gaze taking in his weapon. "You were still working? This late?"

"No, I was having dinner with a woman I met recently. Didn't have time to go home and change before I went to her place."

"A-ha!" Eloisa's pixie face lit with delight. "Now you have to tell me all about her."

"So you can tell everybody?"

She returned his grin. "Of course."

This was why he didn't tell anyone in his family about the women he saw. There would be demands to meet her. He'd once made the mistake of taking a casual girlfriend to Sunday dinner at his mother's, but never again. Not everyone in the family had liked her. Others did and wanted to know why he didn't bring her again. When he'd been driven to admit he wasn't seeing her anymore, they wanted to know why. If he gave them so much as a peek into his personal life, his family would drive him crazy.

Crazier than they already did.

He'd worried that Tia Paloma would have spread the word about the woman he had taken to lunch. Not only taken to lunch but brought to *her* restaurant. He felt certain that everyone in the family would like Beth, and she'd like them. That he could see it happening alarmed him. She'd fit right in. They'd have him married off before he knew it.

It alarmed him that he couldn't think of any good arguments against an ending that had never struck him as happy. But why think about anything like that, anyway? He hadn't even known her a week.

While his mind wandered, his sister had poured him the coffee he didn't want but now couldn't refuse. He had started to thank her when his phone rang. Beth was the only person he'd like to hear from—

The number, although local, wasn't hers.

"Navarro."

"Detective? This is Officer Scott Kelly. I responded to a call that I'm told will concern you. A woman named Bethany Marshall was assaulted behind her townhouse."

What the— "Beth?"

"That's what a neighbor called her."

His body rigid, he said sharply, "Tell me what happened."

A man who may have worn a mask had stepped from behind a parked car and swung a baseball bat she thought was aimed at her head. She'd somehow dodged that swing, but he'd connected with a second that broke her arm. She'd suffered additional, minor injuries from falling. Yes, she was currently at the ER.

Had she been attacked right after he drove away? Tony couldn't think of any other reason she'd have been out back, unless she'd decided to go somewhere.

Heart thudding, he said, "I'm on my way. Keep me informed."

He poured the coffee down the sink, kissed his sister and said, "Next time, answer the damn phone, at least when I'm calling," and jogged out to his pickup.

Five minutes later, he walked into the ER.

BETH KEPT NODDING OFF, but she opened her eyes when she heard the sound of the sliding door that separated her cubicle from the corridor and the nurse's station. The doctor had promised to let her go once he issued a prescription.

But it was Tony who walked in, his gaze locking on her as he came straight to her side, ignoring Matt as if he wasn't there. Then he assessed her, from the gauze wrapping her palms to the cast enclosing her left arm.

"You look out of it."

She worked her tongue around in her mouth before she tried to speak. "They gave me something."

"Damn." The hand he lifted to stroke her cheek had a tremor. "If I hadn't left…"

"You had to go. Your sister…"

"She's fine. Wanting to be left alone, that's all." He smoothed her hair back from her forehead. "Officer Kelly told me what happened. I won't ask you to repeat it right now—"

On the other side of the bed, Matt assumed a cross-armed stance. "No, you won't. This son of a bitch tried to kill my sister. What are you going to do about it?"

"Catch him." His dark eyes met hers again. "Kelly thinks this could have been random. You were standing outside, your door open behind you. A burglar who saw a great opportunity."

"He was right there," she whispered, seeing the dark shape loom, feeling the terror anew. "Behind a car. He was waiting."

She saw him understand. If the man had been after her, he had to have seen Tony arrive. Bided his time until she was alone. Would he have risked rushing her if she'd stepped back inside before Tony was out of sight?

"I tripped and fell down. If I hadn't…"

His face spasmed. "I shouldn't have left you alone."

"You can't be with me all the time."

"I swear, I'm going to throttle Emily," Matt said, violence vibrating in his voice. "How could she be that stupid?"

Beth already knew Tony shared the sentiment. She mumbled, "My fault for—"

Tony laid a hand over her mouth. "We've talked about this."

Looking bullish again, Matt asked, "About what?"

Tony looked straight at her brother. "Beth tries to take responsibility for everything and everyone, and that means the blame, too."

To her astonishment, red stained Matt's cheeks,

and he hunched his shoulders. "Yeah. I guess we've all gotten too used to it."

"Yes, you have," Tony said, with no give in his voice.

To her surprise and embarrassment, Matt touched her face much as Tony had, with a tenderness that made her eyes sting. "He's right," Matt murmured. "I'm sorry, Bethie. You...made it too easy for us."

"That's what Dad said, too."

"Dad?" He stared at her. "Are you sure you weren't hearing things?"

She started to shake her head and regretted it. Had she bumped her head? She didn't remember, but it did ache. "No. He...apologized to me. He said some other things, too." She told him, watching emotions wash over his face. He didn't hide what he was thinking well. *Like me*, she thought, at least according to Tony.

"I don't know if that makes it better or worse," he grumbled.

She didn't either. Right now, she didn't want to think about Dad or—

The sliding door opened again, and the too-cheerful nurse announced she had the prescription and a sample of painkillers to get her through until tomorrow. "An orderly is on his way with a wheelchair."

"Ashley is making up the bed in our spare

room," Matt said gruffly. "I'll go get my car and meet you outside."

"No." Tony. "I'll take her home and stay with her for the night."

Matt's eyes narrowed. "That's a little above and beyond, don't you think?" His gaze dropped to the hand Tony was holding. "Please tell me—"

Tony stared him down. "It's none of your business."

"Yes, but…" His pleading gaze met hers. "What if he arrests Dad?"

"He won't. We both know Dad would never do anything like that."

Her brother's mouth opened and closed a couple times. Finally, he settled for a surly, "He never admitted he was more aware than he let on, either."

Beth couldn't argue with that, except one had nothing to do with the other. Anyway, she didn't want to argue about anything. She wanted to go home, take a pain pill and snuggle into her own bed. Preferably with Tony wrapped around her.

When she thanked her brother for being there for her, he gave way. Relieved not to have to take her home with him? She couldn't tell. Tony went out to move his pickup, while Matt walked beside her as the orderly wheeled her down the corridor.

Outside, Tony helped her into the high cab with exquisite gentleness. Then the two men shook hands, although she didn't get why, and Tony drove away, leaving Matt standing alone, looking forlorn.

Beth turned her head. "He really was sweet. Maybe I should have let him take care of me."

"Not a chance," her detective said flatly.

Someday, she'd have to stand firm against his domineering tendencies—if this relationship lasted. Tonight, she didn't have the spirit, since he wanted the same thing she did.

"There's no way to track the man who attacked me, is there?"

Passing headlights let her see the taut, unhappy line of his jaw. "No. Even if we could get DNA, it wouldn't be much use. Getting results takes forever, and we haven't even come up with a fingerprint match yet."

She'd been wondering. "Because whoever he is has never been arrested."

"Or been required to give fingerprints for any other reason. Unless he served in the military, but getting them to open their databases isn't easy."

"Did any of the men you're looking at serve?"

He shook his head and laid his hand on her thigh. "We'll get this creep."

"I know." But how?

"I'm glad it wasn't your right arm that was broken."

"A silver lining." Despite her overall woozy, hurting state, she almost smiled. "How unlike you."

He gave a short laugh. "It's cover. I'm so angry, if I could get my hands on the son of a bitch right this minute, I'm not sure I could do my job instead of beating the crap out of him. And I'm not feeling so friendly toward your sister, either. Matt was right."

"She'll be horrified when she hears what happened." It was true. Too bad Emily never foresaw consequences.

He grunted, turning into the alley behind her building. "Do you have your keys?"

"Yes, fortunately I'd left them sitting out on the table. The police officer locked the back door and brought them to me at the hospital."

The visitor parking spot near her back door was open. There shouldn't be any reason she couldn't walk—except her knees hurt. And she felt shaky.

Tony would help her.

"Wait until I come around," Tony ordered.

Beth probably rolled her eyes but made no move to get out beyond gingerly freeing herself from her seatbelt. After opening her door, he picked her up and used his shoulder to nudge the door closed.

"What are you doing?" She sounded panicked. "I'm too heavy! You shouldn't be carrying me."

She wasn't a lightweight, not like a couple of his sisters who were as tiny as his mother, but he didn't have any trouble carrying Beth either. "Of course I should," he said, but he gently set her on her feet when they reached the concrete pad in front of her door. "Key?"

"Oh." She dug them out of her pocket and handed it to him.

He unlocked the door, then said, "Do you need to lie down immediately?" When she said she was fine, he nodded. Keeping a supportive arm around her, he said, "Talk me through what happened."

She swept an uneasy glance over the parking area and alley. "I didn't move after you left. The cool air felt good. I was looking after your pickup, when I caught movement out of the corner of my eye." She told him how her flip-flop had tripped her as she tried to turn to face a possible danger. "He came from behind that SUV." She pointed. "It belongs to the guy who lives next door."

"Stay here." After making sure she was steady on her feet, Tony turned on the flashlight he'd hung from his belt before getting out. Now he turned it on and walked slowly around the black Toyota Sequoia, scanning the ground as well as the vehicle. Then he returned to her. "Was he wearing gloves?"

She closed her eyes for a moment, as if to see the scene more clearly, then said, "Yes. Black."

"Not worth more fingerprinting, then." He sighed. "Okay, his first swing missed you."

Beth wrinkled her nose. "Because I was doing

a belly flop. I skinned my knees there—" a smear of blood had dried on the concrete, he saw "—and my hands on some of that loose gravel."

His jaw was so tight his molars ached.

"I started to push myself up, and that's when I saw him going back for another swing. So I threw myself at his legs, and he had to adjust mid-swing."

When the bat had smashed into her upper arm. Tony wished he *couldn't* envision that moment with no effort at all. "Did you get your hands on him?"

"Just for a second." She frowned. "I think he was wearing sweatpants. Something soft. You know?"

"Black."

"He had a black hoodie on, and what I think were black athletic shoes. There might have been a metallic design on the sides. I saw him running that way—" she pointed, just as Officer Kelly said she had for him "—and he passed under the streetlight. That's really the only look I had at him, and it wasn't good because of the SUV in the way." The streetlight was on the corner at the cross street. The city didn't bother lighting alleys.

Tony had every intention of calling the owner of these townhouses tomorrow and urging him or her—strongly—to improve the lighting in the back. Motion-sensitive lights would be good.

"But you didn't see his face at all."

She bit her lower lip as she shook her head. "I think it was covered, but I'm not positive. I mean, I was already falling as I started to turn. And, you know, I kind of was focused on the bat." She sounded apologetic. "And then I was on my face and, when I lunged for him, I didn't lift my eyes higher than his knees."

"Any sense of height?" Not that he expected anything helpful. Victims almost always exaggerated the size of assailants and, in this case, Beth hadn't been on her feet long enough to judge their relative heights. But he had to ask.

"Tall," she said. "But not huge. He was more… lean."

As he would describe both Alan Schuh and Michael Longley. Tim Oberholtzer, the banker, was heftier. Tony had done a search for photos and had found two in the Frenchman Lake newspaper taken close to the time of Christine Marshall's murder. Even then, the guy had some extra padding and a soft jawline. He was a few years older than the other two men, too. *And* still married to the same woman. After Beth's description of her assailant, Oberholtzer dropped even lower on Tony's list of possibilities.

Tony really needed to connect with the senior partner in the accounting firm and ask for names of Christine's male clients, particularly any she might have gotten friendly with.

"Smell?" he asked.

Beth looked startled, then thought about it. Finally, she said, "Nothing I remember except, you know, a whiff from the Dumpster, and some oil or gas."

"Okay." Seeing her sway, he pushed the door open and swung her back into his arms despite her protest, carrying her through the townhouse to her bedroom. There, he helped her undress. She left on her panties, and, doing his best to ignore her beautiful breasts, he was able to work an oversize T-shirt over her cast. It fell almost to mid-thigh.

Seeing gauze taped to her knees had him gritting his teeth again. Bruises were forming, too, and he'd seen her wince as she stuck her hands through the arms of the shirt. Had the doctor X-rayed both wrists to look for additional broken bones?

He piled pillows behind her and pulled up the covers. "Let me get some water so you can take some more of your meds."

"Thank you," she said softly. "Are…you going to sleep with me?"

"I am, if you don't have any objection."

She relaxed. "No. I'm not sure how well I'd sleep if I was alone."

Tony shook his head, smiling. "I think once this pain pill hits, you'll be out like a light."

At her request, he also brought her a couple of soda crackers, which she nibbled without a crumb escaping, as far as he could tell.

"The sister I checked on tonight, Eloisa, seems to be living on crackers right now. Like I said, she's having trouble keeping anything down. Her doctor recommended them."

"See?" Despite everything, she appeared to be teasing him. "They're the best medicine."

Once she finished the crackers and set the glass on the bedside stand, Tony sat on the edge of the mattress, close enough to smooth her hair back from her forehead. He used fingertips and thumbs to massage her temples, careful to avoid touching the beginnings of a bruise on her jaw. Beth turned her face into his hand, her eyes sinking shut.

Only when he felt her body go lax did he leave her long enough to check the locks on the front and back doors, as well as the windows, and to use the bathroom. Then he stripped, leaving neatly folded clothes on a rocking chair in her room and laying his gun and phone on the bedside stand. It looked like she usually slept on that side, but he needed to be within arm's reach of his weapon. He turned off the lamp and slid beneath the covers, half lifting her a few feet over.

When he eased his arm beneath her neck, she made a small sound and turned to nestle her head on his shoulder as if she'd done it a thousand times. As if this was where she belonged. The casted arm she rested across his belly and chest, the plaster cold to his bare skin.

He smiled in the darkness, foreseeing the thing getting badly in the way when he made love with her.

Better think of it as having sex. Love...wasn't yet on the table.

Tenderness he couldn't deny he felt. And, damn, he'd been scared when he'd understood that Beth had been attacked, that her life had been saved by a cheap rubber sandal.

Thank God for flip-flops.

He breathed in the citrus scent of her hair and closed his own eyes. He was here to keep her safe, which was what counted.

CHAPTER THIRTEEN

LEANING BACK AGAINST Beth's kitchen counter, Tony cocked his head when he thought he heard her stirring. Nope, only quiet. Beth had had a restless period in the middle of the night when the pain meds wore off, but once the second pill she swallowed kicked in, she'd been sleeping like—

Not the dead, damn it. Soundly.

Enough coffee had brewed for him to fill his mug. He'd no sooner done so than his phone vibrated. He sighed and, taking the phone, moved toward the back of the townhouse. As he opened the back door and stepped out, he answered his phone.

"Mamá."

He'd tried *Mom* when he was in his defiant teenage stage. It hadn't gone over well. His mother was entirely American, a modern woman when it suited her and not when it didn't.

Without so much as saying hello, she launched in, voice sharp. "You didn't call me. You couldn't find the time, even when you knew I was worried?"

"Eloisa is fine."

"I know that now because *she* called a few minutes ago. I hardly slept a wink," she scolded, "imagining her unconscious on the floor, Jaime crying and trying to wake up his mamá. Would it have been so hard for you to take one minute—"

When he'd first returned to Frenchman Lake after his father's death, Tony had been patient with his family. Everyone sticking their noses in each other's business, the lack of privacy or time alone, those were familiar enough to him, and he'd become accustomed to that again. These past few months his patience had eroded, and he didn't even know why.

Now he snapped, "Eloisa told you why I left, didn't she? Why can't you understand that my job has to come ahead of calling my mother to soothe her nerves?"

"How can you talk to me this way? Didn't your papá and I teach you to respect your parents?"

He tipped his head back to rest against the door-frame. "I don't mean to be insulting, Mamá. A woman who is a witness in a murder investigation I'm conducting was attacked last night, almost killed. I would have let you know if I couldn't get to Eloisa's to check on her. Is it unreasonable to expect you to trust that I did go?"

"A call would have taken you so little time."

He was in no mood for this. "I'm sorry."

"You don't mean that."

He squeezed his eyes closed and held the phone a couple inches from his ear. Still, he heard her.

"Where have you been all week? None of us has seen you. With Carlos away, didn't you promise to mow Eloisa's yard? She's counting on you."

Actually, Mamá had promised he would. And his sister's dry lawn, at the height of summer, could wait until Carlos returned.

"My lieutenant counts on me, too," he said. "I'm expected to work as many hours as I need to on an investigation. The woman who came close to having her head bashed in is counting on me, too." He wanted to say *And I deserve a life of my own, with time for a girlfriend*, but he didn't. The slightest hint and Mamá would insist he bring Beth to a big family dinner so they could all meet her. The idea made him cringe. "Sometimes, unimportant things like mowing a lawn need to wait."

"And calling me? That is unimportant, too?"

He loved his mother. He did. But right now, it took all he had to say, "I drove fast on the way to the hospital. It was no time to make phone calls. I've apologized."

"When will I see you?" she asked.

"I don't know. I have to go, Mamá. I'm at the witness's home and need to speak to her."

"Very well. I'll wait until you have time for me." Guilt inserted like a stiletto, she hung up on him.

He muttered an obscenity and turned to go back

inside. That's when he saw Beth standing only a few feet away, close enough to have heard every word.

Hugging her cast to her body, looking very alone, she said, "*The witness?*"

HE HADN'T HEARD her padding barefoot into the kitchen. Beth almost immediately realized who he was talking to. And she'd heard him call her a *witness* twice.

Yes, it stung.

"I was already irritated enough," he said. "This wasn't the moment to mention that I'm seeing a woman."

Not having known Tony quite a week, she should let this go. But...*witness?* Who—oh, by the way—he'd slept with?

So she said tartly, "Aren't you usually *seeing* a woman?"

"Damn it, don't make this into something it isn't," he said irritably, closing the door and walking right past her into the kitchen. "And, no, I don't tell my mother when I'm involved with someone. She'd insist on meeting her, then interfering."

"But you know my family."

"They're not like mine. Anyway, I've met them on the job, not because of any personal relationship."

That was true but painfully brought home that

he'd met *her* on the job, too. From his point of view, instead of "friends with benefits," this might qualify as an extra job benefit.

She opened a drawer and took out a plastic kitchen trash bag to cover her cast. "I'm going to take a shower."

He didn't follow her. Even humiliatingly aware she might not be able to get her bra on or the tank top she intended to wear over the cast, Beth was *not* going to ask him for help.

She should have gone home with Matt. A teacher, Ashley had the summer off. The two of them had always gotten along well. Ashley wouldn't have minded helping.

It's not too late, Beth thought. She'd rather stay home—but this thing was miserably unwieldy, and she hurt. It was Tony's pampering she wanted, not her sister-in-law's, but Ashley was family.

Trying to keep the spray from getting inside the plastic bag made showering awkward. Plus, she should have taken the next pain pill *before* the shower.

On getting out, she discovered that twisting a towel into place on her head was a challenge with one hand. She couldn't really dry her back, either.

And, oh, she hated feeling sorry for herself.
Then don't.

Beth stuck her tongue out at herself in the mirror before struggling into panties and stretchy pants. Lightheaded before she was done, she sank onto the closed toilet seat and bent forward.

At a tap on the door, she straightened. "Yes?"

"Can I come in?"

The least he could do was fasten her damn bra. "Sure."

He came in and crouched in front of her, eyes a dark chocolate, expression rueful. "I'm sorry."

"There's nothing to be sorry for. What you tell your mother is your business." Beth reached for her bra. "If you wouldn't mind fastening this…"

He took it from her, helping her maneuver her cast through the opening, then scoop her breasts into the cups. He got a few sneaky caresses in there, before she leaned forward again so he could hook it closed.

"Shirt?"

"I'm just going to wear a tank top today."

He managed to slip it on her without jarring her arm, a minor miracle. When he finished that, he gave her head a rub with the towel and brushed her wet hair for her.

"Shall I leave it loose?"

"Do you know how to braid?"

His mouth quirked. "Remember all those little sisters?" He deftly began.

Picturing him getting half a dozen little girls ready for school in the morning, hair braided or decorated, made her smile.

He did the same. "That's better. Now, come

on. I've already poured your coffee and set out your pill."

"I need to get to the pharmacy," she remembered.

"No, I already called to be sure the prescription is ready. Once we have breakfast, I'll run over and pick it up."

His consideration pulled her out of the last of her sulkiness.

A few minutes later, he set a plate with scrambled eggs and toast in front of her, then sat down with his own serving.

"I don't love the idea of leaving you home alone today," he said.

She let her eyes meet his. "I was thinking I should probably take Matt up on his offer." She shook her head when he opened his mouth. "His wife has the summer off. I imagine I'll be feeling better in another day or two, and I'm sure I'll figure out how to get dressed once I quit hurting so much. In the meantime, you have more important things to do than babysit me."

"What if I drop you off there just for the day?"

Beth hesitated. "Tony...are you sure?" She waited, knowing he understood she wasn't asking only about today.

He reached across the table for her hand. "Positive."

"Fine. Although...maybe I should go to Dad's instead. He must need company by now."

Tony didn't look thrilled but finally said, "Up to you. I need to talk to him about the drawing, anyway."

"Let's do that, then."

"Call and make sure he'll be there."

Beth wondered how much use her father would be in defending her against an attack. Sobering thought.

He answered right away, his grave voice betraying some alarm. "Emily just called, hysterical. She said you were attacked?"

"I was." She looked at Tony, who nodded. "Detective Navarro thinks the guy who came after me might be the same man who killed Mom." The formal reference to Tony barely out, guilt poked at her. Her father had met Tony, yes, but she'd lied to Dad about having any personal relationship with him. Of course, her reasons were different from his for not wanting to introduce her to his family.

At her father's urging, she gave a synopsis, then said, "Actually, the detective—um, Tony—doesn't want me home alone today. Can I come over?"

He agreed, and she promised to tell him more when she got there.

Setting down her phone, she sighed. "I suppose I ought to call Emily."

"Why?" Tony sounded uncompromising.

"She's my sister. She loves me."

"Do it later." He didn't have to say *When I don't*

have to hear you. She read him loud and clear. "We can stop at the pharmacy on the way."

She scooped a few magazines and a book into her tote bag to keep herself entertained, brushed her teeth and was ready to go.

The pharmacy had a drive-through window, so the stop didn't take more than a minute or two.

A block from the house, Beth admitted, "I haven't told Dad I'm dating you."

He gave her a sidelong, extremely ironic look.

"It seemed…disloyal," she said quietly.

"We can go on keeping it to ourselves," he offered.

"From your family, maybe. But Matt knows."

"You're right. Since he felt compelled to call Emily, she probably knows, too."

"And would have passed it on to Dad," Beth said with a sigh. And anyone else she talked to.

Tony pulled into the driveway next to her father's aging car. "Handle it however you want."

She only nodded. Dad had the front door open before they reached the small porch.

Her father looked stricken. "Dear God."

"It's not that bad." She let him hug her.

"Have you had breakfast?" he asked, looking at Tony, too.

"Yes. Um… Tony was nice enough to spend the night. He made sure I ate."

In the family room, she sank onto one end of

the sofa. Tony set the tote by her feet. Her father studied Tony more keenly than she was used to seeing.

"You think this man will come after her again."

"It's a possibility," Tony said. "Ah, I have something I'd like to discuss with you."

"Privately?"

"No, Beth already knows. Maybe your other daughter or son have mentioned it."

Her father sat in his usual recliner, his face assuming a more usual expression of perplexity. "Something about a drawing? I couldn't quite follow everything Emily said this morning. I think she was crying."

Beth vowed to call her once Tony was gone. Always emotional, Emily would be hysterical once she understood that she was partly responsible. Or did she already know, thus the hysteria?

Tony sat on the sofa a few feet from Beth. "Mr. Marshall, I'd hoped to spare you from seeing the drawing, but I think I need to show it to you."

"What is it?"

"A rather skillfully done, colored-pencil sketch of your wife naked."

Her father didn't so much as blink for a long time. Too long, or maybe it just felt that way. Then he swallowed. "I...wouldn't have thought she'd do something like that."

"I'm sorry."

He only nodded, but in that minute, he aged another decade. Every line in his face seemed pronounced, his shoulders more rounded, his skin tone grayer.

"Dad?"

He didn't look at her, only reached for the phone Tony handed over. He stared at a photo of the drawing, then moaned. Tony took the phone from her father's suddenly slack hand.

His eyes unfocused, Dad seemed to be seeing another time and place. Tony didn't push him. After a minute, her father said, "As I told Bethie, I suspected Christine was seeing someone. She'd become…less and less content with her life, or maybe just with me. I didn't know how to reach her. How to change. I…hoped she would decide to keep our family together."

Tony leaned forward. "I showed this to you only because you might recall an acquaintance of yours talking about his art. Or your wife mentioning how talented a friend was. It's possible you even saw other drawings done by the same man."

But Dad was shaking his head. "The only artist we knew was…" He looked frustrated at his inability to summon a name immediately. "He taught for a year or two at the community college. I liked his work, but Christine was less enthusiastic. I'm sure we had a couple of original watercolors of his around." Dad, being Dad, turned his head as if he expected them to magically appear.

"Oh! I found three matted watercolors," Beth said. "One was of the columnar basalt."

"Yes, that was his. I suppose we never hung them. I left that kind of thing to Chris."

"You never heard that any of your friends drew as a hobby."

"I'm afraid not." Forehead wrinkled, he said, "I sometimes didn't pay attention to chatter. Chris could have said something, and, well…"

He'd tuned her out.

Beth saw that Tony understood, too. He nodded and rose to his feet. "Then I regret asking you to look at the drawing."

Her father stood, too, visibly trying to square his shoulders. "My marriage ended a very long time ago. It seems it was over even longer ago than I knew." He turned his sad gaze on Beth. "Is Emily right that you think you saw something else this monster drew?"

"I don't know, Dad, but…there's something at the back of my mind."

He looked at Tony again. "I wish I could help, but I never knew who the man was."

Tony inclined his head. "I need to get going. Beth, don't go outside, even to get the mail. You understand?"

She made a face at him. "Of course I do. I plan

to spend most of the day right here on the couch. But…will you call? So I know when you're coming back?"

"I'll call." He took a half step toward her, as if he wanted to kiss her, then abruptly turned away, thanked her father and left.

FEELING MORE TURMOIL than he liked, Tony drove straight to the tax firm. Yesterday, he'd been assured that Keith Reistad, one of two founders of the firm, would be there today. The other founder had retired at some point, although additional partners had since been added.

In the parking lot, he turned off the engine but sat there for a few minutes. Even his stomach churned with tension.

He'd never had a woman he cared about in danger. The pressure to find the killer before he could get to Beth again was a crushing weight. Then there was Tony's personal crap. His mother's refusal to soften her demands on him. The hurt in Beth's eyes this morning when he made it plain he wouldn't be introducing her to his family in the near future. Dealing with his family was stress enough without introducing anyone new. But her expression had served as warning: Beth wasn't a woman who could enjoy a casual dating and sexual relationship with no expectations for a future.

Yeah, this was too soon. But would he ever be ready?

It took him a few minutes, but he finally jammed all the tension down deep, freeing him to focus on interviewing a man who would have known Christine Marshall well.

The first time Tony had come by here, his primary intent had been to gather information on her clients. Since then, he'd done some research on Reistad.

He'd barely been older than Christine when she went to work for him. Like Dr. Schuh and the arrogant attorney, Michael Longley, Reistad had been lean and handsome. Also married, and still was to the same woman. Which didn't mean he hadn't had affairs.

Reistad came out to shake hands and lead Tony to his office. Tony hadn't found a recent photo but saw that the man hadn't changed much. Maybe five foot ten, he had wavy brown hair that, despite what was probably a salon cut, still managed to appear disheveled. He'd stayed fit, like Tony's other leading suspects, and had a broad, friendly smile. He wasn't handsome in the same way the other two men were, with his nose crooked, his whole face slightly out of alignment, but Tony could imagine a woman finding him more appealing.

"What can I do for you?" the CPA asked, after

they were seated in an office that was a whole lot more utilitarian than the partners' offices at the law firm. Walls were bare, the furniture comfortable but understated. While attorneys had to impress potential clients, it was possible any display of wealth would repel clients here, who didn't want to believe their accountant was soaking them.

Tony launched into his usual explanation: as part of investigating Christine Marshall's death, he was trying to speak to her friends and co-workers, and was hoping Reistad would let him see her client list.

He saw the refusal gathering in eyes as blue as Christine's had been. Reistad kept smiling even as he said, "I think you'll need a warrant for that. I can tell you that, in general, she dealt mainly with couples, some steady businesses, nothing too complex."

Keith Reistad could play Puck in a production of *A Midsummer Night's Dream*. Yeah, that hint of mischief in his smile might well have appealed to a woman married to a man Tony suspected was incapable of humor.

"I know that she developed a friendship with at least one of her clients," he said.

"The pediatrician?" Reistad shrugged. "She took her kids to him, too, so that was natural enough."

"What about other clients? Do you become friends with people you meet when you do their tax returns?"

"Rarely." Body relaxed, Reistad didn't look bothered by the question. "You know, nobody likes tax time. We're probably a little like dentists. No pleasant associations."

"Unless you save someone a lot of money."

He laughed. "That does happen. As for Christine…" He gave his head a slow shake. "I don't remember anything like that, but I'm not sure I would, or that she'd have told me."

"Did she have particular friends among her co-workers? I've been able to track down only one close woman friend."

"I want to say she and Andrea… Van something—" he clicked his fingers until his expression cleared "—Vanbeek, that was it. I know they went to lunch together, that kind of thing. I can't tell you where to find her, though. She quit and moved away after a divorce. Six or seven years ago?"

"Perhaps your records include a forwarding address."

"I'll ask," he said pleasantly. "Now, if there isn't anything else?"

"I'd like your impressions of Christine. You worked with her for some years."

A flicker of some emotion passed over Reistad's face too fast for Tony to identify it. "She was upbeat and immensely likable. Pretty, as I'm sure you're aware. People tended to think she was considerably younger than her age. Chris was popular here, both with staff and clients. I'll admit to being shocked when she disappeared. I know the assumption was that she'd run off with a man, but I was stunned that she hadn't given notice. We had to really scramble to cover her work."

"I'm told she was part-time."

"Some of the year. Not when she walked out." He shook his head, as if annoyed with himself. "Except she didn't. Finding out she was murdered... well, that's another shock."

"Very much so for her family."

"Yes, it would be, wouldn't it? I'm told she was...*in* the wall? How is that possible?"

Were details like that common knowledge now? Tony supposed it would be irresistible. "It's an older house," he explained, "built differently than newer ones. And she was a very small woman."

"I see."

If he was disturbed, Tony couldn't tell.

Reistad walked him out, stopping to ask a woman in one of the offices to look up Andrea Vanbeek's forwarding address. She jotted it down and handed the slip of paper to Tony.

He left, mulling over his impressions of the guy. Unless Keith, too, had called Emily to mine for information, was there any way he could know that Beth might be able to identify her mother's killer, if a single memory clicked into place?

As Christine's boss, he'd probably met her kids in passing but wasn't likely to have had much of a relationship with them. Wouldn't even Emily have wondered if he'd called her now out of the blue?

Yeah, but this wasn't that big a town. He could have run into Oberholtzer, the banker, or Longley, the attorney. It would be natural for them to share what they knew, especially if he pumped the well a little, so to speak.

A few phone calls, Tony thought, and he could find out.

EMILY SOBBED INCONSOLABLY. Beth couldn't understand a word her sister was saying.

She broke in, "Honey, you thought you were talking to friends. I know you didn't want anything bad to happen."

The wails rose in intensity.

"Please," she begged. "Quit crying. This can't be good for you."

Her father had slipped away when he realized who she was calling. That being typical of him, she hardly noticed. And, really, listening to this conversation wouldn't be any fun, even second-hand.

It took twenty minutes before her little sister's

sobs changed to hiccups and repeated, "I'm sorry! I'm so sorry!"

Emily announced her intention of coming to stay with Beth and take care of her, since this was all her fault.

Beth winced at the idea. "That's nice of you," she said gently, "but I already have a friend staying nights. It's working out well. I'm actually at Dad's today."

When Beth asked, Emily woefully listed everyone she could remember telling about the drawing and the fact that her sister thought she might have seen another drawing by the same artist. Some of the names were harmless—Emily's friends, Debra Abernathy, and Jennifer Sager, half of a couple who'd been friends of their parents.

"I had to upgrade my phone, and she saw me talking to one of the reps. She still manages the Verizon store, you know."

"I haven't seen her in years," Beth admitted.

"Because your phone is practically an antique," her sister retorted, confirming that she'd bounced back from her emotional storm.

Beth made a face, since her sister wouldn't see her anyway. "It not only works just fine, it's only four years old, which hardly qualifies as antique." Living within her means wasn't one of Emily's strengths. It simply wouldn't occur to her that she shouldn't have the latest and greatest phone, which all of her friends were certain to buy, too.

A couple minutes later, Beth was able to claim Dad needed her, so she could get off the phone. The white lie came so easily, she realized she wasn't as honest a person as she liked to think she was. That was probably no surprise; managing her dysfunctional family meant doing a lot of soothing. Matt was the only one who could take a direct comment. He might blow up, but later he'd apologize and at least understand why she'd said what she had.

A wave of exhaustion swept over her, and not only because of the conversation with Emily. Physical pain, only blunted, contributed, as did the medication. All the revelations about her family that had come out in the past week suddenly seemed overwhelming. And Tony—Tony was going to hurt her, she feared. This was why a smart woman didn't let herself get involved with a man too quickly. Apparently she hadn't had enough experience to *be* smart, at least about men.

It had happened so ridiculously fast, but she'd never felt like this about a man before. But, while she believed he was powerfully attracted to her, this morning suggested that he'd had an end date in mind from the first time he kissed her. Maybe he would never really let himself fall in love. She could understand why, if he didn't want to have children, given how involved he'd had to be in raising his siblings. They still needed him. His pride in his youngest sister's ambition to be a doctor had been obvious. He already had nieces and nephews.

Chagrined at how depressed she felt for no good reason, she lay down on the sofa with her head on a throw pillow. She thought about pulling the throw over herself, but it was too hot in the house already, at not even 10:00 a.m.

As she closed her eyes, she resolved not to be a coward where Tony was concerned. Expecting him to introduce her to his family a week after they met was ridiculous. She didn't want to let her own sense of inadequacy, her fears, rule her. Picturing the tenderness she so often saw in his eyes, she knew she had to take the relationship as far as he was willing for it to go.

CHAPTER FOURTEEN

"KEITH REISTAD?" Michael Longley sounded surprised. "Of course I know him. A number of his clients have come to me when they needed legal counsel."

Counsel. That sounded like a euphemism to Tony, but call him a cynic. Cops in general hated all defense attorneys. Tony knew some he liked just fine, Phil Ochoa being one. Longley was too slick for him.

But, on the positive side, he'd taken Tony's call, despite the way their last conversation had ended.

Leaning back in his desk chair at the station, Tony kept an eye on an altercation across the room, though two detectives appeared to have the furious man under control. To Longley, he said, "I hope you don't mind my asking, but have you seen him or spoken to him recently?"

A short, suspicious silence. "Just yesterday he called with some questions about one of those mutual clients. Why?"

"Did you discuss Christine Marshall or the investigation?"

"Of course we did," Longley said impatiently. "Who isn't talking about it?"

"Specifically, did you pass on what you'd learned from speaking to Mrs. Marshall's daughter, Emily?"

"If I did, is that a crime?"

"No, Mr. Longley, it is not. All I'm doing is attempting to trace the flow of information."

"Then, yes, I believe I did. We're friends who both cared about Christine. Discussing what we knew was natural."

"I understand. Thank you for taking my call."

Replacing the receiver, Tony did some more brooding.

He'd already brought his lieutenant up to date on the investigation, much as he hated admitting to not being sure where to go next with it.

"I'm not a fan of hypnosis," the lieutenant had said, "but that might be one route."

Tony had argued—and still felt—that it would be better if Beth came up with the memory naturally. Prosecutors were reluctant to file charges even partially based on memories recovered under hypnosis, since defense attorneys tended to rip them apart.

"Anything solid tying the artist to the killing will be hard to come by as it is," he'd said. "Just because this guy had an affair with the murdered woman doesn't mean he murdered her. Our best bet will be matching his fingerprints on the replacement sheet of wallboard. I might have been getting to the point of thinking I was wasting my time, if he hadn't tried to kill Beth."

"You're sure—"

"It makes sense," he had retorted. "Why else would an inoffensive woman be a target? This guy wasn't trying to incapacitate her so he could rape her. It's pretty clear his goal was to kill her. For now, that has to be my assumption."

Lieutenant Davidson agreed, leaving Tony no further ahead than he'd been.

He'd been resisting the temptation all day to check on Beth, but with it now being midafternoon, he called her.

"Tony?" Answering, she sounded groggy.

Frowning, he said, "You okay?"

"You caught me dozing."

"A nap is a good idea. You need the extra rest right now."

Her laugh sounded husky. She couldn't possibly have intended to arouse him, but, damn it, she had.

"This was nap number two. I slept away a good part of the morning, had lunch and settled down to read. I think I fell asleep mid-page. How's your day going?"

"Frustrating. I did interview Keith Reistad,

your mom's former boss. He won't hand over her client list without a warrant."

"Can he give it to you, legally?"

"It's not like we're asking for the client's confidential financial information," he grumbled.

"I suspect it wouldn't look good for him if word got out that he'd given you that information."

Tony grimaced because she was right. He did understand Reistad's decision, which didn't mean he had to like it.

"You didn't know him well, did you?" He hadn't asked her as much about Keith Reistad as he should have.

"Hardly at all," Beth said promptly. "Mom would make a quick stop at the office with at least one of us tagging along when we were younger, but she'd make us sit in the waiting room while she went in back. When we were older, we'd sit in the car. That way we could tell stupid jokes or fight or whatever. I might recognize him if we came face-to-face in the grocery store, but mostly his name is familiar because Mom talked about him."

"You get a sense of whether she liked working for him, or if they had conflict, or…?"

"She really liked him, I think. I used to—" Beth stopped.

The unexpected silence made him wish he

could see her face. Tony waited but, when she didn't continue, he had to say, "You used to what?"

"Sort of cringe when she started to talk about this amazing coup her boss had pulled off, or how brilliant he was," she said very softly. "Mom would do it at the dinner table. Dad would just keep eating, but…it must have stung."

Tony had the passing thought that he might have discounted her father as a suspect too quickly. He had a similar build to the other men Tony was seriously considering, if considerably less athletic.

His gut still said no. Everything else aside, it was a stretch to imagine him swinging a baseball bat at his daughter's head. Tony would swear John genuinely loved his oldest daughter.

Beth said, "You're thinking that…*he* could have been the one?"

"I have to consider him." Tony shifted gears. "Did she talk about other male friends that way in front of your dad?"

She didn't answer right away. He liked watching her face when she was thinking, but he had no trouble picturing the little crinkles that would have formed on her high, usually smooth forehead, or the way she'd nibble on her lower lip.

"Maybe not as much," she said finally, "but I remember her talking about how Mr. Longley had bought *his* wife a BMW, and how Teresa was probably the only person working at the middle school with a car that nice."

Ouch.

Had the emphasis on *his* been conscious, or was she mimicking her mother as she took a jab at her husband for failing as a provider?

"Mom loved the Schuhs' home. The Sagers', too. She'd wish we could afford to remodel or even move."

Tony realized how much he was coming to dislike Beth's mother. Had she really been that insensitive to her husband's feelings, or did she just not care? For that matter, she must have been blind to how she was treating Beth, versus petite, blonde Emily.

"And she saw Keith more often," Beth added. "So it's not surprising she'd talk about him more."

"What about other co-workers?"

Silence. Then, "Not as often. Except…she had one friend. I can't remember her name."

"Andrea?"

"Yes! That's it. Have you gotten in touch with her?"

"I haven't been able to locate her so far. She moved away after a divorce." Divorce was becoming a theme when Tony looked at the Marshalls' old friends. Everyone except the banker and his wife—and Keith Reistad and his. "Reistad gave me the forwarding info they had," he continued, "but she moved again. She doesn't have a driver's license in Washington, so I'm guessing she's gone out of state."

"Could she really tell you anything useful?"

"Working with the two of them, she might have had a good idea whether they were involved," he said, hearing the grimness in his voice. Wasn't it lucky for Reistad that the co-worker most likely to have noticed something going on between him and his pretty, blonde employee hadn't stayed in town?

They talked for a few more minutes. He told Beth that, right now, he didn't see any reason he couldn't get away to pick her up by five-thirty.

"Take your nap," he said.

Call over, he wondered if any of the ex-wives would open up to him about their marital problems if he contacted them. Had infidelity been the issue? But he'd become more interested in Reistad paradoxically because he *was* still married to the same woman. Why would a man who ended up divorced in the next couple of years anyway kill Christine because she had threatened his marriage?

Of course, the motive might have been something else altogether, but—what?

Baffled and disliking the feeling, Tony set to tracking the ex-wives of Michael Longley and Alan Schuh.

FRIDAY BROUGHT NO progress on the investigation. Or should she say *either* investigation? Beth wondered. None of the neighbors who'd rushed to her rescue had happened to be coming or going at a time they might have seen the assailant. No witnesses to a man dressed in black running away had come forward. Tony believed he'd been parked on the cross street. Once he jumped in his car and yanked off the mask—if he'd been wearing one—he could drive away without drawing any attention.

This morning, Tony had dropped her at her father's house again. When he picked her up, he said, "I talked to Longley's ex-wife today. She remembered all of you and said to say hi."

"At first after Mom disappeared, Mrs. Longley did call and even stopped by the house a couple times, but... I don't know, Emily and I were still kids, and she was still the school counselor."

Tony smiled. "I think she understood."

"Did she tell you why she got the divorce?"

"At first she said her husband was a workaholic, which led them to sharing the house but not much else. When I pressed her on the subject of infidelity, she did finally admit she'd suspected him of an affair. In fact, he remarried in a matter of weeks after the divorce."

"So he could have had other affairs."

"Yes. On the other hand, he's still married to that same woman."

She thought about it. "He could have had an affair with Mom but not been willing to marry her."

"Yeah." He sighed. "Doesn't sound like he and Teresa had much of a marriage, though. Would he go so far as to kill a woman because she threatened to tell his wife?"

She studied his profile, noticing his hands flexing on the steering wheel. "You sound...disappointed."

He glanced at her, his smile wry. "I don't like him."

Beth had to laugh.

She didn't feel like laughing, or even smiling, when Saturday morning, after helping her get dressed, Tony asked if she could spend today, too, with her father or brother.

"I need to finish mowing my lawn, and do two of my sisters'. Maybe some things for them, too," he explained.

Heaven forbid he should have to introduce her to anyone in his family—*or* let her see his house.

Of course, trailing around after him all day, making conversation with strangers while he worked outside, didn't actually sound that appealing.

Beth smiled as if she wasn't bothered at all. "Sure, no problem. Let me give Matt a call first."

She was feeling better enough that she and her

sister-in-law went shopping. Ashley steered Beth
into buying a couple of front-closing bras and a
few shirts that would be relatively easy for her
to put on without help. She bought a new pair of
flip-flops, too, and some clips she could use one-
handed to get her hair out of her face.

She needed to become independent again and
found she liked Ashley even better for helping
her find ways.

Of course, while they were at the mall, they
checked out cribs and baby bedding and clothes.

"Once I know whether we're having a boy or a
girl, I think I will go through the clothes Matt says
your mother packed away," Ashley said. "Unless
that would bother you?"

"Heavens, no!" Feeling a pang, Beth set down
a soft sleeper with a puffy lamb on the chest. She
didn't necessarily want to have a baby right now,
but she did want children. "You'll find more that's
useful if you're having a boy, though. Between
us, Emily and I put a lot of wear and tear on the
girl's stuff."

"True," Ashley said cheerfully, "but Matt and
I are talking about me taking at least a year off
work, so we'll have to be careful with our money."

She had an ultrasound scheduled in two weeks.
"Matt wasn't sure whether he wanted to know the
gender," she told Beth, "but I overcame all resis-
tance. I don't plan to do all blue or pink, anyway,

but knowing will help when we paint the spare bedroom and buy stuff."

"For everyone who comes to your baby showers, too," Beth said. "I've been meaning to tell you, I intend to put one on."

Ashley hugged her. "Thank you. I think one of the teachers will, too."

When they got back, Matt eyed them. "You look like you had too much fun."

"Baby clothes are so cute!" his wife said, rising on tiptoe to kiss him on the cheek. "And Beth says she's going to have a baby shower for us."

Matt hugged Beth and whispered, "Thank you."

One-armed, she hugged him back.

They had such a good day, she was almost sorry when Tony arrived to pick her up.

He had obviously showered at home, since his hair was damp and his clothes both clean and unfamiliar to her. He and Matt nodded at each other cautiously. Beth introduced him to Ashley, who looked intrigued and mouthed *Call* when he wasn't looking.

Tony raised his eyebrows at the shopping bags full of her new purchases but carried them out to his truck without comment. He suggested stopping to pick up a pizza and, once they agreed on what they wanted, she phoned in the order.

At home, while they sat at the table making inroads into the pizza, she chattered about the shopping expedition and Ashley's intention to go through the baby clothes in her father's garage.

"It would make Mom happy to know she hadn't saved them for all these years in vain," she said lightly.

He smiled. "At least styles won't have changed much. How much can you do to one of those fuzzy things with feet or miniature overalls?"

The next time a silence fell, she said, "I'm so glad Ashley suggested the front-closing bras. I should have thought of it. It'll make getting dressed so much easier."

"I'm happy to help," he said mildly. "In fact, I might miss groping your breasts every morning."

Beth laughed. "Is that what you were doing?"

His own smile spread. "I was more subtle than that."

Given that she hadn't even needed a nap today, she said, "You know, I'm feeling a whole lot better."

His gaze lowered to her mouth, her breasts, before traveling slowly back up. Voice a little rough, he said, "Are you, now?"

"Although… I'm not the sexiest thing going with this in the way." She lifted her injured arm slightly. Supported by a sling, the cast extended from her upper arm down to her hand, the intent to prevent her from doing more than wiggle her fingers.

This smile was wickedly sexy. "Oh, I think we can work our way around it."

"Really?"

"If you mean it."

She bobbed her head.

"Then I think I've had enough to eat," he said. "What about you?"

The glint in his eyes had warmth flooding outward from her core. "I might even want to go to bed early."

"I could go for that," he agreed huskily, standing up.

Tony did put the uneaten pizza in the oven before he gathered her into his arms. The relief she felt, resting against him, was almost as powerful as her response to the soft kisses he pressed to her temple, her forehead, her cheekbone—and, at last, her mouth.

SUNDAY MORNING, Tony woke with a pounding headache. Groaning, he knew he'd gotten too much sun yesterday; he'd spent hours out in the blazing heat mowing, rebuilding—with her husband's inept help—a section of fence in Maria's backyard that her large dog had knocked over, and looking under the hood of Beatrix's 1998 Acura, trying to figure out why it was making a "knocking" sound. Why him? he'd asked. Half the men in the family did automotive engine or body repair and surely knew more than he did about cars.

She had sniffed disdainfully, her hands pressed to her distended belly. "Eddie drove it and says he doesn't hear anything. Which only means he's deaf."

Did she know how much like Mamá she sounded?

She offered him a melting smile. "You're so good at fixing things."

She wasn't smiling when he left an hour later after telling her he didn't hear any knocking either and couldn't find anything obvious wrong beneath the hood.

Last night, pizza and Beth had improved his mood immeasurably. Because of the clunky cast, he'd had her lie on her good side and had entered her from behind, his body spooning hers. They'd started slow, urgency building. The detonation at the end had knocked them both out. He couldn't remember the last time he'd gone to bed that early or slept the night through without waking once.

He rolled over in bed to find himself alone. Damn. How had she gotten up without him hearing? Grogginess settled into the drumbeat of the headache. Tony groaned again and got up, listening for Beth. The sound of the refrigerator door closing was reassurance enough for him to decide to take a shower. But first, he'd search her medicine cabinet for any kind of over-the-counter painkiller.

When he finally appeared in the kitchen, her sunny smile warmed him, despite the headache.

"He's alive!"

"You didn't provide slave labor yesterday." He kissed her.

"But I shopped. You don't know what an ordeal that can be."

Tony swatted her butt. Laughing, she dodged.

Two cups of coffee and a homemade waffle later, he felt a lot better. Until his phone rang.

The caller was his mother—and this was Sunday. Crap.

"I'd better take this," he said and went into the living room, half sitting on the arm of the sofa. Answering the phone, he said, "Mamá."

"Good morning to you!" she said. "Carlos and Eloisa picked me up for church. Miracle of miracles, Jaime is still clean."

So Carlos had made it home last night. Relaxing, Tony said, "Once they start finger painting, he won't stay that way." Older teenage girls, supervised by one adult, ran the childcare that freed their parents to worship in peace. The little ones always had fun.

"No, but at least everyone will see that his mamá made sure he looked nice for church." She barely paused. "Are you on your way?"

"No, Mamá. I won't be there today."

"Tony! This is the third Sunday in a row. What will Father Raimundo say?"

"He'll say Tony is a busy man, and that God understands."

"He might start thinking you're wandering from the faith," she countered. Two hours once a week isn't so much to give."

"And I usually do attend," he said, maintaining a calm voice. "You know that. This has been a difficult week."

"I suppose you won't be coming to dinner either?"

If she'd asked that first, he might have surrendered. Beth could have gone to her dad's again or her brother's. But now he had his back up.

Thinking about Beth, he glanced toward the kitchen. The rustle of a newspaper page being turned allowed him to hope she wasn't listening. He should have gone outside for this conversation.

"I'm afraid not."

Over-the-top mournful, she said, "You're slipping away from us."

"I spent all day yesterday helping my sisters," he reminded her, having no doubt that she already knew exactly how he'd spent his day.

"Beatrix says you didn't fix her car."

He pinched the bridge of his nose hard. His facade of calm began to creak, too. "There's nothing wrong with her car that I could find. She says Eddie told her the same thing."

"Oh, Eddie." Usually she approved of this son-in-law, but not today. "Beatrix was counting on you."

"I'm not a car mechanic." He knew he sounded as tense as he felt, and his voice had started to rise.

"And now you're not a churchgoer either."

"I'm done," he snapped and cut her off. Or had he yelled?

Tony stayed where he was for what had to be five minutes before cooling off enough to go back to the kitchen.

Loading the dishwasher, Beth glanced up. "Are you okay?"

"Sure."

"It sounded like you were having a fight."

"My mother managed to push all my buttons." And he didn't want to talk about this.

"Are you going to church?"

"No." He sighed. "Can we let this go?"

"But…doesn't your family usually do a Sunday dinner?"

"They do." He was afraid he was coming across as curt, but he couldn't help himself. "I won't be there."

At last, she accepted her cue, nodded timidly and wiped down the counter.

Now he felt like a jackass. "Is there anything

you'd like to do today? I'd suggest we go for a swim at the lake, except…" He nodded at her cast.

"That would have felt amazing." Beth came to sit at the table. "What would you like to do?"

"You know, the lake could still be fun. What if we take a picnic? You could wade in quite a ways, at least cool off."

"While you plunge in and swim out to the dock."

Disappointed, he said, "Yeah, that might not be the best idea."

She laughed at him. "I was kidding, Tony. It does sound like fun. I'm not a very good swimmer, anyway. The park will probably be crowded, but who cares? I haven't been in ages."

Tony couldn't remember the last time he'd neither worked nor joined his family on a Sunday. His stress level dropped, while his mood soared.

He suggested they stop at a deli on the way for sandwiches, but Beth insisted she could put together a lunch. He didn't argue too hard but did insist on helping. Since they had plenty of time, she hard-boiled eggs for egg salad sandwiches and produced some homemade cookies from the freezer.

"I usually freeze most of them," she explained. "I delude myself that if I have to thaw them before I can take a bite," she explained, "it'll give my willpower time to grow, and I won't stuff my face."

Tony shook his head. "You're not fat. Your body is perfect."

"I could easily be—"

He silenced her mid-sentence with a single look. In fact, she laughed again. "Why am I arguing? What more can I ask out of life than a man who thinks my body is perfect?"

He snugged an arm around her waist, enjoying her softness and the scent of her shampoo. "I can hardly wait to see you in a bathing suit. Do you have a bikini?"

"Not a chance."

Giving her a little shake, Tony shook his head sternly. "There you go again."

"Well, I don't own one, so you'll have to settle. Although getting a bikini top on over the cast would have been easier."

Their picnic came near to being drastically delayed when he let himself be tempted into squeezing her breasts, even kissing them, before groaning and helping maneuver the cast through the arm of the relatively modest suit.

Stepping back, he decided he approved of it anyway. It fit snugly over her curved body and was cut high enough on the hip to make any man's eyes linger. Just enough cleavage was exposed to tantalize. He might need to be careful not to leave her alone for long at the beach, he decided. Other men might decide she needed help.

She went looking for the suntan lotion while he carried their lunches and towels out to his pickup. He'd have to stop at his place to grab his suit, but it wouldn't take a minute. When he came back inside, he was dismayed to see Beth on her phone, the tube of lotion on the kitchen counter right beside her.

She rolled her eyes toward him and made a face. "Emily," she whispered, then, into the phone, said, "I *am* listening. But I don't understand what brought this on."

Oh, for God's sake. Tony wanted to ask why she'd answered or tell her to hang up. Irritation rose, even as he knew it wasn't justified. Except when caught up in something on the job, he rarely ignored a call from his mother or any of his sisters.

"Emily, don't say that!" she exclaimed. "I got hurt because someone attacked me. It's on *him*, not you."

The conversation went on, Tony able to hear most of what Beth's little sister wailed. Increasingly annoyed, he thought she was playing Beth. Apparently, she was used to being the center of attention and didn't like having the spotlight shift.

"Emily, really—" Beth started to look alarmed. "Okay, okay. If you need me—"

What the hell?

More wailing.

"In just a few minutes. Yes, I promise. I love you, you know." Finally she ended the call. Her unhappiness visible, she said, "I'm so sorry, but Emily is falling apart again, and I need to go over there. If you want to go ahead to the lake, I can—"

"What? Spend two hours patting her back?"

Hers stiffened. "You think I should have told her to suck it up? I might stop by tomorrow, when I don't have anything better to do?"

"I hurt my mother's feelings so I could spend the day with you. Apparently, spending the day with me isn't as important for you."

"She threatened suicide."

"Did you believe for a minute that she was serious?" he asked, incredulous.

Beth hesitated but said, "That's not the point. She needs me."

He shook his head in frustration. "I can't do this."

For a moment, she went so still, he couldn't tell if she was breathing. Then she whispered "This?"

"Us."

CHAPTER FIFTEEN

I CAN'T DO THIS. Tony's words rang in Beth's ears. He couldn't do this.

Us.

Why was she even surprised? There'd been plenty of hints.

"Well, this is the shortest relationship I've ever had," she heard herself say.

He paced a restless circle in the small kitchen before facing her again. "It's not you. It's both of us. We're too much alike, trapped by our families. I love mine, I can't back away, but they drive me crazy enough that I can't take on any more. Every time your sister or father claim to need you, you'll be running to their sides, won't you?"

Beth stiffened. "Claim? I suppose your family really needs you, while mine is just manipulating me?"

"I didn't say that."

"You implied it."

"Damn it, that's not what I mean!"

"So, if I'd told Emily she was on her own and gone to the lake with you, we'd have been fine? You expect to be the center of your girlfriends' lives? No other priorities accepted?" She tried to cross her arms and could only clutch the bulky cast with her good hand. "Well, good luck with that."

"You have to see—"

"I don't have to see anything. You've made your decision. Fine. I'd appreciate it if you'd clear out what you have here and leave."

He looked strangely shocked, considering he'd started this. "You shouldn't be alone."

Hurt and angry, she said, "That's not your business. I have people who care about me."

"I'm one of them," he said quietly.

Beth braced herself. "You need to go."

They remained locked in a stare for what had to be a minute, his eyes dark and turbulent. Then he shook his head and went into her bedroom, where the clothes she'd washed for him sat atop her dresser. His badge and gun were there, too. He hadn't immediately donned them this morning, the way he had other days.

Because it was Sunday. The day of rest.

On the verge of tears, she held herself together. She didn't say anything when he emerged with a duffel bag slung over his shoulder.

"I'll get your towels and the lunch," he said gruffly.

She held herself as tightly as she could. "Don't bother."

After a moment, he gave one more nod and

started for the back door. He opened it but didn't turn around. "Be careful, Beth."

She didn't think she was capable of further speech without bursting into tears, so she kept her mouth shut.

He closed the door behind him. A minute later, Beth heard the roar of his truck engine.

Only then did she let herself dissolve.

TONY DROVE A BLOCK and a half, then pulled over. With a white-knuckled grip on the steering wheel, he sat staring straight ahead through the windshield without seeing a damn thing. A part of him knew how stupid that was: cops couldn't afford to be oblivious to their surroundings.

He'd done what he had to, he told himself. He and Beth, they were a nightmare waiting to happen. Already stretched beyond his limits, he'd have acquired another brother, another sister, a father-in-law. Before he knew it, Beth would have been rushing to his sisters' sides, too, every time one called. That's how she was made. Their own plans, their own lives would always come in second.

This was why he should never marry. Getting involved with Beth, he'd violated his own rules. He'd been perilously close to falling in love with her. The terror he'd felt when he got the call saying she was hospitalized after the assault…he never wanted to feel anything like that again.

An unwelcome voice in his head murmured, *You're not going to feel the same when this guy goes after her again?*

He rapped his forehead on the steering wheel a few times, which only served to re-ignite his headache. He'd left her alone. If he waited another few minutes, kept his eye on his side mirror, he'd be able to see her car turning out of the alley. After all, Emily needed her.

It was too late to go to church—not that he thought the service would help him untangle this ugly knot of conflicted feelings. He could still go to the family dinner. He'd make his mother happy.

Sure. He'd also add to her certainty that she could guilt him into obedience.

No.

Okay, what about driving out to the lake on his own? Too bad the idea now held zero appeal. He felt alone enough without pretending to have fun in the midst of hundreds of other people.

Swearing, he stayed where he was until he saw Beth's car turn onto the street, just as he'd expected. Then he pulled a U-turn to follow her, hanging well back.

Her sister's apartment building was crap, but Beth would be less than thrilled if he appeared to escort her in. So all he did was pull up close to the entrance, roll his window down and listen.

Nobody screamed.

Now what? Did he sit here for hours, while she consoled the spoiled brat? Shit, he'd roast in the truck. And tomorrow...tomorrow he had to work. He couldn't stake out her townhouse or follow wherever she went.

Jaw painfully tight, he drove away. Beth was smart. She wouldn't do anything like stand outside in the dark again. He hoped like hell she wouldn't go out after dark at all. Although he wished she had an alarm system, the dead bolt locks on both exterior doors were good ones. The biggest windows faced a busy street. Only a fool would break in that way. The utility room window was too small for a man to squeeze through. Her kitchen window, looking out at the parking area in back, was the one that made him nervous. Breaking glass might alert a neighbor, though, depending on how well-insulated the units were.

He drove into his own garage and walked into the house. The air was hot and still. Looking around, he felt eerily as if he hadn't been here in weeks, when in fact he'd mowed the lawn and showered here yesterday. Tony used the air-conditioning units as seldom as possible, but he turned both on now, dumped his duffel on his bed and stuck the lunch in the refrigerator. He didn't know if he could bring himself to eat the sandwiches Beth had made such a short time ago, the cookies she was afraid to eat because her mother had convinced her she was fat.

Tony prowled the house, finally persuading himself to grab a beer and turn on the TV to watch a Mariners game. He'd had a six-pack in the fridge for weeks. Given that he wasn't much of a drinker, he could get pretty drunk if he guzzled them all. For once, the idea held a lot of appeal, but he knew he wouldn't. What if Beth needed him?

Resting his head on the back of the couch, he gave a mirthless laugh at the irony. He'd just ditched the woman because he didn't want one more person to need him but, if she called, he'd tear out of here like a crazy man.

But it wouldn't be a problem, would it? Beth wouldn't call him if a killer wielding a butcher knife was chasing her through her house. 9-1-1, maybe. Him, she'd probably already deleted from her phone.

SHE'D SPENT SO MANY years hiding whatever she felt so that she could be the happy center of her family, Beth felt sure Emily hadn't noticed anything was wrong. Red, puffy eyes? Allergies. Couldn't be tears. Beth didn't cry. No, Emily saw her as dull, her life so lacking in excitement or drama, why would *she* be upset?

Usually, Beth even convinced herself. She

couldn't remember ever feeling as if she was having an out-of-body experience. Big sister Beth, serene as always, sat on the sofa holding Emily, who still sniffed piteously into a soggy paper towel. Another Beth altogether stood watching, but it was as if she was looking through glass.

Tony was right: this Beth knew. Emily's tears were real enough because she was good at stirring herself into an emotional state, but she was far too self-centered to try to kill herself. However unconsciously, she was making a point: *she'd* been hurt by any suggestion she'd done something wrong. And her feelings were so much more sensitive, she was so emotionally fragile, Beth needed to say she was sorry. She had to reinforce Emily's belief she was always the victim.

I don't want to do it anymore.

The Beth on the sofa was saying the right things. This Beth, weary, knew she had to make changes, or she'd be condemned to play this same role for the rest of her life. Tony could go to hell, but he was right about this.

It would be easy to believe that, if she was trapped by her family, she'd done it to herself, but Beth knew better than that. Her mother had made very bad decisions that left Beth the only one who could keep the family going. No, Mom hadn't run off, the way they'd always thought, but she still bore a lot of the blame. Dad, too. Maybe he couldn't help being so dysfunctional, but he'd lit a coal of rage inside her when he'd admitted he always knew the load he'd dumped on her and, yeah, he was a little sorry now that he hadn't carried his share of it.

What was she supposed to say? Thanks, Dad, that means the world to me?

She had a right to be angry, too.

As if acknowledging that made her whole, suddenly she was back in her body, patting Emily's back.

She sat up, smoothed messy hair from her sister's face and said, "Go wash your face. You'll feel better. Do you have iced tea? If not, I'll make some."

Emily hid her surprise with a sullen look. "I want a beer."

Beth shrugged. "Suit yourself."

She went to the kitchen once Emily dragged herself to the bathroom. Beth found a jar of powdered instant tea, not her favorite, but it would do. She mixed up a tall glass for herself, added ice cubes and sugar and went back to the couch.

Small and defiant, her sister stopped on the threshold of the living room. "Where's mine?"

This placid smile was a lot easier to summon. "You said you didn't want any."

"You could at least have gotten me a beer," she grumbled and went to get her own drink.

322 BACK AGAINST THE WALL

At least? Because Beth never did anything for her.

Yep. Mad.

Emily flopped onto the other end of the sofa and popped the top of her can. "So everything is supposed to be all better?"

"No, it isn't." Beth set her drink on the glass-topped coffee table. "Emily, you need to get some counseling." Seeing outrage on her sister's face, she held up her hand. "No, listen to me. I love you. When you really need me, I'll always be here for you. But you need to deal with this over-the-top stuff. You did tell a lot of people something you should have kept to yourself. Common sense should have told you that. And, yes, word spread, and that's probably why I was attacked."

Tears glistened anew in Emily's big blue eyes.

"Don't you dare cry again." Beth didn't even recognize this hard voice as hers. "I'm not seriously injured. You've apologized. I wish I thought you'd learned a lesson, but once again you've made this all about you."

A sob broke forth, and Emily clapped a hand over her mouth.

"If you start that again, I'm leaving." Maybe she hadn't merged into one Beth, after all. Maybe the serene Beth who was unfailingly comforting was gone for good. "I had plans today that... meant something to me." She couldn't think about that without hurting more than she could afford right now. "No, it doesn't matter what they were. If you'd been injured, or had a real dilemma, I wouldn't have minded canceling. But I had to come running over to convince you again that *you* didn't do anything wrong. It was mean of me to ever suggest you did. That's what you think, isn't it?"

The stricken, blotchy face looked tragic and very young. Beth stomped hard on the pang she felt. Her sister was twenty-five now, an adult.

"Since we found Mom's body, I've been discovering how her disappearance impacted us all. I know how close you and Mom were, how devastated you were to think she'd left you. I was fifteen years old. A kid, too, and I was driven to take over for Mom. I never thought, *Dad can't cope, we'll end up in foster homes if I don't do anything*, but my instinct was powerful. Matt—he was already angry, and he got angrier. I think that now, thanks to Ashley, he's starting to deal with some of his feelings. I haven't, and you haven't. I've been enabling you because somewhere inside I'm still that fifteen-year-old girl, who did her best but didn't really know how to be a parent. I thought making everyone happy was the way to go. I was wrong."

Emily's shock continued. She didn't say a word.

Beth wanted, so much, to scoot over and pull her sister into her arms, but found the strength to hold on to her determination. "Now I'm going to be the parent I should have been a long time ago. I'm not sure you ever grew emotionally from the twelve-year-old girl you were. That's not your fault. It's not even mine because I did do my best. If it helps, you can blame Dad, or Mom."

Fury flashed over Emily's face. "Someone *murdered* Mom. How can anything be her fault?"

Beth repeated what she'd recently understood to be the truth. "She was a married woman sneaking around to have an affair with a man who was probably also married." Some of her anger leaked through, but how could it not? "She posed naked for him to draw that awful picture. She lied to Dad and to all of us. She didn't deserve to be murdered, but she broke our family and left us damaged."

"That's...that's a horrible thing to say."

"Do you think she was entitled to have an affair? Lie?"

"If she wasn't happy—"

"She should have talked to Dad. Insisted on counseling. If nothing else, she should have left him before she started sleeping with another man."

Okay, she'd apparently stunned her sister into silence. How often did that happen?

"I've been enabling Dad, too. I won't stop altogether. For the most part, I think he did his best. He supported us, he chauffeured us when we needed it, he put us through college." Oops—

shouldn't have said that. The fact that Emily had dropped out after two quarters was a sore point. Too bad. "I'll keep doing some of what I have been for him, but not all of it. I think he's more capable than I've always believed."

"And me? You're pushing me out of the nest? Bye-bye, sis?"

"Of course not." Now Beth let herself speak gently. "What I'm going to do is get recommendations for the best counselor in town, and I'll help you pay for visits."

Emily flounced to her feet. "What if I don't want to go?"

"That's your choice. But I won't be rushing over here every time you work yourself into a fit either. I especially won't be if you refuse to help yourself."

Emily cried.

It took every bit of willpower Beth had, but she kept her distance. She repeated, "I love you," and "I'll always be here when you really need me."

And then she left, heartsick, exhausted, wishing for numbness.

Not until she was halfway home did she realize she hadn't paid any attention to her surroundings when she walked out of the apartment complex. She hadn't even locked the car doors after getting in. And if someone was following her, it was too late for her to pick out any particular vehicle.

She heard Tony's voice, rough with—not regret, more likely relief—saying, *Be careful, Beth*. She hadn't been careful at all. What did she think? He'd always rush to her rescue?

He had said he still cared about her. Beth winced away from the memory. Maybe he did—but not enough.

THE NEXT FEW days sucked. Tony made no progress on any front. The only word he heard about Beth was from her brother when, on Tuesday, Matt called.

"Tell me you've done some actual detecting and are closing in on the scum that tried to kill my sister."

"I'm investigating." Tony really hated to admit the rest, but wouldn't lie. "I don't have much to work with."

"You're an asshole. You know that?"

Dead air. Matt was gone.

Yeah. Tony did know that.

He'd caught another case that he had to work, however frustrated he was not to be able to focus on Beth's assault a hundred percent. This was a domestic, no mystery, but he still had to be able to lay out for a jury who did what and, so far as he could determine, why. The *why* would determine what charges the prosecutor's office brought.

The ex-Mrs. Schuh did return his call at last.

She'd moved to San Juan Island, about as far as she could get from her ex while staying in the state, and had opened an art gallery.

"I have plenty of competition," she told him cheerfully, "but a lot of artists live on the islands, and tourists arrive ready to buy."

After expressing her shock once she heard about Christine's body being found in the garage wall, she said. "I could never understand—" She broke off.

"What couldn't you understand, Ms. Inman?" She'd gone back to her maiden name.

"How she could leave her children. Or maybe I should say, I didn't believe she would. She cared more about appearances than I ever did—thus my divorce." The last bit was said drily. "But she loved her children. I'd have sworn she did."

She listened in silence as Tony explained that they had reason to believe Christine's killer might have been a man with whom she was having an affair. "I'm sure you'll understand that we have to look at any men who were friends at the time."

"You wonder if Alan might have been sleeping with her."

"He's only one of many possibilities."

"I want to tell you he wouldn't have slept with a married woman—one *I* considered a friend— but I can't. Killing a woman, though? No. Killing anyone, really. He's a doctor who truly does care about his patients, I think. Sleeping with her, that's different. Pretending to be concerned about my health, he gave me frequent lectures because I'd 'let myself go.'" The quotation marks could be heard. "I put on weight. I didn't torture myself at a health club to uphold his standards. I had a wheel and kiln in the garage—and wasn't that a battle—and was even selling some of my work. I couldn't have cared less that I was getting a few gray hairs. He did."

"Did you suspect he might be seeing another woman?"

"Yes," she said flatly. "Eventually—a couple years after Christine's disappearance—I hired a private investigator. He supplied me with photos that helped me get a generous settlement in the divorce. Enough to allow me to open my gallery."

How could a man quit loving a woman because she got a little plump, went gray, developed wrinkles on her face? That was life. A betrayal like that was unimaginable to Tony. If Beth—

He gave his head a hard shake.

"Ms. Inman, did you ever have reason to suspect he and Christine might have been involved?"

"No, but, in retrospect, I have to say I wouldn't be totally surprised."

"One other question. Did your husband have any artistic ability?"

"Artistic?" She laughed, a rich sound. "Not that

I ever saw. He let me choose the art for our home, as long as he deemed it attractive. Nothing experimental. He had to be able to tell what he was looking at. Otherwise, he had zilch interest in gallery showings, art fairs or my pottery." Sadness infused her voice now. "Not the kind of thing you think will come to matter."

"Most people marry someone they don't know anywhere near as well as they thought they did," he agreed.

"With luck, they'll both work at bridging their differences," she said. "If not…well. I'm happy with my life now."

"I'm glad. And thank you for your time."

Tony put down the phone, braced his elbows on his desk and dug his fingers into his hair. It was hard to imagine how Dr. Alan Schuh could have been a skilled artist without his wife—an artist herself—knowing. Did that mean he could now eliminate Schuh as a suspect?

Maybe. Probably.

Which left him with any number of faceless, nameless men the victim would have met at work, at PTA meetings, in the stands at her son's baseball games. Hell, at the grocery store, or in the waiting room at the dentist's or the pediatrician's.

And then there was Keith Reistad, who didn't have an ex-wife willing to talk about his flaws.

Without more reason to suspect the guy, Tony couldn't approach his wife.

Back to the people at the accounting firm, he decided. If he was artistic, wouldn't you think he'd have showed off one of his drawings at some point? Even displayed his work?

Tony had an uneasy recollection of the empty walls in Reistad's office. What if he'd taken down some of his own work after hearing through the grapevine about the discovery of the body? Or even just because Christine's body had been found? He'd have known investigators would dig through her stuff. Whoever had drawn that portrait must have worried for years that someone in the family would come across it. It had been long enough he might have relaxed. But no longer.

Tony sometimes paired with a fellow detective in his unit, but most often they handled investigations on their own. As Frenchman Lake had expanded, the department funding hadn't kept pace. He could talk this over with one of the others, most of whom he liked and respected. But laying out what he did know would take too long, when they were all overworked. And the truth was...he wanted to talk to Beth. He shouldn't have shared as much as he had with her, but he'd trusted her, found she had a way of arrowing straight to the point.

He missed her.

No—ridiculous. Although he would miss the best sex of his life. Her family, not at all.

He did still care enough to feel a driving obsession to find her mother's killer. He'd have hated to have to put the murder investigation on the back burner. Pursuing it after Beth was attacked was a given, though. Which made the assault the act of a fool—unless the killer knew for a fact that Beth had seen something he'd drawn.

Was she even trying to remember? Frustrated, he began a search for Andrea Vanbeek in neighboring states. Nothing new about this—he spent most of his days on the computer or the phone. In fact, he jotted a reminder to himself to call the medical examiner's office to find out what the holdup was.

BETH SMILED AT the middle-aged woman who sat across the desk from her. Kim Brubaker had dyed blond hair that needed a touch-up, huge bags under her eyes and twitchy hands.

"I hate the idea of putting Mom into a nursing home," she exclaimed, for at least the third time. "But I just don't know what to do."

Beth gently extracted more information. Kim had two teenagers at home, one heavily involved in sports, the other in community theater as well as the high school plays. The oldest had a driver's license but was too busy to chauffeur his sister.

Kim's husband was a long-haul truck driver, a willing helper when he was home, but gone for days at a time. They'd taken her mother in to live with them a year ago, after she was diagnosed with Alzheimer's. She had inevitably deteriorated, and Kim was afraid to leave her alone.

"I've always been involved in my kids' lives," she said. "Having responsibility for Mom limits the time I can give them."

Her mother did have nursing home insurance. Beth suggested checking to find out whether it would also cover in-home care.

Finally, she said, "First, let me say that the likelihood is high that you'll eventually find caring for her beyond your ability. When that time comes, I encourage you to look at memory-care facilities instead of nursing homes. There are two here in town." They went on to discuss the possibility of taking advantage of an adult daycare that wasn't a mile from her home. "That can be full or half day, or even for a couple hours. You'd have some time each day to do errands or just relax. But they close at five, I believe, so I don't know if that would still free you to drive your kids to after-school activities."

The hope on the other woman's face warmed Beth. She loved her job, despite the sadness inherent in helping people make these decisions. Dementia was the worst, she thought.

She also gave Kim numbers for the two agencies that sent workers into people's homes to care for elderly or disabled patients. "Setting up a regular schedule works best but, by planning ahead, you might be able to arrange for someone to come on an evening when you want to go see your daughter in her play. If you choose to keep your mom at home long term, you can have help twenty-four hours a day, if that's needed. Of course, your decision almost has to be weighted by whether her insurance coverage supports that, or only a nursing facility."

It was after five when she ushered Kim out, sending her off supplied with a pile of reading material and inviting her to call with any questions.

Beth flipped the sign on the front door to *Closed*. Ramona, the receptionist, was already turning off her computer, her purse on the counter.

"Thank goodness you're back," she said. "We've been scrambling to get by without you. Barbara decided we should ban vacations, except then she felt awful when she heard the real reason you'd taken time off."

Barbara had already told Beth the same. Virtually every tidbit of information about the Marshall family and the investigation had made its way to the offices of the Council for the Aging.

People had been clucking over her all day. She'd rolled her eyes and joked about being clumsy for the benefit of clients who exclaimed over the cast.

Worn out and hurting, she couldn't decide if returning to work so soon had been a good idea or an awful one. It kept her busy, kept her from thinking about her own problems, but she was more wiped out physically than she'd expected.

And, of course, she now had to go home to an empty house. She was being stubborn, not wanting to be a guest at Matt and Ashley's place for who knew how long.

Beth walked out to her car with Ramona, the others having already left. Really, she could have gone out safely on her own, since the nearly empty parking lot didn't offer many places to hide, especially in daylight.

She'd intended to stop at the grocery store on her way home but decided she was too tired. Surely she could find something to eat. Or she could pick up a pizza—but that only reminded her of the last few times she'd had pizza, when she wasn't alone.

Home. Scrape up some dinner, find something mindless to watch on TV, take a pain pill to knock herself out in hopes of sleeping better than she had last night. Oh, and pile dishes in front of windows and doors, so she'd at least hear a warning crash if an intruder broke in.

This could go on for weeks, months. She couldn't hide out 24/7. Being careful, however, *that* she could do.

CHAPTER SIXTEEN

TONY DIDN'T WANT to call what he felt loneliness, but it was close enough. Wednesday evening he found himself reaching for his phone. When had he last talked to Ross, the cop who'd saved him when he'd been a rebellious teenager? Still in uniform then, Officer Ross Taylor had even come to Tony's graduation from the police academy.

Time had gotten away from Tony, but that was no excuse. He'd suggest they plan to get together.

Ross picked up right away. "Well, if it isn't Detective Navarro himself."

Sprawling on his couch, Tony grinned. "Hey, just checking up on you. Heard rumors you're in a wheelchair, decrepit old man that you are."

Ross snorted. "*I* played a full-court game of hoops at the Boys and Girls Club today. Did you ever heave yourself out of your desk chair?"

Barely.

"Actually, I was thinking we should get together, shoot some baskets. Have dinner."

"Sure. Any time. Not like my social calendar

is booked. Old man that I am." His tone changed. "Given your age, yours should be."

"Off and on." Tony grimaced. "It's off right now."

"Tony, Tony," Ross scolded amiably. "Why aren't you married and thinking about starting a family?"

"Family is a sore subject with me right now," he admitted. "You know how overwhelmed with family I am. Count your blessings."

Pause, followed by a quiet, "No, son, I won't be doing that."

Tony closed his eyes. Damn, that had been tactless. "I'm sorry." He drew a deep breath. "Have you ever thought of remarrying?"

"Never met the right woman. I have a lady friend now, I guess you could call her, but it's not the same. We don't spend the night together. You know how that is."

He did. In fact, Tony made a point of not staying after sex. A few times, he'd made the mistake of bringing a woman home. It would have been crass to suggest she head out in the middle of the night. He slept restlessly, and each time had changed the sheets once she was gone in the morning.

He'd tried living with a girlfriend when he worked in Portland, but that hadn't lasted more than a few months. He didn't talk about his job, she cut hair for a living, and that didn't leave them with a lot to talk about or really anything in common except sex.

This thing with Beth had been different.

"Rumor has it the dead-woman-in-the-wall investigation is yours," Ross said.

"It is." They talked about it for a few minutes, but with Ross retired now, Tony didn't feel as if he could name names, and there was a lot he didn't want to say about Beth and her family, so the conversation wasn't productive. They made plans to get together, and Tony hung up feeling strangely hollow.

Frowning, he went to the kitchen to pour himself a second cup of coffee while he tried to decide what this odd mood meant.

Beth. Of course, it was all about Beth.

He was beginning to think he'd screwed up, bigtime. No, he *knew* he'd screwed up. He shouldn't be able to miss someone he'd known such a short time, but he'd figured out that they had spent more time together in those eight days than dating couples did in months. For him, she'd clicked immediately. Everything about her.

Because they were too much alike, he reminded himself. Somehow, though, the ache beneath his breastbone didn't show any signs of going away. Imagine Beth *not* committed to her family. Could he really care about a woman who went home for holidays only because she felt she had to and wouldn't inconvenience herself if someone in her family needed help? As irritated as he'd been at his mother lately, Tony still saw his family as bedrock. What could matter more?

Shame, he discovered, twined tendrils around the ache in his chest. If the call Sunday morning had come for him instead, if Beatrix, say, had been sobbing, he'd have made the same choice Beth had. Of course he would have. And she'd have understood. Kissed him and said, "We can go next weekend."

Tony wished he *didn't* understand why he'd been such a prick, but no such luck. Panic was easy to diagnose. Panic because his mother had been pushing him hard, until it seemed as if he had no free time. And panic because what he felt for Beth was new and in opposition to his life plan. He hadn't believed in love at first sight, but something close to that had hit him, and he'd run scared from that moment on, even as he pursued her in defiance of both departmental policy and common sense.

His mother had been perplexed by his talk of never marrying. She'd thrown up her hands and exclaimed, "*Está loco!*"

Yeah, Mamá, he thought, *you're right; that was crazy talk.*

Tony poured the coffee down the sink, rinsed

the mug and put it in the dishwasher. Another cup now would just keep him awake. More awake. He hadn't been sleeping well.

He wandered to the living room, picked up the remote then tossed it aside without even looking to see what was on. Was this really what he wanted? A house to himself? No one waiting at home for him? A lifetime of nothing but "lady friends," a necessity so he could scratch an itch? Remembering lovemaking with Beth, even just sleeping with her warm, soft body draped over his, he shook his head.

The conversation with Ross, that single, pain-filled pause, gave Tony an insight.

Had he envied his mentor because he seemed so free?

Yeah, probably, considering that when they'd met, he'd been at his wildest and most resentful. Tony rubbed his jaw, thinking about it. He hadn't been a teenager for a long time. Why hadn't it ever occurred to him that when Ross bailed kids out of trouble, encouraged them, befriended them, he'd been filling an emptiness in his own life?

There were people who liked living alone, having few obligations to other people. That wasn't Ross—and it wasn't Tony, either.

As long ago as Ross had lost his wife, he still missed her. He'd never said as much, but Tony knew he would till the day he died.

Tony gave a humorless laugh. Yes, he was an idiot. He'd run like a jackrabbit when he should have been holding on tight. He could be with Beth right now instead of being home alone, restless—and worried because she was also home alone.

The family stuff—it was something they'd have to work on. Tony couldn't believe he'd simmered so long instead of sitting down with his mother and saying, "I love you all, but I need to set some boundaries." Why had he had to mow Eloisa's half-brown lawn, when Carlos was due home in only a day or two? Most of his sisters had husbands. Except in rare circumstances, they shouldn't need him as anything but a brother. Tony suspected that, half the time, Mamá had used him to make those men feel inadequate, and he'd let her. For that matter, having him showing up the second any of his sisters expressed the slightest need kept them from finding solutions themselves. Tony doubted that had been his mother's intention, but he couldn't be positive. She was a controlling woman. With so many children, she'd probably had to become one, but somehow she hadn't gotten the memo about backing off when your children became adults. Nudging Mamá that way wouldn't be a bad thing, not for any of them. Eloisa, for sure, would appreciate it.

The fact that he'd let his resentment build instead of talking to her suggested he hadn't been thinking like an adult himself. He wasn't proud to know he'd reverted to a defiant sixteen-year-old without realizing that's what he was doing. There was nothing like coming home.

He finally checked the locks, turned out the lights and went to his bedroom. Stripping, he took his second shower for the day, keeping the water tepid. He stayed under the stream for a long time, thinking about Beth. Knowing he had to talk to her, apologize, beg if he had to, but feeling uncertain about the outcome. He remembered her accepting his invitation to dinner even after he'd chickened out once. He could hear what she said, word for word, see the seriousness in her hazel eyes.

But, Tony? If this is some kind of trick, or you back off again, that's it.

He brushed his teeth and padded to bed, where sleep was slow to come.

THURSDAY, WHEN EMILY hadn't called, Beth tried her. Of course, she didn't answer. No point in leaving another message.

Between appointments, Beth kept trying. She even phoned the chiropractor's office, where Emily worked.

"I'm sorry," she was told. "Ms. Marshall books appointments three days a week—Mondays, Wednesdays and Fridays."

"Oh, right. I'm sorry. I'd forgotten which days she worked."

Emily also filled in at several other places, which Beth called, but nobody was sure where she was today.

What if her threat to kill herself had been real? Oh, dear God, what if she *had*?

Hyperventilating, Beth didn't know what to do. Driving around town hunting for her sister wouldn't help. Matt, she decided.

"What?" he said, after she reached him. "No, don't be ridiculous. I talked to her last night. She's still mad, but swinging around to thinking it wouldn't hurt to talk to someone like you suggested, especially if you'd pay for it."

"I offered to *help* pay for it."

"Come on, you know Emily."

Her whole body sagged as the fear vanished with a *poof*, leaving her muscles weak. "I hope you re-inforced my message."

"Sure, I did. Meant to call and tell you that you surprised me. It's way past time, Bethie."

She'd have been annoyed, except...he sounded gentle, the way Tony did sometimes. "We're changing. All of us."

"That's good."

"Have you talked to Dad? This has been really hard for him, you know."

"You sound like Ashley," her brother muttered.

"Listen to her."

He grunted. "I'll think about it. And you need to think about moving in with us until the cops catch Mighty Casey."

"*Who?*"

"Uh…you know. Mudville? Casey stepping up to bat?"

Her mouth fell open. "You're making a joke about a man who tried to *kill* me?"

"Well. It's just…you remember how the poem ends, don't you? '…mighty Casey has struck out'? Since he missed…uh…"

Beth astonished herself by bursting out laughing. She laughed so hard she dropped the phone, so hard she had tears in her eyes. She heard Matt's alarmed voice coming from a distance, but giggles kept erupting.

After a quick rap on her door, it swung open, Barbara popping her graying head in. "Are you all right?"

Still laughing, Beth waved her away. Picking up the phone at last, she said, "Thanks. I needed that."

"Uh, you're welcome?"

After letting him go, she dug in her drawer for a tissue to wipe her eyes. Mighty Casey. It *was* funny, in a macabre kind of way. So why did she still feel so sad?

As if she didn't know. She'd get over it—get over him. Time, she told herself desperately.

By five, she was wiped out. A broken arm shouldn't have her feeling like this, but it didn't take a genius to understand that, really, it was the combination of stress, lingering pain, depression and anxiety.

Once again, she made sure to leave at the same time as Ramona, who stopped dead the second she stepped out the back door.

"Will you look at that?" she said, then made a humming sound of approval.

"What?" Her key in the lock, Beth looked over her shoulder at the man leaning against her car, his legs crossed at the ankles. Tall, dark, handsome, the personification of confidence—and a plain-clothes cop. Her heartbeat revved, wiping out the tiredness, but not the sadness that felt like grief.

"It's okay," she told Ramona. "I know him."

Ramona grinned at her. "I wish I did." Her head kept turning, but she headed straight to her car.

Seeing Beth, Tony straightened, his hands dropping to his side, but he waited where he was. She walked toward him, wishing he was here to tell her he'd made an arrest, that she was safe, but suspecting otherwise.

He didn't smile and, closeup, tension showed on his face. "Beth."

"Hello, Tony." She had her keys in her hand,

but he stood between her and the driver's door. "More questions."

"Not about the investigation." Lines creased his forehead. "I've mostly eliminated Michael Longley and Alan Schuh, although I can't be a hundred percent sure. Don't trust either of them."

"Okay." Beth wasn't exactly brimming with trust for anyone these days.

"Reistad is my best bet at the moment. But…" He hesitated.

Finishing his thought for him was no problem. "It could be someone neither of us have ever met, whose name we've never heard."

"Unfortunately, that's true." His gaze sharpened. "It hasn't come to you?"

"No. I just…keep coming up with a giant blank. I think I'm trying too hard."

He grimaced agreement, then hunched his shoulders. "Beth, I came to say I'm sorry."

The words were naked, as was his expression.

Even she heard how stony she came across as when she asked, "About what?"

"You know what. Losing my temper after Emily called. Implying there was anything wrong with you needing to go to her."

"Implying?"

He flushed. "Saying. You had to go. I…panicked."

The exhaustion hit her again. Pride was all that

kept her from crumpling. She had to get rid of him. "You're forgiven. I understand your reaction. I even…took some of your advice."

"My advice?"

"I talked to Emily. I'm pushing her to get into counseling. I can see that I've spoiled her past the point of being healthy for either of us. So you did that much good."

"I'm glad." Now he took half a step forward, his dark eyes searching hers. "Beth, I miss you. I probably don't deserve it, but will you give me another chance?"

She locked her knees and gripped the hard shell of her cast with her right hand. "No. You've had me on a roller coaster, and I hate roller coasters. If I agreed, I'd find myself tiptoeing around you. Sneaking away when I wanted to call Emily, or lying about where I'd been when I went to Dad's house to change his bed and make sure his kitchen is stocked. I'd be waiting for your next bout of second thoughts. You said, 'I can't do this,' and I think it was a good call. Now I'm saying the same."

"You don't understand." He leaned toward her in his intensity. "I meant it when I said you're right. I'd have made the same decision." He spoke faster and faster. "I swear I won't expect you to abandon your family, any more than I'd ditch mine. We can work it out. Support each other."

"But, you see, I don't believe you. It was… unreasonable of me to be so hurt, since we'd barely started anything personal, but I guess that's how I'm made. Which should tell you how wrong I am for you. You're a man who doesn't want more family, while me, I do want that—a husband and children. See the disaster in the making?"

"I've been falling for you. Hard."

"I'm sorry." She kept her head up, and her eyes stayed dry. "Tony, I'm really beat. If you don't mind…" She gestured toward the car.

He moved aside. Even as she unlocked the door, he said, "How can I convince you?"

"I don't know." Sitting behind the wheel was an enormous relief. She reached immediately for the door. "Goodbye."

Beth didn't want to look at him but, even from the corner of her eye, she saw how stunned he looked. That hurt, knowing she'd done it to him, but her instinct was to run. And, of all people, he should understand. Wasn't that exactly what he'd done?

He hadn't moved when she drove away.

THAT WENT WELL.

Even after Beth turned out of the parking lot and disappeared from sight, Tony stood where he was.

In one way, he'd known how she'd react, but he still hadn't really expected her to say *No way, I'm done with you*. During the night, he'd convinced himself she'd been falling for him, too. Feeling desolate now, he realized she had. That was why he could hurt her as much as he had. Good going. No wonder she wasn't up for more.

Shit. Now what?

Trying to find a grain of optimism she hadn't stamped underfoot, he latched on to her answer when he asked how he could convince her to give him a chance. She could have said a flat *You can't*. She didn't. There might be a small opening. *I don't know* wasn't as final as *You can't*.

No matter what, his first priority was doing his job, arresting her mother's murderer and allowing Beth to feel safe stepping outside her door. The strain on her face had almost killed him. He wanted to kick his own ass for making what was an already horrendous week worse. It had taken remarkable strength for her to decide to return to work, to spend her days helping other people solve their problems. He imagined her warmth, how she'd comfort complete strangers, supply common sense and resources, without ever letting them see the shadows over her own life.

Hearing himself making an odd sound, Tony let his head fall forward. His shoulders and neck ached, as if he'd spent the day hauling hay bales, as he'd done one long-ago summer.

Finally, he took the few steps to his truck and got in. Tomorrow, he'd do his job. Tonight, he needed to talk to his mother like the man he was, not the boy he'd been. And then he just might spend the night in his truck outside Beth's townhouse. He wasn't sleeping anyway, and his gut said her assailant had to be freaking as the days passed.

His mother was so delighted to see him, Tony felt a stab of guilt.

"And for you to bring dinner, too!" she exclaimed, speaking Spanish which, even after spending all of her life in this country, was still most comfortable for her.

Embarrassed, he said, "It's not as if I labored in the kitchen for hours. All I did was stop at Tia's."

"*Ropa vieja*? I smell it."

"With rice."

They sat to eat at the table in the kitchen of his childhood home. A typical ranch style built in the late 1970s, it wasn't so different from his own. Despite having lived here, he marveled at how his parents had raised such a large family in a three-bedroom house.

When he looked around, he could see the wear and tear. Flooring had all been replaced, courtesy of one of her sons-in-law, but otherwise not much had been done. Mamá resisted change and didn't like accepting what she considered charity. His role was to mow her lawn or paint the exterior of the house, but she couldn't accept new kitchen cabinets.

Tony was conscious of the wear and tear he saw when he looked at his mother, too. She had always had such a straight back, and now her spine was developing a curve. Gray streaked her thick hair, and the wrinkles on her face seemed deeper than he remembered from even a few weeks ago. His gaze fell to her hands, increasingly knobby with arthritis. She was a short, stocky woman whose skin was darker than his. Tony's height had come from his father.

Mamá chattered about the girls and complained about how seldom she heard from Isabella. "It was foolish to let her go so far from home. She could be in all kinds of trouble, and we'd never know."

He smiled. "Having sex, you mean?"

Mamá scowled at him. "Don't even say that."

"I didn't like the idea either but, before she went, I had a talk with her about men and birth control. I know you don't approve, but she's smart. She won't get pregnant and have to drop out of college."

"But becoming a doctor will take so many

years," his mother worried. "She'll never come home."

"Summers." Maybe. The college had hooked his baby sister up with a job at a medical clinic in Monroe, a town not that far from Seattle and near the size of Frenchman Lake, if you didn't count the enormous state correctional facility there. Even Tony tried not to imagine an inmate escaping, taking Isabella hostage... No, he had enough to worry about here at home. And, for all Mamá's complaints, his sister did send emails at least weekly and posted even more often on Facebook.

When they finished eating, his mother didn't leap up to clear the table the way she normally would. Instead, she looked at him with eyes even darker than his own and said, "I think you have something to say."

"I do," he agreed. He'd spent the past hour mentally rehearsing what to say, not wanting to hurt her feelings.

Her mouth thinned, but she listened. Finally, she said, "This is about a woman."

"No, Mamá." Why bother saying *Yes, I met a special woman, but I hurt her, and now she doesn't want anything to do with me*? His resentment predated Beth, anyway. "I love you all, but I need you to respect the long hours I work. How will I ever meet a woman if I'm always mowing my sister's lawn or standing in her garage with my head under the hood of her car? I was with someone when you insisted I check on Eloisa. I understand why you were worried, but did you call anyone else in the family first? She might have talked to one of them five minutes before. Carlos wasn't home, but Eddie and Diego probably were. Why is it always me?"

"Because you're the big brother," she said, as if it were obvious. "They trust you. Not everyone does what they promise. You do."

"Thank you for saying that."

"So you don't want to help your sisters anymore."

He shook his head, smiling. "That's not what I said, Mamá, and you know it. I will always help when they *need* me. When you need me. But not when they can fix their own problems. Do you understand?"

He could tell she'd rather not but did. Tony left a half hour later, after a big hug, knowing she might believe she was trying but would fall back into the same habits if he let her. But he'd told her what he felt, so she couldn't say she didn't understand when he said no to requests that he would no longer let himself feel were demands. Change went two ways, after all.

It wasn't yet dark when Tony drove to Beth's, turning into the alley and parking in a spot marked for visitors. He didn't take the one closest to her back door, in case she did come out. Here, she wouldn't notice him, but he had a good line of sight to her unit. He'd see when she turned out her lights, see anyone approaching. And with his window rolled down, he had a chance of hearing the sound of breaking glass, or a scream.

WITHIN TWENTY-FOUR HOURS, Beth had doubted her decision a few hundred times.

She'd vowed to take the risk of a relationship with him, then opted out after the first speed bump. A giant one, sure, but she could have foreseen it. He had issues, she'd known that. And... he'd been right about her having allowed—or encouraged? Awful thought!—her sister and father to be dependent on her.

Roller coaster. She'd twice ridden on one and hated every clanking second, from the climb with the people down below shrinking into miniatures to the plunge, when she was sure the thing would fly off the rails. The only good part was getting off. Remember?

Then she'd picture him standing alone in the parking lot, his very stillness making him look desolate. Her heart cramped.

She could love him. Until Tony, she'd never met a man she could.

Up, down, all around.

Beth made it through another day of work, this one especially challenging because Barbara had called in sick. Her heart had been fluttering, she said. Later she called to tell them that her doctor had asked a cardiologist to see her as soon as possible, which probably wouldn't be until next week. She was glad today was Friday, sure that by Monday she'd feel fine.

One more person to worry about.

But it *was* Friday, so Beth, too, had a couple days to recuperate.

She did stop for much-needed groceries. At home, as she unloaded them from the trunk, she spotted the young guy from two doors down who'd raced to her rescue. When she waved, he came over to ask how she was, giving her the chance to thank him again.

Inside, even before she put away the groceries, she walked through the house, as she'd done every day since Tony had left, peeking in closets and anyplace else a person could hide. Silly, but at least when she was done she could be absolutely positive she was alone.

She made a giant potato salad, enough to give her lunches and maybe dinners, too, for several days. Tonight, a heaping serving was all she wanted.

She wasn't even tempted to watch TV because then she might not hear the tinkle of breaking glass or a soft footstep. Instead, Beth tried to concentrate on the book she was reading, but without success. Finally, she let it fall to her lap.

Aloud, she said into the silence, "Keith Reistad." What did she remember about him?

She'd had to call him Mr. Reistad because it was polite, but Mom had always said Keith. And she did talk about him a lot. Too much, maybe. Yes, he was one of the partners, and she worked directly under him, but she must have spent most of her hours at the office with clients or on her computer. She should have gone days at a time without seeing him.

Had there been a spark of excitement in her mother's voice or expression when she talked about him?

Mostly what Beth saw was Dad's face, not so much vague as blank. He'd built a wall—

Her phone rang, making her jump. Emily, at last.

"Emily?"

"Hi." Her sister sounded almost shy. "Are you still mad at me?"

Beth sighed. "I wasn't mad, I was worried about you."

"I, um, made an appointment today. With the woman counselor. I can't talk to a *man*. So I hope you're happy."

Hearing the return of a whine, Beth shook her head but only said, "I am."

"I was wondering, well, if you'd come over. So we could talk. You know."

Don't wanna. But how could she not, when Emily had asked nicely? Except—"Detective Navarro asked me not to go anywhere after dark. Can you come here instead?"

"But what if that guy thinks I'm you? No, that doesn't make sense. I mean, even in the dark anyone could tell the difference between us, couldn't he?"

Because I'm a hippo compared to your dainty self. "Gee, thanks."

"I don't mean that in a *bad* way. You're too sensitive."

Maybe she was.

Hesitant, Emily asked, "Is it really okay if I come?"

"Yes, you can still come. If you're hungry, I made potato salad."

"I *love* your potato salad. See you as fast as I can get there."

It would be good to have company. Maybe she could even talk Emily into spending the night. The sofa pulled out into a bed.

Relaxing, she put on a pot of coffee and went back to thinking about Keith Reistad. He had a quirky, nice face, she remembered that. Mom was the one to insist her kids stay in the waiting room. It wasn't like he'd made a rule or anything. He'd sometimes been nice enough to sit down and talk for a minute. Of course, she'd been tongue-tied, but Emily would chatter away to him. Once he'd whipped a deck of cards out of his pocket and amazed them with some tricks. Mom had watched, too, smiling. Then there was the time Mom had gone to her office and he had come in the front door, looking surprised to see Beth. Emily hadn't been with her. Beth's momentary puzzlement cleared. Because elementary school didn't get out as early as middle school, of course.

Mr. Reistad had raised his eyebrows at the sight of her daypack at her feet. "Bored, are you?"

Beth remembered wrinkling her nose. "Not bored enough to do homework. Most of it's math, and I hate math."

It ran like a movie in her head.

His smile was so open, not like most adults'. "Well, I can entertain you for a minute."

"How?"

"Wait and see."

He'd reached behind the reception counter and come back with a clipboard and plain white printer paper. Oh, and a pencil. "You have an interesting face," he said. "I can always tell what your sister is thinking, but not you."

He sat, studied her with his head tilted and began to draw.

The movie cut off, with the suddenness of a skipping CD, and jumped jaggedly to another scene.

"Oh, my God," Beth whispered. While he drew, she'd gone back to being bored. That's why she'd dismissed the scene from her memory. She thought he was doing some silly cartoon-like thing, as if she was a dumb little kid. She hadn't paid any attention to what he was drawing, until...

She spun toward the counter, looking for her phone. Her hand shook as she picked it up. It took a minute to scroll to Tony's last call, a week ago. There. Hearing the first ring, the second, she whispered, "Please, please answer. Please."

"Beth?"

"I remembered. It was Reistad. He started to draw me because I was bored waiting for Mom, only she came back and was in a hurry, and he shrugged and said he'd do it another time. He balled the sheet of paper up and tossed it into the wastebasket. I went to get it, but Mom got mad and hustled me out."

"Did you get a look at it?"

The knock on her back door made her jerk. "Oh! Emily's here. Yes, at the end. I didn't pay attention until then, but...it was really good. And I'm sure it was the same—" She reached to unlock.

"Don't open the door until you're sure it's

Emily," he said urgently. "I'll be there in about two minutes. Be cautious."

"Yes, okay." Beth dropped her phone on the table and sidled to the side, where she could look out the window. Emily's puff of short blond hair couldn't be mistaken.

Another hard rap. "Beth?"

She hurried to open the door.

"What *took* you so long?" Emily stepped inside.

Focused on Emily, it took Beth a second too long to see the blur of movement behind her.

CHAPTER SEVENTEEN

THE BLACK-MASKED FIGURE from her nightmares was suddenly there, rushing toward the doorway behind Emily.

A cry caught in Beth's throat. Desperate to slam the door in his face, she lunged forward. Too late. His shoulder slammed into it, and he bowled into Emily. She went sprawling, and he leaped right over her, going for Beth.

It all happened so fast. She dodged to the side and swept the counter with a desperate gaze. No butcher block with knives. The sole thing within reach was a ceramic bowl filled with apples and bananas.

Behind him, Emily began to push herself up. *No, no! Stay down!* Beth didn't know if she got the words out. He was already spinning toward Emily. Now Beth heard herself screaming like a banshee as she clutched the bowl in her good hand and swung it at him, hard. Fruit flew, and the bowl bounced off his back as his booted foot lashed out and smashed into Emily's head. She dropped with a thud and lay still.

Rage seemed to sweep away Beth's terror. She wanted to kill this man.

With a ceramic bowl?

I'll be there in two minutes, Tony had promised. If she could hold out that long...

Watching the intruder, she backed away. Eyes glittered from the cut-outs in the mask. Until now, she hadn't seen what he held in his gloved hand, and she wished she still hadn't. Instead of a baseball bat, he'd brought a knife with a wicked blade and a black rubber hilt.

It was hard, so hard, to tear her eyes from that blade, but she had to be able to read his intentions.

Not looking away from her either, he used one foot to shove Emily's limp body to the side so he could shoulder the door shut. Beth retreated as fast as she could going backward, while he took the time to flick the dead bolt closed. Out of the kitchen. *Run*. If she could make it to the front door... But he'd catch her, she knew he would, and if she turned her back—She shuddered involuntarily. No.

Her mind scrabbled for anything she might reach that could be a weapon. Trying to find a knife of her own in the drawer would have been hopeless. She had a sudden, absurd image of them fencing. *En garde*. The bowl felt silly, useless, but without it she'd have nothing. If she could get that far, there was an African sculpture in the living room, tall and heavy. Ebony, she'd always thought, or ironwood. She could use it as a club.

But she wouldn't get to it in time. Unless she could shake him up.

"Why the mask, Keith?" Except for a rasp, she almost sounded conversational.

He froze in the middle of a prowling step forward. She shuffled back two.

"Sorry," she said, "but this scene is too late. I've already told the detective."

"He won't be able to prove a thing. I'll be long gone."

Two minutes. Had it already been two minutes, or only seconds? Beth had no idea.

"If your little sister hadn't blabbed, I'd have had no idea you remembered."

"If my sister hadn't blabbed—" she kept inching back, sliding her feet to stay balanced "—when the police came, you could have said, *Sure, Christine and I were lovers.* How could they have proved you'd killed her?"

He shrugged as he took a longer step than any of hers. "Who knows what they found with her."

"I do."

"Really?" There was a smile in his voice. "I was careful, you know. But forensics keeps improving. Better safe than sorry."

If Tony looked in the kitchen window, would

he be able to see Emily? Dear God, what if he'd taken the key to her place from his ring?

He could break the window.

"Why did you kill her? What could possibly—"

He sprang forward so fast, she stumbled but still swung her clumsy weapon. By some miracle it connected with his arm enough to deflect the knife but not to stop him. He kept coming, thrusting toward her torso. This time, she lifted her broken arm to use as a shield. The blade slid off the cast. Beth lurched back, realized she was in the living room.

Please come, Tony.

TONY WASN'T HAPPY that Emily would be there, but he needed to get Beth's story. He could use it to justify asking Mrs. Reistad for an interview. Was it enough for a warrant to look for Reistad's pencil drawings—and the bat that had come in contact with Beth's bare skin? Probably not, he thought ruefully, turning into the alley. But they were getting there. Beth had thought the bat was wood, so the chances were excellent that the state lab could lift enough skin cells to confirm it was the weapon used in the attack. Maybe fingerprints. The assailant had worn gloves, but people often forgot they'd had to touch a weapon when buying it or stowing it at home or in the trunk of the car.

Tony's usual visitor slot was occupied. He recognized the Volkswagen Golf from that first Sunday. Damn it. He had to back up to get to the one open parking place he saw. He was taking it even if it said residents only. No, he'd gotten lucky— it was the same one he'd used during last night's useless bodyguard stint.

More out of anticipation than urgency, he jogged to Beth's unit, where he rapped firmly on the door.

He didn't hear a thing. Nobody came to let him in, which was strange. Frowning, he raised his hand to knock again but checked himself. The prickles on the back of his neck were probably premature, but he didn't like what he was thinking.

Then, tipping his head, he identified something he'd been hearing. It sounded like a far-off train whistle...except it was coming from behind this door.

Now adrenaline shot through his body like a bolt of lightning.

"Shit!" He tried the knob and realized the dead bolt was thrown. He dug in his pocket for his keys.

THE KNOCK ON the door made Beth jerk, although she didn't know how she'd heard it through the roar in her head and the sound of her own screams.

Reistad froze. "Who is it?"

Backing away slowly, she let out another earsplitting scream, praying Tony would hear her even though she knew how well-insulated her townhouse was. She was almost to the bookcase where the African statue of a tall woman carrying a basket on her head was displayed. A real weapon. Except she couldn't swing it effectively like a bat, not with one hand.

There was no second knock. A new crest of fear struck at the possibility that Tony had been annoyed and gone away. If so…she was dead.

Looking wild, Reistad rushed her again.

This time, she slammed her cast downward on the hand holding the knife, although she felt a sting across her belly. Using ugly words, he threw himself forward again as she dodged to the side.

They both heard an exclamation from the kitchen, then a roar of rage.

Reistad turned from her and ran for the front door. Beth didn't hesitate. She grabbed the heavy statue and went after him.

TONY COULDN'T BELIEVE he'd almost fallen over Emily's body, after his nearly silent entrance. God, he hoped she wasn't dead.

Another enraged scream came from the front of the townhouse. Gun already in his hand, Tony ran forward, yelling, "Police!"

A black-clad figure and Beth seemed to be struggling by the front door. No—Beth was pounding him repeatedly with something. He was trying to get away, hunching against the blows.

As Tony snapped, "Freeze, you son of a bitch," Beth bashed the guy in the head. He staggered, momentarily stunned, and Tony closed in. Seeing the knife in the scumbag's hand, he wanted—like he'd never wanted before—to pull the trigger.

He shoved the barrel of his Glock to the creep's neck. "Hands against the wall! Do it! Now!"

As he used his body to flatten Reistad, something whistled through the air and smacked his shoulder.

"Beth! I have him. Stop."

From the corner of his eye, he saw her back away, trembling. Some long, dark object dangled from her good hand. Blood soaked the front of her T-shirt.

Swearing, he twisted Reistad's wrist until the knife fell, then slapped on plastic cuffs and shoved him to the floor. Knee in the middle of his back, Tony groped for his phone with his free hand. Reaching dispatch, he barked out orders. *Ambulance. Backup.*

Then he went to Beth. "Sweetheart. God. You're bleeding."

She let him pry the weapon from her hand—a statue of some kind, and damn, it weighed a lot more than it looked—and propel her to the sofa.

She sank down with a muffled sob, then tried to spring right up.

"Emily!"

"Sit. You're hurt."

The eyes that met his were scarcely human. She'd gone to a desperate place he recognized. Her whole body shook. Blood now smeared the cast sling and her other hand, after she touched it to her stomach.

Keeping an eye on the man who lay unmoving, Tony lifted her shirt. Blood didn't geyser out. With a sick feeling of relief, he tore his own shirt over his head and pressed it to the general area of her wound.

"You're safe now," he said. "You're safe."

She looked at him, but he didn't know what she saw.

He went to the kitchen, determined that Emily was breathing, and returned to reassure Beth. Then he crouched next to her assailant, yanked down the hood, pulled the mask over the man's head and stared at Keith Reistad.

"You are under arrest," he began.

BETH STARED UP at the strips of fluorescent lighting on the ceiling of the emergency room cubicle. The local the doctor had injected before using a combination of sutures and butterfly bandages on her laceration seemed to be wearing off because she felt the burn again. The doctor had told her she was lucky because the cut wasn't deep. Lucky? Right now her anxiety had ratcheted so high, she was *this close* to exploding out of the cubicle and running through the emergency department until she found Emily.

At the soft scuff of a footstep, she turned her head.

Tony came straight to her, his gaze raking over her. "You're okay?"

He'd had to let the EMTs take her away earlier. Instead, he'd accompanied Reistad to the hospital, to be examined for a possible concussion. Vengefully, Beth wished she'd caved his head in. Why did Tony have to stop her?

When Tony got close enough, Beth grabbed a fistful of his shirt. "Emily. Nobody will tell me anything!"

"She's awake." He gently closed his hand around hers. "I borrowed this shirt. Don't ruin it."

"Oh." Flushing, she let go, but his hand stayed wrapped warmly around hers. "Where is she?"

"Across the way." He nodded toward the nurse's station set up as the hub of the department. "I had a feeling you'd demand answers, so I went by there first. She asked about you, too."

"She was unconscious."

He nodded. "My guess is, they'll want to keep her overnight, but that's no reason to worry. I had the impression she was flirting with the nurse or orderly or whatever he was who brought her back from having an MRI."

Her fingers bit into his. "They could find something. Like…like a blood clot."

"They could, but they probably won't." He smiled at her with warmth and humor. "Were you like this when she was younger? Sure she had the plague if the school called to tell you she was sick?"

Beth stuck out her tongue before conceding, "Of course I was. Especially the first year because I didn't have a driver's license and couldn't rush to her school. And, yes, when she got older, I freaked whenever she was five minutes past her curfew, too."

He laughed, lightening an expression that had been grim. "Is that how you learned to be a wild woman?"

"I sort of was, wasn't I?" If anger hadn't been part of the mix, would she have been able to fight back as effectively? "I really wanted to kill him. I've never felt anything like that before."

She saw understanding in his brown eyes. "Thank God you did."

"It was partly seeing what he'd done to Emily."

"But if not for Emily, you wouldn't have opened your door."

Indignation had her trying to pull her hand free of his. "So now it's *her* fault?"

He laughed again, white teeth flashing. "No, Beth. Sharing everything she knew with the world was her fault, but nothing else is."

"Well." Her momentary pique couldn't last. "Did he talk to you?"

"No, he lawyered up right away." He frowned. "I hope we can get him for your mother's murder, but I can't promise. I know he admitted to you what he did, but a defense attorney will claim you're lying. It would be good to have physical evidence to support your word. There's a chance his fingerprints, now that we have them, will match one on the inside of that wallboard, for example."

"He told me he was careful."

"Tonight?" Tony said in surprise.

She nodded.

"It's next to impossible not to leave a little piece of yourself behind. At the very least, we have him cold for attempted murder." Satisfaction hardened his expression again. "We got a warrant for his house. Another detective is executing it right now. He called to tell me he found a baseball bat in the garage. No glove or ball. His wife didn't remember seeing it before."

"But I didn't bleed on it."

He explained why techs were likely to find flakes of skin, invisible to the naked eye, embedded in the wood. "Not that we need that," he added, "except to add a charge for the first assault. This time, I caught him in the act."

Beth shivered. "I was so afraid you wouldn't come in time. Or that you'd have gotten another call and decided talking to me could wait."

"Hey." He half sat on the edge of the bed, a foot braced on the floor. "You're thinking about my mother and sisters."

She didn't answer. Didn't have to.

"I swear to you that I will never break a promise to you without talking to you about it first." His eyes had darkened again, and his voice was deep, serious. "When I say I'll be there, you can count on me."

Beth searched his face. He had come to her rescue tonight. He'd rushed to the hospital the other time, scared for her. He'd moved in with her to keep her safe.

Well, and for sex.

Yes, but he would surely have gone home afterward had he not been afraid for her. Essentially moving in was…above and beyond.

She nodded at last. "Will you go check on Emily again? And…has anyone called Matt?"

"I did a few minutes ago." He stood, looked imperturbably at her for a long moment, then walked out.

The next footsteps she heard coming fast were

her brother's. His hair was wildly disheveled, and she saw that he hadn't stopped to put on socks with his athletic shoes. The sight of his bare ankles made her eyes sting.

"Damn, Bethie." He grabbed her hand, much as Tony had, and bent until his forehead rested on hers. "You keep scaring the shit out of me."

She struggled for a smile. "I keep scaring me."

"Navarro said the guy's behind bars."

"The last time I saw him, he was lying on his stomach with his hands cuffed behind his back. Did Tony tell you who it was?"

"Reistad." He shook his head in disbelief. "Unbelievable. He got away with it all these years. If he'd just sat tight…"

"I told him that tonight. I guess he's been watching stuff like *NCIS* on TV because he was afraid that new investigative techniques might find something."

"What, you stood around chatting?"

She made a face at him. "We exchanged a few words in between him trying to stab me."

"Jesus."

Beth hoisted her cast a few inches in the air. "This saved me. It made a good shield. Without it—" She shuddered.

"Tony said when he got there, you were beating the shit out of Reistad. With some kind of wood statue?"

Ashley had been with her when she found it at an antique store, of all places. Beth reminded him, and he said, "Oh, yeah. I remember that. Damn, Beth. That was smart."

"I wouldn't have had a chance to get to it if Tony hadn't charged in so that Reistad tried to escape out the front door. If Tony hadn't come—"

Matt's hand shook a little as he smoothed her hair back from her face. "But he did."

She bobbed her head and fought the urge to burst into tears.

"Bethie!" Another voice.

Her father rushed into her cubicle. "You're all right?"

Surprised, she looked at Matt, who shrugged. "I thought Dad needed to know."

"I can't believe this." Her father's eyes were damp. "That monster attacked you."

"Emily, too." She let go of her brother's hand and reached for Dad's instead. "She's conscious."

"Your detective called after Matt did and told me that. Both my daughters. And it's my fault." He blinked hard.

"What? Don't be ridiculous." The guilt virus was really going around.

Matt said, "Knock it off, Dad. Your marriage imploded. That doesn't make this nutjob your fault. Who could predict anything like this?"

Her chest felt odd, as if her heart was being

constricted. Beth smiled at Matt. He shifted uncomfortably and muttered, "It's true."

She was pretty sure the byplay went right by their father, as usual, but he fussed over her for a few minutes before Tony reappeared at the door. There was definitely not room for three large men in this cubicle.

Seeming to have developed an unexpectedly sensitive side, Matt said, "We should go see what's up with Em," then escorted Dad out. He and Tony did exchange a stare, although she couldn't see Matt's expression. To her amazement, Matt and Dad seemed to be talking as they walked away.

Tony came to her bedside. "What was that about?"

She shook her head and said, "You asked for another chance." Her heart was getting a workout tonight, her pulse racing again. Was she really thinking about taking another risk?

Yes.

"I wouldn't have called it *asking*," he said gruffly. "*Begged* is more like it."

"I guess—" this was really awkward, so awkward she looked away from him "—what I need to know is what you were asking *for*."

The silence went on so long, she sneaked a peek. The lines carved in his face had deepened. "You mean, did I think we were good together in bed and wanted to keep that going for a while, or am I open to the possibility of marriage and kids?"

"It's not like I expect a proposal or anything like that." She made herself meet his eyes and tried really hard not to sound apologetic. "But I don't want to waste my time if there's no hope of a future. And you've sounded like…"

"Beth." He sat on the side of the bed again, where he could take her hand and look at her with those dark chocolate eyes. "I'm not that big a jerk. You made it clear what you need. Thanks to you, I've had to do a lot of thinking."

"Was it a strain?" she asked politely.

His grin warmed her, head to toe. "Actually, it was. I got somewhere, though. I figured out that my role model was the cop I told you about, the one who saved my ass. It went further than me becoming a cop like him."

She clung to his hand watched his face.

"I saw him as free. Nobody weighing him down. That impression…solidified, even though I should have known better once I was older. I called him yesterday, and while we were talking he told me I was a fool if I wished for less family. His wife died of cancer before they could have kids. I don't know if I said that." At her nod, Tony kept talking. "He admitted he's never met anyone who could take her place. For the first time, I let myself hear how lonely he is. I felt like an idiot."

"That's sad," she murmured.

"Yeah, it is." His mouth twisted. "I also realized I've let myself revert to old habits since I came home after Dad died. I sat my mother down and had a talk. I think she understood."

"Really?" Beth said in surprise.

He laughed. "She'll forget, but I laid down some rules, and I'll stick to them."

"I've made some resolutions of my own," Beth confessed. "Long past due."

Tony tipped his head. "Ditto." He hesitated. "This is a roundabout way of telling you I've been seriously falling for you. I've never come close to feeling the same about any other woman. When you kicked me out, I felt like you'd—God, I don't know—torn a hole into me. Chopped off an arm or a leg or something."

Yes. She'd felt the same.

"I know where I want us to go." Anxiety mixed with tenderness in his gaze. "We can take it slow—you need time—but I'm hoping you'll feel good enough to come to Sunday dinner at my sister Maria's house."

She blinked. "This Sunday?"

"We could put it off to the next Sunday," he said hurriedly. "Or…longer than that, if you're not ready. I don't mean to get pushy."

Beth laughed in relief and joy and a whole lot

else, not caring that her wound twanged a protest. "*Pushy* is your middle name."

Shoulders she hadn't known were tense relaxed as he smiled at her. "Maybe." This smile dimmed. "I can work on it."

"No. *Pushy* is another word for strong." Past a lump in her throat, she said, "I can hardly imagine what it would be like to sometimes be able to lean on someone else." No, not true—she'd already learned what it felt like.

He momentarily looked away. "Mamá said something that surprised me. I asked why she always called me instead of one of the others, and she said it was because everyone in the family trusts me. Not everyone does what they promise, but I do."

He sounded bemused, as if he hadn't known how trustworthy he was. It made her eyes sting again. "You do. I want that. I want *you*."

Tony planted a hand on the pillow beside her head and bent to kiss her softly on the forehead, then on the tip of one cheekbone, the bridge of her nose. "God, Beth," he muttered, just before he reached her mouth. "I've been…" He didn't say what he'd been. He kissed her instead, his mouth gentle but his hunger for her close to the surface.

Beth closed her eyes and let herself drink in every sensation. She laid her hand on his jaw, savoring the roughness and hard bone. Then she slipped her arm around his neck and held on tight as the kiss deepened, as she, at least, forgot where they were.

He was the one to pull back, although dark color in his cheeks and a gleam in his eyes suggested he hadn't been far from losing it.

"If you'll put up with my family," he said huskily, "I'll put up with yours."

Beth managed a shaky smile. "Deal."

"Your brother is actually growing on me."

Something like a giggle escaped her. "Me, too."

He was suddenly serious. "Your place is a crime scene, you know."

The idea of yellow tape wrapping her doors made her queasy.

"Will you come home with me?" he asked.

She swallowed and nodded. "I want to see Emily first, though."

"Thank you," he said, voice low, "for letting me try again."

"I let myself get scared." Looking past him, she smiled again. "Just so you know, here's your chance to put up with my family some more."

He grimaced. "You'll have plenty of chances to put up with mine."

"Starting Sunday."

His eyebrows quirked, but then Matt and her father crowded into the cubicle. It all hit her at once. The two of them so relaxed together. Dad rushing to her side. Emily being okay. Tony open to a future with her.

Connected to him by firm grip on her hand, Beth soaked in an astonishing state of happiness. She could get used to this.

* * * * *

If you enjoyed this story by
Janice Kay Johnson,
you'll also love her most recent books:

THE HERO'S REDEMPTION
HER AMISH PROTECTORS
PLAIN REFUGE
A MOTHER'S CLAIM

Watch for her next book
coming in April 2018.

All available at Harlequin.com.

Get 2 Free Books,
Plus 2 Free Gifts—
just for trying the Reader Service!

Get 2 Free Books,

Plus 2 Free Gifts—

just for trying the Reader Service!

Get 2 Free Books,
Plus 2 Free Gifts—
just for trying the Reader Service!

HARLEQUIN

HEARTWARMING™